THE MAN SHE FELL IN LOVE WITH

"Don't you want to see what's in the box?" Anthony made the little velvet box dance in his palm to the rhythm of the music, bouncing it around to make it hard for me to grab. But I did get hold of it.

I bit my lower lip and slowly opened it on its silent hinge. There they were. The platinum wedding bands we picked out. Our wedding bands. Simple, smooth, unadorned platinum. Traditional and elegant. None of those "it opens up into a timepiece" gadgets or Black Hills gold tricolored rings various mail jewelers tried to push on us. No diamond channel set for me. No birthstones or laser etchings in a lace pattern. No dual-tone metals with a gold edge in case gold jewelry comes back into style. We went simple. Beautiful.

I pulled mine from its slot and held it at an angle. And it was there. The inscription Anthony kept secret from me when he ordered it: *E.—Forever—Love A.*

And that was the first time I had cried in days. The first time I had cried tears of joy in months . . .

Books by Sharon Naylor

IT'S MY WEDDING TOO

IT'S NOT MY WEDDING (BUT I'M IN CHARGE)

Published by Kensington Publishing Corporation

It's My Wedding Too

SHARON NAYLOR

KENSINGTON BOOKS
KENSINGTON PUBLISHING CORP.
http://www.kensingtonbooks.com

KENSINGTON BOOKS are published by

Kensington Publishing Corp.
850 Third Avenue
New York, NY 10022

All Kensington titles, imprints and distributed lines are available at special quantity discounts for bulk purchases for sales promotion, premiums, fund-raising, educational or institutional use.

Special book excerpts or customized printings can also be created to fit specific needs. For details, write or phone the office of the Kensington Special Sales Manager: Kensington Publishing Corp., 850 Third Avenue, New York, NY 10022. Attn. Special Sales Department. Phone: 1-800-221-2647.

Kensington and the K logo Reg. U.S. Pat. & TM Off.

ISBN-13: 978-0-7582-0923-8
ISBN 10: 0-7582-0923-1

First Trade Paperback Printing: June 2005
First Mass Market Paperback Printing: March 2007
10 9 8 7 6 5 4 3 2 1

Printed in the United States of America

Chapter 1

No one ever told Delilah Winchester that nothing in life is perfect. When you have more money than several royal families combined, and a well-adapted ego that's aware of every penny, coddling each cent like a pedigree pet, there's very little "perfect" you can't create somehow with the whisper of a check torn from its Prada holder. Perfect can be bought. Perfect can be demanded. And perfect can be pulled from others at first by a threatening stance and a proverbial ax held over their livelihood, and then over the years with just a raised eyebrow and pursed lips. *Perfect, my dear, is the goal. Those Buddhists are wrong, you see. It's the only theory they can hang on to when they have no good shoes or clothes.*

Delilah Winchester wasn't always Leona Helmsley's evil twin. She wasn't always sour-faced and held together as if screwed too tightly by a too-often-insulted surgeon inserting titanium rods into her spine, neck and hips. And she certainly didn't start life off looking down her nose at others (tough to do when you're 5 feet 2 inches tall, by the way) with an overly applied scent of disdain. *Spritz disdain into the air and then walk through the mist so as not to overapply. One never knows when one will walk into an elevator with a wealthy Somebody inside, perhaps.*

Not too many people remember anything of her other than this icy power bitch in heels, who would pull out a wad of hundreds as a big show in front of a homeless person to fan through for a single (of course, doing this only in front of an admiring fan who would later go to the fan-based chat room to report Delilah's act of benevolence and then call the gossip rags for a quick $100 finder's fee on the tip).

Not many people remember when she shopped at retail stores, and not many people remember the softness of her pre-successful cheeks, the smell of apples on her hands from the pies she made at Thanksgiving, the simple silver chain she received as a wedding present from her groom that hung a cross demurely on her chest and the cotton shirts she wore with her sleeves rolled up, the Mary Kay lipstick she bought only at friends' cosmetics parties, the sound of the laughter when her best friends from high school gathered once a year at her place and drank $8 bottles of wine by the fireplace, talking about their old high school days and rock concerts and wondering what happened to their ex-boyfriends.

She was young and pink then, a radiant Madonna woman in the days when that meant nurturing and peaceful, with hair dyed from the box with a few chunks mistakenly untouched by the auburn shading in the back when she pulled her hair up. Not many people remember when she went by her real name of Donna Penks. *I can't go by the name Donna Penks anymore! Donna Penks sounds like a name for the*

woman who calls Bingo at the church and runs coat
drives for the needy. Donna Penks shops at Target. Donna
Penks is the housewife who sits at home, cleaning the fish
tank and wondering why her husband is three hours late
coming home.

So—and not many people remember this either—Donna Penks was symbolically cremated with
a bonfire on the kitchen stove to make ashes out of
her old driver's license, library card, PTA card, old
postcards from vacations, twelve years of journals,
a handkerchief, some old underwear, and a hand-
made sign that said "The Penks Family Welcomes
You to Our Home." Donna Penks was dead. Delilah
Winchester rose out of the ashes in the skillet, after
being sprayed a few times by the fire extinguisher.
Delilah Winchester became the phoenix rising from
the flames, once the burnt plastic fumes cleared
away. Not too many people know that story.

Not too many people remember when her Mary
Kay bubble gum pink lips magically morphed into
$50 MAC red, and not too many people remember
that she used to smile readily, laugh heartily, hug
mightily, sing when she thought no one was looking, laugh when she burned a pot roast, playfully
tossed a handful of flour at her kids while making
Christmas cookies, stayed up all night with a sick
family dog and dried the tears of her husband.

No one's really left here to remember that person. She got rid of them all. The friends, the husband, the Mary Kay consultants. She cut them off
her life like the Greek cooks cut the lamb in strips
off the rotating meat roaster in the window of the
gyro restaurant. Slash. Slash. Slash. Anything Donna
Penks had to go.

Except me. And I remember every ounce of
Delilah Winchester back when she was Donna Penks.

Every scent. Every line of her face and soothing word, the warm, peaceful feeling of cuddling up with her to read a good book when I was four. I remember it all.

And that's why it's hard to hate her now. It's hard to hate what my mother has become, because I know Donna Penks is still in there somewhere, trapped in a cocoon among all those memories of fabulous garden parties, book premiere launches, celebrity weddings, interviews on *Entertainment Tonight,* flights to Rome and back, designer clothes and shoes, and letters of praise from Steven Spielberg. Donna Penks is sandwiched way deep in there with her lips still smoothed over in bubble gum pink, her hands all plump and soft and smooth, with a lilac-smelling handkerchief ready to soothe away someone's tears.

I can't hate her now. Because I can see past my mother's outside to that little bit inside of her that I still love. Donna Penks, the best mother in the world. The mother all my girlhood friends once said long ago they wished they had of their own.

And Donna Penks is the one I wish I was hurrying toward right now with my left hand held behind my back to hide the sparkly new ring that hasn't even had a full day to find its comfort zone on my hand. I wanted Donna Penks there to clasp her hands together at her chest, envelope me in her arms, and cry embarrassingly loudly for joy at my good news. Donna you could predict. You could paint her like "what would Maya Angelou do?"

Sometimes I choose not to remember that most of Donna Penks is buried in a non-sealed plastic baggie beneath the willow tree out back. Sometimes I think she'll materialize in a puff of silver smoke and recapture my mother's packaging; that the little seed of her punching back all those bub-ble-wrapped memory cells of Gucci shopping trips and drinks with George Clooney and Tom Hanks would rise up victorious to win the competition to come back out and re-assume her life. Actually, I think that a lot of the time.

And I really, truly, stomach-sinkingly wished that it was Donna Penks I was about to announce my engagement to. If you took a picture of that mo-ment, like I take pictures of moments automati-cally as part of my job, you would have seen me with wide, nervous eyes holding up a shaking hand for her to inspect and waiting . . . just waiting . . . for the inevitable letdown. The only question was . . . what form would it take?

Delilah Winchester smiled the kind of smile where you don't see teeth. She took my hand into her own, softened of course by today's paraffin peel, didn't look at my eyes and said flatly, "Well, if he wasn't going to buy the one I showed him at Tiffany then why did he waste my time by bringing me all the way out into the city?"

I wonder if stomachs actually physically detach from their positions when you feel them sink.

The worst part was . . . that was a better response than I expected.

During the half hour ride from our place in Hoboken to her place in Basking Ridge, with my mind spinning what-ifs as a way to steel myself, as a well-practiced way to keep me from actually getting the wind knocked from me with the unexpected response, I imagined these Delilahisms: "Your hand looks too big now." "My engagement ring was a lot bigger than that, and your father was just a fire-man at the time. I'd think Anthony could have done better than that." And my favorite, "Well, it

shows how much he loves you." Fantasies, all of
them. Protective fantasies.

Donna Penks would hate Delilah Winchester,
I'm sure. But she would wish her the best anyway.

And so began my first moments as an engaged
woman. The best time of my life. The magic was
about to begin.

"Emilie," my mother called out as I began to walk
away upon command at the sound of her trilling
cell phone. Her world was calling. "I'm happy for
you," she said, using the side of her manicured finger to click TALK on her phone. "Really I am," now
a bit more animatedly, as we had a listener now.
Her fake voice. Her television voice. Her audience
voice.

My turn for the no-teeth smile, the stiff stance.
The words she said were fine. Flat as day-old un-
corked White Star and they came from a face that
could have said the same sentence to a stranger
whose kid just won a three-legged race. But I like
to think that was the best Donna Penks could do
from way inside there, blowing a message up out
through the cold cavern trails of her like a bubble
and not being able to twist the Botox forehead and
eyes into a warm, maternal smile.

At least I know Donna Penks heard it somehow.
And that was who I'd really come to tell. And before my heels made three clicks in retreat across
her marble kitchen floor, Delilah's higher pitched
"social voice" filled the wide rooms and high ceil-
ings, wrapping around marble columns and bouncing off priceless paintings, brushing over the leaves
of enormous floral arrangements on the hall tables and making them quiver just so slightly.

"*Tasha, darling!*" Delilah tinkled her voice like
ice prepping a martini glass. "I have the most glo-

rious news! My daughter Emilie is *engaged!* . . . I *know!* . . . Oh, of *course!* We're just *thrilled!*"

And I shut the door behind me just as she was showering Tasha with her enthusiasm, but still heard through it. "Of course it's going to be a *fabulous* wedding! We're having Vivienne design the whole thing. . . ."

Anthony hadn't even turned off the car. When I slumped into my seat, pulling my jacket up to clear the door frame, he touched my leg right at my hem. "Marriage Lesson Number 1," he said with a smile. "Never expect things to be other than they are." And he kissed me. He had just had an Altoids too, in preparation for the emergency kiss I was sure to need. Pretty soon, he'd need to stock the car with Altoids for him and Valium for me.

We had a wedding to plan.

Chapter 2

And now we were headed for Carmela's. Back on the road to Brooklyn, with speedy teenagers in their little red Mustangs zipping through traffic like they're playing a videogame, SUVs swerving when the ring of an inevitable cell phone calls the driver's eyes off the road, and the reliable bumps of potholes. Our Starbucks jostled and spilled in the cup holders.

Anthony knew well enough to let me lean my head against the cold window, staring out over the asphalt and bridge landscape, listening to one song after another on the radio as my mind floated from concern to concern, really wanting to back up and stay on the memory of our engagement. Of that amazing night Anthony gave me last night ... turning the corner on high heels, flipping my burgundy silk wrap and looking up to see the colors dancing by the fountain at Lincoln Center. It was the ballroom dancers, professionals most but not all, dipping and floating as if on water, dancing clockwise around the blue-lit fountain. An orchestra in tuxedos set up on the square, their music floating around them, and us, captivating like a gentle waft of perfume. The rest of the city just four steps away distanced, retreated, became silent.

And there was that music box scene, the dancers with their long arms emphasizing dramatic dips as the men's strong arms supported them at their backs. The crisp contrast of black-and-white tuxedos with glittery ball gowns in magenta and cerise, pale lavender, black and gold. Feathered accents in the women's upswept hair, peaceful smiles on all.

And Anthony took my hand, leading me expertly into a waltz, his hand on the bare small of my back, and that half-grin I fell in love with the first time I saw it as we watched the Fourth of July fireworks from Frank Sinatra Park. We hadn't danced much in our five years together, but somehow we just knew the steps. He led without leading, and on some turns so did I. Three steps a turn, my hair bouncing over my shoulder with every change of direction, the strong curve of his shoulder under my hand.

At the fountain's edge, Anthony lifted my hand straight up, signaling me to turn once . . . then again . . . then again . . . and on that last turn, with me turned away for only a split-second, less than a split-second, he had pulled from his coat pocket the little blue box. And he asked me. With that half-smile, with eyes that reflected the water fountain's motion, and wiping off a tear before I might see it, he asked me. . . .

And not even twenty-four hours later, here I was freshly snubbed by Delilah and on my way to see Anthony's mother. Carmela. The Smother, my friends and I called her at first. *Would you believe that she actually KNOCKED ME OUT OF THE WAY so that Anthony could put sunblock on her back?! And he DID IT, too!* I almost broke up with him that day, I remembered, smiling a little out the window and hearing myself breathe out a little laugh. Anthony turned his head and smiled. I smiled in return and patted his hand on the gearshift.

Anthony was a reformed Mama's Boy. Normally, you can't reform the true mama's boys, but he was willing to be reformed. That makes all the difference. *There are men who never want to let go of their mothers, who want you to cut the London broil just like their mothers do or make marinara sauce with the same kind of sausage their mothers buy from the same deli. And then there are captive mama's boys who really want the road out. Their mothers have super-glued the apron strings where the boys cut them. They're just back-stepping little by little, one grain at a time, so the mother bear won't notice.* How my friends and I tried to figure it out, tried to imagine why my strong, silent-type Anthony, with his strength of character, his smarts, his humor, his independence, would slap SPF30 on his mother's wrinkled back while she looked way-too-creepily pleased at the massage from her thirty-year-old son. The Smother, my friends and I called her.

But Carmela was kind to me. Kind enough, considering I kept Anthony's attention away from her, cut his affection in half. She couldn't avoid the reality of what I was, so that meant I got the first heaping dish of manicotti, the thickest slice of braccioli, the last meatball. She hugged me warmly whenever I arrived, and she offered me coupons she'd clipped for me just because. Coupons for Anthony's sinus medication in addition to the raspberry jam I adore, but I'll let that slide. Kindness is kindness, no matter what the motivation. At least she wasn't dangerous.

"Anthony!" She threw open the door like our arrival was a surprise party, and latched her arms around Anthony's back, swinging herself from side to side but barely moving him. He kissed her gallantly on the cheek and stepped aside so that I could get my own rib-squeeze. The woman had tremendous upper-body strength.

"Ah, my Emilie!" she sang, rocking the same way and nearly toppling me off my heeled boots. Anthony put a hand to my shoulder to steady me.

And this was just hello.

As soon as she saw that rock on my finger, I'd need protective padding, shin guards and maybe a helmet.

"Skinny little thing," she said, though admiringly, and stepped aside to let us into her warm and always-scented home. Anthony's father Vic was, as expected, lounged out on the couch, reading the paper at arm's length with his neck craned back trying to make out the small print. Wordlessly, he lifted his hand in greeting and went back to the sports pages.

Their home was immaculate, but in a human way. With pictures on the walls in a nonstyled, haphazard way—not lined up with a level like my mother's—solemn religious icons in the window frame, thick fluffy pillows on the couches, coats on the chairs, and always something bubbling on the stove in the kitchen. Always fresh bread baking in the oven—for the family, and for the birds outside if no family shows up in time. Coffee always ready on the counter, the little TV always on and turned to the Food Network. Looks like Emeril would be bamming in the background when we broke the news to Carmela.

"Hey, Ma," Anthony patted her on the waist. "We have something to tell you."

Carmela crossed herself and looked to the ceiling, her automatic response to anything in preparation for both good and bad. She had a dot of flour on her jaw, which I smoothed away from her.

"Calm down, it's good," Anthony assured her, and stepped back to lean against the counter. Protecting himself, no doubt. "Show her, Em."

And proudly, I held out my left hand, with my fingers poised in a gentle ballerina lilt, middle finger pointed down further than the rest of my graceful hand gesture. (Ironic, I think now that things have gotten this bad.)

She looked at it. Then up at me.

Nothing.

She looked at it again, then looked at Anthony, who was beaming.

Nothing.

Both our faces fell. What the hell was wrong with this woman? Did she not *see* the two-carat, three-stone ring? Was she checking out my manicure?

Then she held out her hand, shaking as it was, to touch my fingers, then walk her grip up to touch the ring itself, to *push* on the diamond like it was a gag toy that would shoot water into her face. I looked over with concern at Anthony and shrugged. He was just blinking and pulling his crossed arms a little tighter over his stomach.

"Ma?" he ventured.

Carmela jumped a little, woken out of a daze, pulled back from some reverie.

"Ma, what do you think?" he tried again. "Emilie said Yes. We're getting married."

Carmela actually *worked* at forming a smile. Her lips quivered, her cheek flinched, tears came to her eyes.

Is she having a stroke?

And after a moment of this silence, this facial contortion, what looked like a short in her wiring, she burst out into a cry and flung herself against me, knocking me against the table so that my legs shot out from under me and I only remained upright because of her weight against me. *Was that a hug or a tackle?* I kicked my legs a few times to get some traction with my boots, caught my weight on one leg and tried to stand straight again. But her weight was against me and I couldn't rise. Anthony laughed later in the car about the look on my face, like I was being mugged, how my arms flailed for a second before I patted her on the back, and how I slumped into a chair seat when she finally unclamped and delivered her fullback love to her son, who could handle the body weight.

"But she was *crying,*" I argued as we drove through the tunnel, home to our place on 14th Street in Hoboken, the moderate income annex to Manhattan.

"Tears of joy," he nodded, hypnotized by the yellow lines on the road and the green lights spaced on the tunnel ceiling ahead of us.

"That wasn't happy crying. That was panic with a smile."

"She was happy, trust me."

"Didn't sound happy."

Anthony patted my leg. "Did she cut you a piece of coffee cake?"

"Yes."

"Then she was happy."

I just shrugged and looked for the blue and red sign on the tunnel wall, announcing the precise moment you crossed the boundary from New York to New Jersey somewhere under the Hudson River. My ribs hurt and my brain hurt. I had been snubbed by one and mugged by the other, and neither reacted as I expected.

I looked at my own rock and smiled, making it dance with light with just the slightest adjustment of my hand. Even underwater, practically, it was the brightest thing imaginable. I leaned over as far as my seat belt would let me go, and I thanked Anthony with a kiss on his neck.

Chapter 3

Normally, Anthony and I disagree about the term "fashionably late." He thinks it's fine to show up to any event a half hour later than promised, while I think of that as inconsiderate of others and just generally bad taste. But tonight he's switched over to my side of the coin. I've never seen him dress and groom and grab his coat and keys so quickly. I've never seen him look with such wide eyes at his watch, then at the clock on the wall, as if expecting one of them to give us fifteen minutes extra. So shifty. So nervous. Dropping things. Imploring me with a raised eyebrow to hurry up and get that last earring in so we can go. I had to suppress a smile, because this was no time to get into that argument again. Especially because I knew exactly why he'd thrown his previous position out the window and now resembled *me* urging him to get a move on so we can make the 9:15 movie.

"Ready yet?" he asks again, probably thinking

I'm deliberately fumbling with my necklace clasp now just to annoy him.

"Just about," I sing, a little too happy and casual for his tastes tonight.

"Come on, Emilie. I don't want them there without us," he pleads, sounding like a little boy. It's so rare to hear him like this, I actually think it's adorable. This is a man who bosses multinational corporations around and scares the living daylights out of CEOs with just a glance and the readying of his pen. This is a man who commands the best tables at restaurants on the power of his name alone. And here he is whining like a six-year-old boy who doesn't want to miss the ice cream truck.

"I know," I lower my voice and now make more of an effort to hurry through spraying my perfume in the air and walking through the mist, during which I, of course, forget to close my eyes and cost us a valuable ten seconds of time while I wave both my hands furiously in front of my face, hoping the slight whiff of air will keep the tears from forming. It doesn't. Even with my head tilted back, as if that would help, my eyes immediately fill with protective droplets. Now I have to touch up my makeup again.

"Em, come on," he pleads again. We have a long ride to my mother's house, and I am half blind and tearing like I've just cut onions as I stumble out to the car, arms outstretched and feeling for the door handle.

When we arrive, the cars are all in line in Delilah's circular cobblestone driveway. Candles are lit in each window, which gives the house some appearance of warmth and charm in the darkness (otherwise it quite resembles a haunted mansion with its dramatic stone cuts and gables, the gargoyles on the corner eaves like a classic Old World New York City hotel). Anthony skids the car into an available spot while the red-jacketed valet looks on in stunned and insulted silence. He hurries forward and for a minute forgets that I am with him.

"Are they here?" I call out from still inside the car, with the door swung open, trying to arrange my skirt so that I don't flash the valets as a little compensation for us speeding right by them. I stand finally, tottering on my heels on the cobblestone surface of the driveway.

"I don't . . . I don't see it . . ." Anthony is tall, but he's rising on his toes to try to spot the Mazda among the Lexuses (Lexi?), Mercedes and, inexplicably, minivans.

"Good," I release my shoulders down a half inch and breathe fully for the first time in an hour. Anthony has driven like a—

"Oh God!" Anthony deflates, physically sinks to what looks like two inches shorter than usual, then turns to me with a white face and dull eyes. "It's here."

"They're *here*?" Now I'm stricken and white with anxiety, the blood sound rushing in my ears as I'm sure his was as well. Pure panic. His parents are like him, never on time to anything. And now we were out here in the driveway and they were inside my mother's house, at my mother's party, having probably met her already. Without us. That could *not* be good. Worst case scenario.

"Disaster," whispers Anthony and after a split second to lock eyes in mutual silent planning, together we run for the front door. Running in stilettos is never pretty, but try it on a cobblestone driveway. You need ankles of steel. I must have looked like I was running over hot coals, all flailing and awkward-legged, moving forward and trying to stay upright, not being able to focus on much but seeing the back flaps of Anthony's jacket waving at me as a fashion taunt. And did I mention that it's hard to come to a stop while wearing stilettos and running? I'm sure the guests inside heard the *thud* when I hit the door, and only much, much later, when perspective allows you to look back and laugh at a moment of pure mortification, did Anthony admit that he thought I was actually trying to break the door down with my shoulder.

Locked.

We ring the bell, and the door magically slides open by no one in particular that we could make eye contact with, because the moment we were inside we snapped into reconnaissance mode. Scanning the crowd for his parents and my mother, marching forward with dead-serious purpose, we wove around anything in our path to find them. Time was moving in an off-kilter pace, with edges blurred and no sound seeming to come from any of the partygoers' mouths. Adrenaline apparently makes you deaf too. People smiled at us, and in our fierce tunnel vision, we looked right through them, ignored them. We really know how to make an entrance.

It was our engagement party. We were the guests of honor, and we all but plowed through groups of our well-wishers, elbowed away gushing and smothering great-aunts, snubbed adorably dressed little girls with bows in their hair and a starstruck look in their eyes, twirled tuxedo-clad waiters in our wake as they pirouetted to save their trays of champagne and salmon crudité from our forceful and focused path. We were actually running now. Anthony pulled me by the hand through any open pathway, slaloming around groupings of chairs, turning corners around marble columns, and scanning the crowd with osprey vision for any sign of two somewhat short Italians undoubtedly hovering in the corner in an overwhelmed daze.

Room to room the search went on, with us blowing through in fast-forward with the sound off. And just before we took the stairs two at a time to search the bathrooms and bedrooms upstairs, I saw it happen. My eyes stopped in mid-scan and locked on the scene, zooming in with the clearest of precision. It was, of course, the first thing I saw clearly all night.

At the doorway to the kitchen (where else would Carmela be?), there she stood.

I could only see her upswept twist of a hairdo, home-done and with some flyaways poking out of her hair clip, and the red-flushed side of her face, her mouth open, slack in disbelief. She wore a black dress with a white cameo pin at the neck, which explains the confusion. She was looking down at her hands, at the fur coat she now held loosely in them. And her face rose blankly when Delilah's publisher, Roger, dropped his hat in her hands and kept walking toward the bar, deep in conversation with Delilah's publicist. From the side, another guest draped a fur over Carmela's now full hands, and Carmela's head turned again in a slow, dumbstruck way as it all started to add up . . .

They think she's the maid.

"Anthony!" I pulled him by the back of his jacket, depending on his old soccer days' agility to keep from tumbling backward into a certain head injury on the marble floor, and pushed my way through more guests to reach her. Anthony was paper white when he arrived behind me.

"Carmela!" I hugged her while Anthony deftly slid the jackets out of her hands. The hat he let drop to the floor. "Sorry we're late, we had a terrible time with traffic, and we tried to call you but you'd already left . . ." My plan of diversion was just to keep talking nonstop. Confuse her so she doesn't remember that she's just been mistaken for the help.

"Some museum this is!" Anthony's father, Vic, appeared from the kitchen, chewing on a biscotti that he'd stolen from the not-yet-ready-to-be-served dessert trays. "Jesus! Look at this place!"

"Dad," Anthony warned and with a stiff shake of their hands and a silent male reminder through the eyes, the men were behaving and calm and ready to get drinks at one of the three bars spread throughout the downstairs of the house.

"You grew up here?" Carmela asked with her deep brown eyes narrowed ever so slightly, like she didn't even want to hear the answer.

"No," I said with an enormous smile, showing her that I was *glad* not to have grown up in splendor. "We lived in Nutley before this."

The magic word. Nutley. Carmela softened. I was back to size with her again.

"This is quite a . . ." Carmela couldn't find the words.

"Yes, it is," I stopped her, not even knowing what I'd answered. Anthony formed the international signal for *do you want a drink?* and I held up four fingers. And keep them coming.

Carmela stood with her back to the wall, fingering the leaves on a potted ficus tree, and pulling her hand back slightly when she figured out by touch that it was real. The edges of her mouth lowered slightly, and she looked at the china cabinet. Nothing fake there either. I heard her sigh, then wondered what level of hell this evening was going to sink to.

Quite the thought for a bride-to-be at her engagement party. *What level of hell will this evening sink to?* And right on cue, there was Delilah. She stood still when she saw us, didn't rush forward for a hug. She wore an off-white, tailored suit dress with clear Swarovski crystal beading on each lapel, an off-white rose corsage with pearl accents, quadruple-strand pearl necklace, bracelet and drop earrings of pearl and diamond. Her hair was pulled up expertly and flyaway-free in a tight chignon with pearl pin accents at the gathering, and she looked young and fresh and radiant . . . like a bride herself. No one could keep their eyes off her, and I heard three "Delilah, you look *fab*ulous!'s" as she made her way over.

She stopped four feet away, close enough only for a handshake, and she was looking down. I followed her gaze, which is hard to do from the side, and focused first on Carmela's hand. No big rings on it, not a big deal. Maybe she's looking at her manicure. Home-done, again no big deal, and Delilah wouldn't stare unblinkingly in shock at a rather benign manicure. What was she looking at so intently?

My eye traveled down and my stomach lurched. White shoes.

Carmela had on white shoes. After Labor Day. *Where the hell is Anthony with my drink?*

Carmela had her eye on something too. The quadruple strand of pearls? The smooth Botox work on Delilah's forehead? Delilah's nuclear-white teeth?

Carmela was narrowing her eyes, trying to see something without her glasses, and Delilah instinctively brought her hand up to her mouth. Was it her breath? Lipstick on her teeth? Parsley caught there?

Carmela would tell me much later that she hadn't been looking at *anything* in particular. She just wanted Delilah to feel self-conscious about something. *Who is this woman?* I remember thinking when the truth came out. Mother Earth has an insidious side.

"Mother," I started the official introductions after the showdown at the Insecurity Corral had ended. "This is Anthony's mother, Carmela Cantano. Carmela, this is my mother, Delilah Winchester."

The women shook hands icily, broke out the no-teeth smiles, and simultaneously tilted their heads while chirping out hellos.

"This is a lovely party, Dinah," Carmela complimented, nodding over her shoulder at the vast display of grandiosity she saw. Crystal, china, small and classy servings of butternut squash risotto presented on individual silver spoons.

"It's Delilah," my mother purred, deflecting the shot and rising further above. "And thank you. It's the least I could do for the kids."

The least I could do. Even I winced at that one.

"Well, it certainly is *grand*," Carmela said quickly. "So . . . Emilie tells us you write romance novels?"

Delilah lifted her chin. "Not romance novels, darling . . . romance *epics*."

Anthony arrived with our drinks just in time. *How am I going to find some common ground between them?* I wondered, draining my pomegranate-colored champagne in two swallows. The only thing these two women have in common are that they both have their original sets of ovaries and they both hate Mayor Bloomberg for being a poor imitation of Mayor Giuliani, like he's just filling in for the *real* one.

"Mother," I tried again, silently pushing away any talk of ovaries and premenopause. "Carmela volunteers at the hospital. She cradles the preemies, to give them human contact."

Delilah immediately turned to barrel-chested Vic, who had sidled up at the wrong moment. "Well, that must make you feel secure," she said, and I think we were all stunned. "That she spends her time with infants . . . you know where she is all the time."

God, Mother, stop.

Blank stares only pushed her on, and I heard the champagne's effect on her tongue. "Because sometimes you don't know . . ."

Was she flirting with Anthony's father? Could that slurred nonsense be called flirting?

"Right," Anthony said. "*Anyway . . .*"

"Mother," I started to try again, thinking something *gardening* would work. But Anthony nudged me, the international sign for *give it up, babe.*

"Yes, darling?" Delilah sparkled, her eyes flat.

"Um . . ." Nothing. I had nothing. "This is a lovely party."

For the rest of the night, I was the Jane Goodall of my own engagement party, always tracking, observing, keeping a keen eye on the interactions between the two females of the species, noticing the dominance displays, the avoidance. As Carmela circled through the living room, touching and eyeing everything from the ornate molding of the mirrors to the gold bookends that held Delilah's library (and she *is* the Tom Clancy of romance novelists . . . each book is more than 500 pages), I always knew where Delilah was in relation to her. I tried to see this ballroom of a living room through her eyes, wondering what she was thinking about the artwork, the sculptures, the photos of my mother with the actresses who have played her roles in TV movies.

And I watched Delilah, getting more drunk by the minute, running her hand over the collar and bicep of every man she spoke to, even the waiters. Tucking a fallen curl behind her ear and laughing like a teenager. I hadn't seen her eat anything all night.

"Korean duck?" Anthony appeared out of nowhere, with a plate full of Asian eats and aromatic noodles.

"No thanks," I sighed. "I'm skipping the main courses and going right for the dessert."

"Ahh . . . it's a chocolate ganache moment," he teased and kissed me on the ear. I melted slightly, leaned against him, untensed for a moment to smile at yet another guest I didn't know wishing us well. At least this one got our names right. I've been Amy, Allison, Emmeline, and Emsy all night. Twice I've had my cheek pinched, twice the *other* kind of cheek pinched, three times hugged until breathing was difficult, and about six times told what Viagra can do for our sex life and a happy marriage in the future. All I knew was that there were entirely too many smiling elderly gentlemen in the room. Made me want to hide the tray of oysters . . . and my mother.

"They're not clicking," Anthony said, and for a moment I associated the comment with these old men's false teeth. Ah, pomegranate champagne, deliver me from reason.

"Huh?" I stepped back onto my other heel.

"The mothers."

"Ah, yes . . . the mothers."

The mothers of all evil, the mother hens, the mother—

"So what is it, do you think?"

"What is what?" I blinked a few times and tried to focus on the love of my life, who with a reassuring hand on my shoulder told me he knew I was tipped.

"What is it that's making them act this way? So hostile. Some kind of class warfare?"

I looked up at him, to see if that was a joke, or if he was serious. He was serious.

And before I could open my mouth, his mother approached us with a thin smile and her husband yawning behind her. "So . . . Emilie . . ."

I created a smile for her. "Yes?"

Cautiously, with an eyebrow raised, she said, "You don't have fur coats too, do you?"

How blessedly perfect a moment, right then, for the chefs to light the bananas flambé, sending giant lines of orange flame in dramatic, balletic curls to the top of the room. Perfect. Just perfect.

Chapter 4

"We could elope," I ventured, not blinking and mesmerized by the dashes of white lines coming one after the other on the highway's surface. Anthony was driving, amazingly dedicated enough to stay sober that evening, and I was silently chanting driving directions inside my head: *Stay on the right side. Stay on the right side. Stay on the right side.*

"You know you don't want that," Anthony yawned and gave his upper back a stretch with a backward curve of his shoulders and a quick flick of his head to the side to crackle his neck bones.

"It would be easier."

"Ah, but it wouldn't be right."

"I know."

Anthony put his hand gently over mine, and only then did I realize I had been death-gripping the sides of the leather seats.

"It's going to be okay," he said. "They'll warm up eventually." And I had this fleeting moment of fantasy: me standing next to an enormous glacier in Alaska, with its ruts and turns and chipped-away floes, with a green Bic lighter and a dumb level of optimism.

"And if they don't?" I whisper.

"We encase them in ice blocks like that David Blaine guy and make them a fabulous art déco performance art centerpiece in the reception hall." My love gave my hand a squeeze. It was probably the first time I genuinely smiled all night. I couldn't remember. "Mothers on Ice . . . sounds like an ice skating special on TV, doesn't it?"

Only Anthony could make reference to a figure skating show and still impress me with his virility. I needed him bad right now. "Hey, A," I said with a dash of suggestion in my voice. "Can you find someplace to pull over?"

His look turned to concern. "You going to be sick?"

I took a moment to let a mischievous smile grow across my lips. "Nope."

Tires screeching, we pulled into the back end of a crowded parkway rest stop parking lot. And got a pair of Starbucks white chocolate mochas and a Mrs. Field's brownie to split when we were finished.

Chapter 5

"She's burning that incense crap again," Anthony waved his hand in front of his face once we'd pushed open my apartment door, forcing it with all four of our hands to fight the weather strip the landlord had put across the bottom edge. Rather than get us a door that doesn't have a two-inch gap on the bottom, she stapled on some insulation stripping. Now every time we try to enter my home, it's an upper-body workout.

My roommate, Leah, had lit not one, not two, not three, but four sticks of patchouli incense. Thick swirls of smoke rose up from the coffee table, and over the entire top half of the room hovered a cloud so dense it resembled one of those old French bordello and dance halls. Leah was nowhere to be found.

I looked up and saw the familiar plastic shower cap covering the smoke detector in the living room, and shook my head. "A, could you open the screen door?"

Shaking his head but with a half smile, Anthony assumed his usual task. Air circulation.

"Leah?" I called out through the place, but received no answer.

"Sorry, I can't take your call right now. I'm reading my aura and consulting with my past selves. But if you'd like to leave a message at the beep . . ." Anthony teased, helping himself to a Corona out of my refrigerator. He has his own shelf in there . . . Coronas, string cheese, and V-8 Splash. If I'd been a stranger behind him in a supermarket checkout line, the inevitable analysis of his food choices would leave me no answer as to his sexuality.

"Stop teasing," I nudged him, helping myself to an iced tea from my own shelf. All woman, it is. Yogurt, hummus, Dasani water, carrot sticks, and a roll of Pillsbury cookie dough. And my undereye concealer in the egg compartment.

Anthony just shrugged as if to say *but she makes it so easy!* And she does. I'll be the first one to admit it.

Leah's heart broke open last summer, after her fiancé left her almost at the altar. Actually it was the rehearsal dinner. And he left her for what we think might have been a man. Tall woman, large hands, hairy knuckles, and either a thyroid problem or a definite Adam's apple. Bright red hair, matching red lipstick and too pale skin, went by the name of Kiki and listed her occupation (says Leah's P.I.) as exotic waitress. We're not sure if that means exotic dancer, or if she was trying to jazz up her position as a waitress in a Thai restaurant as something a little bit more enticing. We saw nothing enticing about her when she broke into Leah's rehearsal dinner with dark mascara tears running down her face, leaping across a chair to dive into Leah's fiancé's arms, crying out in broken English, "Don't marry her, she's too short!"

I remember I had a mouthful of carrot cake at the time, which I promptly choked out almost through my nose. As did everyone else, with various sprays of red wine, water, beer, and potato-leek soup flying out of their noses or in sprays out of their lips, or just shooting down the wrong pipes. And there was poor Leah, standing there in her designer navy blue wrap dress, her hair up, her nails done for the next day, drained white, speechless, and at one moment so obliterated that I swore she looked translucent.

Her fiancé (whose name we don't utter) took the lowdown ego boost and ran from the room with Kiki, leaving the truly good woman behind. It's not exactly how it goes in all the best romantic movies. John Cusack would never run off with Kiki. John Cusack would have started off with Kiki, then found his spine and run off with Leah.

Fast forward through Leah's six months of isolation, mourning, daytime television, quitting her job (she says), and a trip to France to find herself, and what returned to us was a glassy-eyed shell of what she used to be. And the glassy-eyed shell called Leah had discovered Eastern arts. Feng shui. Mysticism. Native American rituals.

I didn't ask about colonic cleansing, because I have to use that bathroom too.

She flirted briefly with changing her name to Amaya Feather Lighthorse, upon the advice of a Native American healer she'd bunked up with in New Mexico, done the sweat lodges naked with, and embarked on vision quests. But she stayed with the name Leah for professional reasons. And also because as lost as she was, as much as she turned to Eastern philosophy to answer questions she'd never be able to answer with straight logic and common sense, she wasn't completely gone. She just needed this magical thinking to give her some kind of sense, some sense of control in her life. She'd left it up to chance and trust before . . . now she was going to partner with the universe for meaning and fate to come to her with an engraved invitation from the forces that be.

I found it harmless for now. It gave her some semblance of control. And while it was amusing to onlookers, it really was harmless. Plenty of people believe in feng shui. Corporations pay feng shui consultants to come in and move their furniture around, hang up mirrors and red banners where they can redirect the energies of the space, and all of a sudden their lives were in balance and their balance sheets had some life to them. Don't knock it, Leah says. Feng shui is real.

Our apartment has been rearranged, by Leah. Tables moved, mirrors hung or removed, bamboo shoots in glass bowls bring luck to her Personal Growth corner, a trickling fountain (that I really enjoy, actually) brings renewed energy to her money corner. And this being my apartment too, hey, maybe the good luck charms will swing some extra accounts my way.

Anthony has some trouble with this, of course. He doesn't like being one of her icons. Apparently, a feng shui book told Leah to fill the Love and Romance corner of the house with images that would attract true and everlasting love for her. Heart-shaped pink quartz stones, pairs of candles (always pairs, never single anything!), and framed photos of Anthony and me as the symbols of the kind of love she wants. I find it harmless, but Anthony doesn't like to be on anyone's altar.

Leah has added a crystal figure of two bodies entwined sensually, plus flower seeds. I don't ask. Must be a fertility thing.

Whatever she's discovered, she's been happier. She has a new interest other than replaying her fiancé's departure over and over in her head and refusing to use words with "ki" or "key" in them. That's why she didn't sign up for reiki classes. I don't even know what reiki is, so no explanations are necessary.

"Leah?" I called again, and her door pulled open. No smoke in her room. "Hey, it's so smoky in here," I waved my hands in front of me, while Anthony used a magazine to sweep some of the fog out of the room.

"Sorry, I was on the phone inside," Leah apologized and shrugged sheepishly. She wore a pink tank top with a white sports bra underneath, at my suggestion weeks ago because the no bra look wasn't working for me and Anthony, and gray boxer shorts. Her hair was up and braided.

"Try to light just one, okay?" I suggested. "The neighbors are going to think you're smoking something in here."

"I'm not smoking anything," she defended herself. "But okay, I'll keep a better handle on it next time."

"Hi, Leah," Anthony waved from the dining room.

"Hey," she said. Anthony is the only man Leah trusts, in a big-brother kind of way. I don't blame her for being cynical right now. She's twenty-five and she got blown right out of being trusting and innocent into questioning everything anyone says, studying body language books to see if someone is lying, and watching a hell of a lot of Dr. Phil. I'd be the same way if I were her. It could take years for her to get back to normal. If she ever does. That part of her from before . . . it's been killed. "How was your mother's party?"

"We could have used some of your good luck charms," I laughed.

"Or two crosses and some garlic," Anthony laughed.

"That bad, huh?" Leah bounced onto the couch, crossed her legs, and pulled the soft gold-colored throw over her. Gold is for protection, apparently. Or riches. Or fertility. Who knows?

"Worse than bad," I said, then swigged out of my iced tea bottle. "His family met my family."

"Oh, you had a Delilah moment?" she asked, then leaned back into the cushions.

"Several," Anthony said, and I was a bit pinched on that. *Hey, your mother wasn't exactly the model of restraint and cordiality, buddy! And what about your Dad stealing all the food?*

"They clashed?"

"We need the U.N."

Yes, we need the U.N. As in UN-invite them to the wedding. That's the only way.

"Delilah was drunk?"

"Pickled."

"And the food, how was that?"

As Anthony and Leah discussed the finer details of the quail eggs, endive leaves with goat cheese and caviar, pistachio sorbet, and venison medallions with Madeira sauce, I checked out of the Food Network review and looked hard at Leah. She was invited to the party but opted out. Said she had a date. She obviously didn't. She could have gone.

"We would have brought you back some," An-

thony was saying, sweet as he is to her. "But we just
wanted to get the hell out of there."

"Thanks," Leah smiled. "But I ate. I'm all set."

I looked to the side table, at the Korean marriage dove sculptures, the red candle, the aro-
matherapy oil burner with the sandalwood vial
standing at the ready, the feather sitting next to it
to signify how love can float into your life at any
time. I think she got that one from *Forrest Gump*
and not Lao Tzu, but hey, it gives her hope.

"Well," I said, clapping my hands a few times.
"It's been a long night, very tiring . . ."

"Yes, very tiring," Anthony said not so subtly—at
least not subtly enough to slide the reference of
our pit-stop tryst by my very intelligent roommate.

"Long ride?" she asked the loaded question,
and I loved seeing that tiny glimpse of the old her
again. The girl who could be playful and light.

"Night, Leah," I said and gave her a smile.

"Night, Em, night, A," she said and grabbed a
magazine to drift off to.

"Is Leah okay?" Anthony's voice was quiet,
drifty, on his way to sleep. He cradled my head in
his arm as I lay across his bare, smooth chest. My
leg wrapped automatically over his, and I could
hear his heart beating slowly, calmly, rhythmically.
My favorite sound on earth.

"Yeah, she's okay. She just needs some time . . .
it hasn't been that long."

"Isn't all this feng shui stuff a little weird?" he
asked with full disclosure that the answer should
be Yes.

"She's immersed herself in something that
helps her," I shrugged. "It's harmless."

"You think her keeping a picture of us on her altar is normal?"

"We're her model of the ideal relationship," I shrugged again. "How sad for her," I laughed, and he did too.

Anthony drifted off again, with deep breathing, those little quakes of his nervous system in his arms and legs that once frightened me ("Oh, he's got Tourette's!") but now just a shaking signal that he's letting go of tension. As he drifted away into a dreamland where there's no wind chimes in the corners of rooms, no dueling mothers, no work stress, no competitiveness with the boys, and no worry about his quickly thinning hair, I lay awake wondering two things: will Leah ever get back to normal? And can I plan a wedding with Delilah and Carmela, the two mythical beasts of wedding planning lore? And a third thing: *Remember to ask Leah if there's a "protect me from my mother" corner in feng shui, or some talisman like a little statue of a mother figure with open arms.*

I only had to look to my own nightstand to answer the last one. It's a little white, two-inch statue of the Virgin Mother, my own talisman. We all have our good luck charms, our icons, so I wasn't going to begrudge Leah hers. It was only temporary, after all.

"Em?" Anthony whispered. "Don't worry, hon. It's all going to be fine."

And he kissed me on the top of my head.

Heaven.

Chapter 6

The doorbell ringing at 6 A.M. on Saturday morning can only mean two things: either the building is on fire, or some Jehovah's Witnesses *really* want to save my soul. Preferring the former, I pulled my leaden legs out from under our down comforter, pulled down my nightshirt from where it had bunched at my waist, and padded in a slump to the door.

"Good *morning!*" At the sight of Delilah, I wished for Jehovah's Witnesses. Almost for the fire.

She breezed past me in a too-heavily-applied cloud of citrusy perfume (*perfect for morning-appropriate events, she'd say*), arms filled with a stack of folders and papers and a box of some sort. Decked out in designer black pants, a black-and-brown striped sleeveless shirt and a string of black pearls, with her hair pulled tight in a chignon, Delilah must have started her beauty ritual at 4 A.M., probably waking her makeup artist at 3.

"Mom, it's early," I whined, wishing for some percentage of coffee in my system.

She made some sound like air escaping from a tire, which was a dismissal signal she'd picked up from her foreign rights agent in London. I just tried to blink my puffy eyes and pushed my hair back behind my ears.

"I picked up a few things at the bookstore," Delilah sang, fanning out a pile of bridal magazines like an expert card dealer in Vegas. The house always wins, some small voice whispered to me in my head. I twisted my engagement ring around my finger, which I've done so often in the past twenty-four hours that I have diamond-burn on the inside of my other finger.

"You want to do this now?" I gestured toward the clock shaming us with 6:07 in bright red numerals.

"What better time?"

"Umm . . . *afternoon*? A week from now?"

"Don't be petulant." And again with the sound of the tire leaking air. "Let me show you what I've found . . ." She flipped open several of the *Bridal Guides, Modern Brides, Martha Stewart Weddings,* and the fat, heavy coffee table book of Vera Wang's. All with pages flagged with bright pink Post-it arrows, notes scratched on some of them in silver swirly handwriting. Was she up all night? Lay off the amphetamines, Mother.

"You've picked out wedding gowns for me?" I smoothed my hand over the glossy magazine pages, looking at six-foot brides with pouty, miserable expressions, holding their bouquets limply at their sides like hypnotism victims at their arranged weddings.

"Just a few ideas," chirped Delilah in her media voice, as if Katie Couric was sitting here miked for sound and a camera rolled this "bridal segment" to the television viewing community. She never turned it off, that media voice. That fake voice.

I flipped one after the other closed, the pages slapping shut. Delilah looked up at me, shocked.

"Thank you for bringing these over," I said politely, in my corporate boardroom voice, diplomacy with the client. "I'll look over them and I'll get back to you."

"Emilie," she said, tilting her head. Perhaps a petulant five-year-old would quake for fear of a time-out, but I just mirrored her tilt and looked amused.

"Mother?"

Having lost the battle of the bridal magazines—for now—Delilah turned and in one quick motion flipped open her laptop and set the button to whir its gears and display a bright blue screen. A picture of my mother with Oprah Winfrey was her screen saver. Some quick, lightning-fast clicks of her nails on the keyboard, and the screen lit up with a NASAesque collection of boxes, spreadsheets, and some kind of stock market-like chart with three different colors of indicators tracing the rising and falling status of something.

"What the hell is this?" I laughed.

"Emilie!" Air escapes tire.

"No, seriously," I laughed. "What is this?"

Anthony came out of the bedroom, with lines from his pillow etched into his cheek, bare-chested, his boxers riding low. "Jesus!" he jumped when he saw her, and disappeared back into the bedroom. I could hear him grumbling from behind the door, but couldn't make out the words. Although I distinctly heard the word "crazy." He'd better be talking about her.

"I've set up a system," Delilah beamed. "You're busy, I'm busy, time is of the essence. Who has time for the grand production, and we both know we're not hiring a wedding coordinator to have all the fun."

And this is the woman who has Colin Cowie on her speed dial for tea parties.

"Good morning, Delilah," Anthony emerged again, this time in a gray T-shirt and actual shorts. He'd smoothed his hair over to hide what he imagines are balding indentations on his scalp. Questioning me with a raised eyebrow, and getting my closed-eye "you don't want to know" shake of my head, he went to the kitchen to put the coffee on. As always, I had to watch him walk. I never missed an opportunity to see those shoulders and those thighs moving across my living room.

"Planning a wedding is a formula, my dear," Delilah continued, oblivious to Anthony's form and the shoe-melting effect he still had on me after all these years. "Just like a book . . . you just key in the minor details."

Ah, so gowns, flowers, cakes, vows, rings, and lifetime commitments are minor details.

"Look," she clicked one button, and an offset pile of formally printed letters appeared. "Here are our letters of interest to send out to a dozen or so of the top caterers in the New York area. I have them all coded and formatted, and with just this one . . . click . . ." she hit the button and clapped her hands in delight. "There!"

"You've erased them?" I humored her.

"No, they've all just been auto-faxed out! Done! Cross that off the list!" Delilah has turned efficiency into an art form. Two dozen caterers have just been alerted to the great romance writer's daughter's wedding, and any moment now her cell phone would start ringing with a chorus of *"Darling!"* and *"fabulous!"*

"Stop that," I tried to shut her laptop, but a shrieking alarm went off.

"That's my system," Delilah said, shielding her laptop from my encroaching fingers. "I've had it set so that it can't be accidentally closed."

She should install such a system for her *mind*.

"Mom, this is . . ." The look stopped me. "Mother, this is crazy."

I heard Anthony drop something in the kitchen and curse loudly. Delilah pursed her lips. Only she could find him distasteful for being a real person. Donna Penks would have loved him.

"You have all the letters of interest for all your florist and catering friends ready to go," I summed up. "And you're standing here now in front of me, showing me how techno-smart you are by e-mailing experts for my wedding day."

She saw no insult in there.

"And you're telling me that you have my wedding gown selections narrowed down . . ."

"And categorized by whether it's a New York City or international designer . . ." She flipped through layers of screens, showing me an itinerary for several weeks' worth of gown shopping at the big New York salons, Vera Wang, Michelle Roth. "I had this made up, too . . . to save time."

Of course, Anthony has to come into the room and look over my shoulder as Delilah clicks one of her magical buttons to show a 3-D rotating figure of me, with my exact measurements keyed in to show almost a perfect digital likeness of me with arms held slightly out, my hair up, and a blank expression on my face. I was wearing a white strapless bra and panties, bare feet, and I spun around on a platter waiting to be virtually dressed.

Anthony laughed out loud. And I admit, I had to suppress a smile too. She'd made me into the dress-up Barbie CD-ROM. One click, I imagined, and I'm an airline pilot. Another, and I'm in haute couture with a feather boa and big, dark, Audrey Hepburn sunglasses. Virtual Emilie, the home game.

"Are you making one of those action figures out of Em?" Anthony teased. "Like they do with the professional wrestlers and the Star Wars figures?"

Delilah looked back over her shoulder without making eye contact with him. "It figures you'd make such references."

Anthony pretended to quake with fear and looked back with a smirk at Delilah's video arcade of wedding exhibitionism, featuring me. I spun on a platter! Turn me sideways, and it's Rotisserie Emilie! Ready for the basting.

"Watch," Delilah literally rubbed her hands together and clicked a series of buttons that now had me in five-second increments of display in a selection of different wedding gowns and veils. There! I'm marshmallow puff bride! Slinky sexpot bride! Vegas-wouldn't-have-me bride! Princess Diana bride! Big train, super-big train, no train. Beaded bodices, square-neck tops, lace sleeves. A-line beelines right into a sheath. I am a puppet show, a dress-up Internet doll.

There is just something so wrong with this picture.

Alarm or not, I snapped the laptop shut.

"Emilie!" Delilah cried and caressed her beloved

laptop like it was a prizewinning poodle at West-minster. "I went to a lot of trouble . . ."

"A lot of trouble is definitely the right phrasing," I lifted my chin a little. Anthony rubbed my lower back, as if my spine could use a little help from him. "This is ridiculous, Mother! We're not turning my wedding into a computer-generated virtual playroom with every wedding expert faxed and e-mailed within three seconds! This isn't how it's done!"

"This isn't how *you* do it, you mean," Delilah said and then caught herself. Better change tacks. No leg to stand on here.

"How did you get that model of Em made?" Anthony, of course, focused on the technical design aspects, missing the larger picture.

"Stop," I looked right into her aqua-colored-lens eyes. "Just stop."

And she packed up her laptop and tossed her head, forgetting that her hair was in a chignon so the usual effect wasn't there. And she marched out of our house carrying the nerve center of our wedding plans. All tucked under her arm.

"Unbelievable," I collapsed into a chair and flipped through some of the bridal magazines. *Why do all these brides look so miserable? They're all pouting and standing in positions that only scoliosis sufferers know as a comfort zone, or collapsed onto couches with their shoes half-dangling off their feet. The very picture of a post-mugging or post-traumatic stress syndrome. Dead eyes. Limp arms.*

"Yes, she is," Anthony rubbed my shoulders, which came down about two inches from top tension position, and I realized that I too had a bit of that post-mugging gray shade about me. I was slumped in my chair, and yes, my fuzzy slipper was half-dangling from my foot. "But that action figure of you is going to be amazing," he joked, and the gray was gone with one appreciative smile and one more very appreciated squeeze of my tight shoulders.

Chapter 7

This is how lawyers must feel when they know they're facing a tough case, and they're waiting for the smooth-talking opposition to sweep in with their dramatic easel and charts and laser pointers and expert witnesses dressed up in smart suits and sensible pumps. Anthony and I sat in a corner booth at the Oak Room silently sipping our cabernet, waiting for the showdown to begin. Delilah and Carmela were both running late, giving us plenty of time to whirl around imagined scenarios and preplan our comebacks and diplomatic goalie blocks to every shot they take at each other, and at us.

Carmela, we knew, could hold her own.

Delilah, despite the inches of makeup and plastic surgery beneath it, had the thinner skin. She was more fragile, thus louder and more dangerous.

"Time," I said, and he knew it was a question and not a request.

"Two-forty-five," he exhaled, watching water droplets race one another in slow motion down the stem of his wineglass. Then he started humming the theme from *Jeopardy*. I stepped on his foot under the table.

"Emilie," Delilah arrived behind us without our noticing. We missed the puff of green smoke, apparently.

"Mom," I said, sitting up straighter and trying to look as cool as ever.

"Anthony," she said and nodded her approval of his presence and his wardrobe.

"Mrs. Winchester," he stood for her seating, holding his tie back from its precarious dangle near the open mouth of his wineglass. That would have been perfect. A cabernet-soaked silk tie.

"I suppose we'll have to negotiate what you'll call me after the wedding," she said without looking at him.

Negotiate? With that, my blood went into a slow simmer. *Is this where we come up with suggestions for what to call you, because I have a few to start with.*

Anthony, ever the negotiator and corporate diplomat simply said, "Well, have your people contact my people." And he didn't crack a smile. God, I loved that man. Delilah blinked one slow blink. In my mind, I heard that Spanish soccer announcer screaming *Gooooooooooaaaaaaaal!*

Carmela arrived like a human. She clutched her standard black purse with both hands at her waist, looked admiringly at the tables and leather banquettes upon her approach, and smiled at her son as she made her way to the table. Delilah moved at that moment from her position on the banquette to the chair at the head of the table. The head chair. Somewhere, she probably heard that soccer announcer bleating for her expert chess move. Carmela didn't notice.

"Emilie, honey, hello," Carmela gave me a warm hug when I stood for her, and she reached out to squeeze her son's hand. "Delilah," Carmela attempted, no venom in her voice, a warm smile. She was trying.

"Carmela," Delilah said and held out her hand in one of those handshakes where it's the tips of fingers that touch only. Some kind of Junior League secret handshake. Carmela raised an eyebrow for just a second before lowering herself, albeit a bit ungracefully, onto the banquette next to her son.

"Thank you for coming," Anthony opened the meeting, and after ordering the mothers their drinks and leading the small talk until not one but two wines were sipped through by both, let the games begin.

"We know you both want to help with the wedding plans," I said, putting an intentional emphasis on *help*. "And you both have brought up some good suggestions already." Emphasis on *suggestions*. "So we thought it would be great to just meet for a friendly lunch and start talking about it."

I forgot to put an emphasis on the word *friendly*.

Delilah sighed and Carmela shifted on the banquette, crossed her legs again to the other side, waiting for me to continue.

"Well . . ." Where were the words? Where was that great speech I had all mapped out? A single drop of sweat ran down my lower back and I shivered a little. That was all Delilah had to see. She poised herself to speak, lifting her arm and pointing a manicured nail at Anthony, but I stopped her by barreling onward.

Goooooaaaaaaal!

"We're going to have a long engagement," I started and didn't stop. "We're thinking two years so that we can save up the money to have a beautiful wedding *and* buy our place, pay off my student loans from grad school, and *then* have plenty of time to do all the planning, check out reception halls, do all the planning and enjoy the planning." Yes, I did say the word "planning" three times in one sentence, and I didn't breathe once during it.

"So you want to be on your own?" Delilah said, relishing the threat of her words.

"No," I started. "That's not what I said—"

"That *is* what you said," Delilah huffed and pushed her wineglass away from her, ready to signal the waiter for the check.

"No, it's not what she said." Anthony looked right into her eyes on that one, strong and supportive and unmistakably fierce in my defense.

Delilah curled her lip a little and turned to me. "Does he always need to speak for you?"

It only took a moment for that to sink in, for me to meet her eyes with my own fierce defense. Carmela and Anthony froze. "Mother," I started, searching for the words. "I'm going to ask you right now to apologize both to me and to Anthony."

She looked like I slapped her.

"I'm serious," I glared at her, all business. And I saw it. Her eyes rounded, and there was Donna Penks. My old mother came out to rescue Delilah.

"You're right," she said quietly and folded her hands in her lap. She looked down at them for a moment before breathing a deep one and delivering a genuine. "I'm sorry. You're right."

Carmela looked at Anthony, who silenced her with a barely perceptible shake of his head, and

Delilah looked at me to break the unbearable quiet at the table. I just let it hover there, so they'd remember it.

"Now," I exhaled. "As I was saying . . ."

It went well. When we left the restaurant with polite hugs all around, Anthony put his arm around me to lead me into Central Park for a head-clearing walk. I didn't even see the mothers off into their own cabs but just wanted to get the hell out of there. I don't know to this day if Carmela and Delilah exchanged any chitchat as they waited for their rides, or if Delilah had a limo circling the block to await her return ride home. I don't know if they made any attempt at peace, or if they pretended each other did not exist like the rest of the anonymous crowd hurrying on the streets of New York at any given moment. I didn't know, and I didn't care. All I could think of, and celebrate, as Anthony and I walked hand in hand through the park was that I had set the foundation. Both mothers knew they were involved, but not in charge. They knew it was going to be a long wait for this wedding. They knew they'd better at least be civil to each other, and to us, if they knew what was good for them. They knew we'd be footing the bill for the wedding and so they could just forget about their family legacies and fully loaded laptop programs, the cameras from *InStyle* and the fifty relatives from Italy coming over for the big event. They knew that we, Anthony and I, were in charge, and they were going to have certain responsibilities so they could be a *part* of the plans, not in charge of the plans. They would not steamroll, cajole, blackmail, emotionally sabotage, level, or guilt-trip their way into anything.

And that was that.

Period.

The next day, my mother suggested that we go to Vera Wang just to look around, and I said Yes. She offered to pay off my student loans and give us the full down payment for our house as a wedding present if she could just have a *little* bit more to do with the wedding. "It's just a suggestion," she said before hanging up her phone and strutting back out through the French doors of her estate and lying back down by the pool in her white bathing suit and waist wrap, slipping her black sunglasses onto her nose, picking up her vodka-spiked iced tea and smiling up into the sun while I sat there mute in New Jersey with the cordless phone sitting like a dead bird in my hand. And for my mother, that Spanish soccer game sportscaster yelled, *"Gooooaaaaaaaaal!"*

Chapter 8

I am a wimp.

I am definitely a wimp, but I am a wimp who is trying on wedding gowns and veils at Vera Wang. I am a stylish wimp. I am a fashionable wimp. I am a complete sellout, but I look *incredible*.

Delilah had called ahead to Vera Wang to let them know we were on our way, and we were greeted by three smiling fashionettes who not only knew my name but spoke to me like we were old college roommates. Delilah had e-mailed a dozen pre-picks from Vera's gown line—hopefully not the rotisserie version of me on CD-ROM with various Vera wear on—and the fashionettes had already pulled each of them in my size and had them displayed—spotlit, even—in a wide, mirrored palace of a dressing room. I could practically hear Delilah purring in the background as I stepped from dress to dress, letting my fingers brush barely against the silk and illusion netting, the beaded bodices and crisscross straps. *These are real Vera Wangs!*

I caught my own expression in the mirror—how could I not since we were surrounded with them—and saw the same slack-jawed expression and wide-eyed awe that Anthony had the time he met Michael Jordan. If Vera Wang herself had walked into the showroom, I might literally have passed out. The fashionettes disappeared for a moment. I'd assume they enjoy seeing the dumbstruck look on future brides' faces just being in the same room with a Vera Wang, and I could imagine them imitating the dopey eyes and twitches of the badly acclimated like myself. They returned all smiling and chipper, with their jet black hair perfectly parted down the middle as if with a ruler, their eyebrows done to perfected arches, makeup flawless, manicures flawless, and—as I unfortunately noticed as one bent over to move a pair of strappy white try-on sandals out of the way—apparently wearing very good lingerie. The bender wore a G-string with its unmistakable flash of skin below the string. The other arrived balancing a silver platter on her too-tiny hand, offering both Delilah and me a glass of champagne with a single raspberry in the bottom of each glass. Leave it to Vera.

And with my first sip, I was initiated into the sisterhood of the Wang. My mother had never been so proud. I was finally moving toward her end of the spectrum.

"Hmmmm." One of the fashionettes took a stance in front of me, jutted out one bony hip and brought her knuckle to her lips. With one wave of her hand, which I inexplicably understood as a message to spin slowly in place, she proceeded to catalog me. "She has to take it off," she said.

"Excuse me?"

"The top. Take off the top," Fashionette Number 1 waved circular motions that reminded me of a belly dancer's handwork.

Okay, this was a dressing room, not a hidden camera show, so I peeled off my top. Despite worrying that the fashionettes and my mother would notice that my bra was not designer, I stood taller, sucked in my stomach a little bit, and waited for my next command. As expected, "Zee bottom off," from Fashionette Number 2. Off came the skirt, which left me in my bra and panties (no G-string, thank God) and black socks, which I stripped off of my own accord. I was now a slowly spinning underwear model, having assumed exactly the same position and appearance as on my mother's spooky CD-ROM. Rotisserie Emilie. This was definitely something the fashionettes laughed about afterward. It was perhaps their humiliation payback to all the "princesses" who could afford to shop here. As long as I wasn't spinning in my underwear like this with a Pomeranian tucked under my arm and cradled like a baby, I was okay.

"Good shoulders." Fashionette Number 1 still had her knuckle at her lips, and I noticed she had smudged some of her ruby red lip gloss onto her front tooth. Which gave me some satisfaction. I'll analyze you right back. "Good back. She lifts weights, no?"

"Yes," my mother said, without knowing if I did or not.

"We have to do somesing about zee skin," Number 2 said, pushing at each blemish or beauty mark she found as if she was ringing a doorbell.

Number 3 stood to the back with a creepy smile on her face and no helpful analysis.

"Okay, zee skin needs zee help." Number 2 whipped out a BlackBerry and made notes with a pointer. "Arms, they are good. Hold out your arms, dear."

I did as instructed and held my arms out to the side. She flicked the bottom of my upper arm and looked mortified that a little pooch of skin there actually moved.

"I wasn't flexing," I heard myself cry out.

Notes were made on the BlackBerry.

Hey, where's the royal treatment I'm supposed to get here?

"Waist is good."

What? No calipers so you can measure and announce my body fat percentage?

"Hips are good."

My mother looked proud on that one, and she may even have said "Thank you." I'm not sure. By this time, with my head spinning in the opposite direction of my body, I wasn't doing much listening.

"Legs are good, but they are not seen."

The silent and eerily aroused Number 3 in the back of the room chose this moment to speak up. "Lift her hair," she said, and did her own version of the belly dancer's hand swirl. And in a moment, 1 and 2 had pulled my loose hair up into a pile on top of my head, which allowed Number 3 to simply go, "Hmmmmmm" and then leave the room.

"Can I try on a dress now, or do you want to take a Pap test too?" I snapped.

Once the air cleared of my outburst—which doubled Leah over and made her fall off the couch when I told her about it later—I was allowed near the gowns. Number 1 helped me slide the delicate silk sheaths over my head, or helped

me step into a zip-up ball gown, adjusted the illusion netting across my chest or along my arms,
arranged the beaded crisscrosses when I was about
to get tangled in them. And just generally made
me look a bit more graceful during the stages of
dress and undress. More so for their own comfort
than mine.

I twirled, I floated, I walked on my toes to watch
the skirts swish and to see how that sheath fit my
back view. I stood between opposing mirrors to see
myself coming and going at the same time. Number 3 would probably have dipped me if I'd asked
her to, in order to see how I'd look dancing in this
particular dress with my husband. All of them felt
wonderful on, but where was that electric message
you're supposed to get when it's The One? An old
saying goes, "When your mother cries over the
dress you have on, that's the one." *Well, I'm screwed,
because my mother never cries.*

Dress Number 11 and dress Number 12 were on
and off, and still no electric tingle. No tears came
to my eyes. And then came lucky Number 13. Fashionette Number 3 walked into the room with a big
white bag, unzipped it, and gently uncoccooned a
dress that shot electricity throughout the room. It
had a fully beaded bodice, a princess neckline that
angled down to show my bare back in a sexy
plunge, a straight silk skirt with a tiny and undra-
matic train. "Once I saw the back of your neck, I
knew which one was for you," Number 3 said.

Numbers 1 and 2 busied my mother, who was
visibly agitated that this renegade dress was not on
her original list. I could hear them cooing at her,
feeding her her lines: "Doesn't she look beeee-you-
tiful?" and Delilah had to agree or suffer the
image of not having "in" tastes for fashion. That's

when she squeezed out a few tears, but those were probably only because Number 3 deprived her of being able to tell her seven hundred closest friends and Katie Couric that *she* chose my wedding gown.

As Delilah dabbed her eyes and turned away, I watched her in the mirror. She was definitely not holding it together. Five minutes ago, she sat straight-backed with her legs folded under her properly, sipping at her champagne, and now she was turned in her seat to hide her face as best she could being surrounded by mirrors, digging through her purse for some Visine, and pushing the tears back into her eyes with the sides of her fingers. She turned then, and smiled. Donna Penks was there. Just a little bit, but my mother was there. For a second.

"Emilie, you look beautiful," she said, and that's when I lost it. Numbers 1, 2 and 3 dived at me to remove the gown before I got tear stains, mascara or lipstick on it. As they stripped me, I sobbed. And I hadn't even seen the price tag yet.

In fact, I never saw the price tag at all. Delilah had it all taken care of by the time I put all my original clothes back on and checked out my own back to see just how bad a skin problem I had back there. "Thank you," I said to Number 3, who I now understood as the silent one who knows more than the other two combined.

"You're very welcome," she said and shook my hand. "You're going to be a beautiful bride."

I smiled and felt much better then about selling my soul for a Vera Wang wedding gown. I'm sure anyone in my place would do the same thing.

"Happy now?" Delilah pushed open the doors and led me out into the sunshine of an October afternoon in the city. And I got a little chill. Must have been the air.

Anthony didn't know anything about this little deal with my mother yet. That was coming.

On the train headed back home, that short hop on the PATH, I felt like Diane Lane in *Unfaithful*. What I'd just done came at me in waves. For one second, I was giddy and excited, and then my eyes changed. Self-loathing. Guilt. Fear of being found out. Then some pride that I looked so great in those gowns and my Pilates classes were paying off. Then some more guilt and dread. No one was going to hand me an Oscar nomination for my performance today, but the dress . . . the Vera Wang dress . . . it was gold to me.

Chapter 9

"Why are you so happy?" Anthony moved my hair out of his eyes as I leaned over him from the back. He was reading on the couch, wearing red plaid cotton pajama bottoms that only he could carry off as sexy because he has a great chest and defined abs. His glasses were low on his nose, knocked lower by my chin with my bad aim and my need to just be close to him.

"No reason," I said. "Just glad to be home."

He lifted his arm and cradled it around my head, let me kiss his temple, down the side of his cheek to his jaw, giving me that great "mmmmm" he does when I'm hitting the right spots. Which means it's time for the ear. I know his body like a map. I know every part of him and how each part responds, that he likes the insides of his elbows lightly dragged by my fingernails. He likes the side of his neck kissed with an open mouth and not just with my lips. He loves it when I flutter my eyelashes on his cheek.

And he can always tell when I'm doing all of the above because I'm on a mission.

"Hon?" he said, in something of a moan, I was doing it all so well.

"Mmmm?" I said, climbing over the couch to drape myself across his lap and close my lips over his top lip.

"What did you do?" he said with a smile in his voice. He knew.

"Hmmmm?" Keeping it nonverbal and going for his ear would do the trick, I thought.

He laughed out loud, which couldn't offend me like a game-playing girlfriend, because we both knew I was busted. "What did you do, Em?"

I played along, because I had no other choice. He knew me like a map too. "What makes you think I did something wrong?" I laughed my answer and looked, to him, adorably guilty.

"Because it's Tuesday."

I laughed.

"And because you usually check your messages before jumping on me."

I brought my hands up over my chin and my mouth, laughing still, leaning into his chest as I giggled through my own ridiculousness.

"Did you crash the car?" he asked, still amused.

"No."

"Bounce a check?"

"No." Still playing coy, going almost as far as twirling my hair around my finger, but I'm not the typical bimbo-esque manipulator. I could never pull that look off.

"Did you sell out to your mother because she offered to pay for the wedding, your student loans, our house and a designer wedding gown?" he said right into my ear, then grabbed me in a playful and loving tight hug. I yelled out in delight and relief and love and confession. He saved me from having to say it to him.

Once his kiss let me breathe again, I managed to sputter, "How did you find out?"

Now it was his turn to work *me*. "I have my ways."

"Come on," I poked him in the ribs, then straddled him. "How did you find out? Did Leah tell you?"

"Leah knew?" Anthony nodded, impressed with Leah's restraint.

I nodded. "And your answer would be . . . ?"

"Your mother made the offer to me too," he said. "Except for the gown part."

I blinked. Wow, Delilah was good.

"And you said . . . ?"

Anthony sighed and looked to the ceiling, bringing his hands up to clasp behind his head. Then brought his hands down again so as not to hasten his imaginary hair loss. "I took the deal before you did," he confessed. "I wanted you to have the nice wedding, and get your debts paid without working your butt off, get us a house, set us up."

This was a very strange version of the *Gift of the Magi*, only without hair loss and watches. Instead we had Vera Wang dresses and . . . well, imaginary hair loss. My eyes teared up, which is also a strange reaction to the fact that we now had proof that both my future husband and I were willing to sell our souls to my mother for money.

"You put up with a lot with your mother, and you supported her for a long time," he explained. "You don't live off her wealth, which a lot of people would, and you haven't sold out to her lifestyle. That's why I love you so much."

His eyes are the warmest and most soulful I've ever seen.

"So I took a shot and told her yes, I'd work on you," he sighed. "Just because I wanted you to get something in return."

"And . . . ?"

"And because there was no way we were ever going to stop your control freak mother from trying to run the wedding," he laughed. "No way at all."

"I know," I shook my head, beaming and kissed him again. "That's why I took the deal. She'll never change."

"Well, that's how you're alike," he said. "You have that quality too."

I sat up, a bit shaken by the comparison.

"I mean," he saved himself. "You're both strong women . . . but you have the ability to think of others. And you're not going to change that."

He pulled me in close to him and held me in those big arms. I listened to his heartbeat. Heaven. The safest place on earth. And I thought about what he said, wishing he had gotten the chance to meet Donna Penks. To know how much like her I am. Why my mother killed her off is a mystery to me. Why she doesn't let Donna Penks out more often, like she did for a second today, is also a mystery to me.

But Donna Penks was quickly floated out of my mind when Anthony started mapping me with his hands, with open mouth kisses, brushes of his lips and flutters of his eyelashes on my stomach. And we were lost to the world of weddings and everything else for hours and hours.

Chapter 10

Smoke filled the apartment from knee-high level to the ceiling.

"Leah?" I called into the opaque gray fog, squinting my eyes from the burning scent of sandalwood. "Leah!"

"Over here," Leah was already by the window, fanning some of the smoke outside with one of my bridal magazines in one hand and a paper plate in the other.

This was beyond ridiculous. I bumped the dining room table with my hip and did a double step to move toward her. "That's enough with the incense already, Leah," I said without my usual understanding. Pyromania is not an acceptable form of mourning for a loser fiancé with bad taste in "the other woman."

"I know," she whimpered. "And I know I promised."

The air started to clear just enough for me to see tears in her eyes.

"He called today," she said, then stopped fanning and stooped down to rest her hands on her knees, hung her head and shook it from side to side in defeat.

Hearing his voice was the last thing she needed. She was just starting to come back, and with one of his hellos she was back to square one.

"Did you talk to him?"

"No, he left a message," she sniffled. "Why?" was all she asked.

"Why did he call?" I tried.

"No, why wasn't I here when he did?" she gurgled, choking back tears and probably choking a bit on the smoke.

"Okay," I said, then took her by the arm to lift her back up to her size. "So you're burning the incense to . . . accomplish what?"

She didn't answer.

"Leah, the smoke thing . . . it's not going to accomplish anything," I tried to be gentle, but I have a dry cleaner bill that's sky-high to get all those mystical scents out of my drapes and jackets. The light-a-match-adjust-the-universe train of thought has just pulled into its last station.

"I know," she whispered. "I just wanted to get rid of his . . ."

Energy, I know.

"Leah, the only thing that's going to help is for you to move past it," I clicked on the table fan, reached over and pulled a dryer sheet from the Bounce box on the table, and laid it across the back grate of the fan. An old college dorm trick to remove the smell of smoke. It works rather well. "So get your coat, and let's go walk down by the water." I tried a smile and couldn't pull the same from her. "Come on, let's go get a drink, see if the firemen are playing softball at the park."

If "firemen playing softball" didn't work, then it was time to call a doctor for her.

It registered. She needed just a second to imagine the guys from the station in their blue shirts, gray shorts showing that great curve of their muscles just above their knees, the way they'd pull up the bottoms of their T-shirts to wipe the sweat from their foreheads, thus exposing their stomachs. If you have an ounce of estrogen, that alone can put you in a better mood.

"Come on, let's go," I smiled and playfully squeezed her shoulder. "If we go now, we might catch them stretching out before the game."

"Okay," she said, but it only came out as "K." She grabbed her knapsack and pushed it back across her ribs with her elbow, keeping it tight against her. We walked the nine blocks downtown, passing the pottery store, the dress shops, the outdoor cafés packed with eight-to-a-table revelers and their bright red frozen margaritas, with their dogs on leashes tied to the terrace gates, waiting for a charity-tossed tortilla chip or a chunk of burger thrown by its owner. Kids Rollerbladed past us, deaf to the world with their headphones on. Motorcycle cops ticketed the line of double-parkers, and the music from the pubs spilled out onto the street. The pulse of Hoboken.

We turned the corner at 5th, wound through the playground, then took the steps down to the waterfront park. With the sun beginning to set, the water glistened in dancing gold crescents, the city skyline across the Hudson was clear and unclouded, reflecting the yellows and golds of the setting sun. Kayakers were just pushing off from the rocky shoreline, shifting to find their balance and synchronizing their red paddles. Somewhere above, a kite danced in the sky, but I couldn't quite trace the line back down to the ground. Sunbathers and readers lounged on towels and short beach chairs to soak up the last rays of the day, and—as hoped—the firemen's softball team was just warming up.

"God bless the person who invented hamstring stretches is all I have to say," I joked, nudging Leah, and she grimaced a smile. I took my first step onto the bleachers, waving at someone I recognized across the way, and Leah was not behind me.

"I just need a second," Leah said, squeezing out a quiver-lipped smile, and she walked away quickly with her knapsack still hugged tightly to her. I feigned "no concern," waved her on, but watched closely as she walked down the promenade to the railing overlooking the water and stood there for a second. I tilted my head and squinted into the yellow glare of the sun. *If you jump from there, it's about six feet to the water level and about six feet deep. Diving boards are higher than that. I, of course, was surprised by my own callousness.*

Leah unzipped her knapsack and pulled out what looked like two balls. No, they were oranges. Or grapefruit. Something big. Either balls or fruit. And she hauled back and threw them into the river. One at a time, with a pretty impressive windup and some serious arm-power. Even one of the firemen who happened to be looking her way made a comment about having Leah pitch for them instead of the, and I quote, "fucker who's up there right now, right, Eddie? The dumb 'fucka who couldn't hit the side of the station with a ball." What a charmer, that one. I silently thanked God for Anthony.

Leah padded back, seemingly cheered by her

launch of whatever it was she just contributed to the collection of whatever it is sitting at the bottom of the Hudson River. I happened to know that her engagement ring was one of those things resting at the bottom of the Hudson. A watery grave for a useless trinket, she had said. Never mind that the trinket was a $6,000 ring from Tiffany, but it was worth more to her down at the bottom of the river. I didn't even question that choice of hers. I'd have probably done the same thing.

And I watched for it. I watched the firemen and their opponents, the players both on and off the field, check Leah out with her every step. They watched her coming and going, from the front to the back view. Her black hair swinging over the top of her shoulders, her long legs leading up to her stylishly faded and frayed-edged denim shorts. They nudged each other and nodded to their friends that they, too, should take a look at the "in-coming." I saw it, but she was oblivious to her fans on the field.

"Hey," I said when she climbed up the aluminum bleachers to sit one level below me. I moved my purse to give her room.

"They start yet?"

"No."

I tried to let it go. I really did. But I had to . . .

"So what was that you just tossed in the drink?" I asked, tilting my head and smiling. Nonjudgmental.

"Nothing," she answered. Noncommittal.

Whatever it was, it seemed to brighten her a bit, and the players took the field.

Chapter 11

"**S**o, we meet again."

It was an inauspicious start to yet another attempted group meeting about the wedding. Carmela and Vic took their seats across from Anthony and me, and, of course, my mother took the chair at the head of the table, as was her custom.

"This is the restaurant where Anthony and I had our first date," I beamed my announcement to our parents, who nodded their approval and looked around at the décor and the flowers in bud vases on the tables, the candles in their glass holders, artwork on the walls.

"It's all about the atmosphere," Anthony kidded. "With the right lighting, she's quite beautiful." He winked and I wrinkled my nose back at him with a smile. Under the table, he gave my hand a squeeze.

"Okay, small talk's over," I announced, morphing into CEO mode and getting ready to lead the discussions. The parents adjusted their positions, either folded their hands on the table or brought their drinks up to their mouths. I'll give you one guess who had the drink, by the way. "We've talked it over, and we've decided that planning this wedding will be a team effort."

Please don't say anything about The Deal, Mother. Please.

"We have our wedding date picked out already, we know where it's going to be—"

"Are you getting married in a church?" Carmela bleated, her eyes wide, like she'd been dying to get that out of her system since Minute One.

Anthony and I looked at each other. We thought we'd get a little further before the controversies started flaring up. "Um . . ." I shuffled through my notes. "We haven't decided that yet."

Actually, we had. We wanted to get married outside under a willow tree in Central Park.

"How can you plan the reception before the ceremony?" Vic shot out, all of a sudden the Italian Colin Cowie.

"Dad, we're still working on the details," Anthony tried.

"And you skip the first thing? The most important thing?"

Carmela started to cry. First a sniffle, then a sob. Her son and his future wife are heathens.

"See the pain you cause to your mother?" Vic pushed at Anthony's hand on the table, and Anthony stiffened, gave him a "don't go there" look.

"No church wedding?!" Carmela sobbed. And we hadn't even gotten to the menu yet. That's where my money was for the mother of all wedding battles as far as Carmela was concerned. But God took precedence over the cannoli.

Delilah sat silently through this one. Not a

churchgoer. No vote. As long as there would be good lighting for the cameras, we could get married anywhere.

I looked at Anthony, panicked, and mouthed "change the subject."

"Okay, we'll think about the church wedding," was what came out of his mouth. He is either a bad lip-reader, or I still have some work to do on the Mamma's Boy thing. But who am I kidding? I caved in to my mother for a gown. "We'll have to find some sort of compromise."

Carmela stopped crying on the spot. Her red nose the only evidence that it had happened. She smiled properly again and lifted her eyebrows to wait for the next topic. It was the only time in my entire history of knowing the woman that I silently called her a bitch. So the waterworks are the key, lady? Vic looked proud at his effectiveness, bending his thick knuckles under to give the table a sharp knock. Code for "what can we help you with next?"

"Um . . . uh . . ." I blanked, shuffling through my papers and my index cards, each with a different task written out on them, plus notes on what we must have, what other ideas we have in mind, and what's a definite No for each category. Sometimes I am too like my mother.

"What are those, Emilie?" my mother spoke up for the first time, jutting her chin—the perfect angle for her new heart-shaped face—toward the pack of purple 3x5 cards in my hand.

"They're all the things we have to plan for the wedding, like . . ." I flipped through them, fanned them. "The wedding cake, the music, the photographer . . . the things we want . . . just to keep us organized."

On the word *organized,* my mother lifted an eyebrow. My system versus her computerized and mail merging system? No comparison. This was absolutely Cro-Magnon level to her. She hadn't seen an index card in years and probably thought they stopped making them in the 90s.

"We thought we'd start by—" Anthony attempted to bring up the first topic . . . the reception hall.

"Let me see those," Carmela pounced and grabbed the entire stack of cards from my hands. Mugged again.

"Here!" Delilah snatched a handful of cards from her, and Vic came to his wife's defense by snatching three or four back from Delilah. Anthony and I sat back in our chairs at the same time. We listened to *tsks* and sighs as they read over our notes, watched squints as Delilah attempted to read my handwriting. (*Didn't they teach you cursive in school? This looks like an architect's handwriting, dear!*)

Vic started the game and quickly moved to leading it. We sat by, stunned into silence for the first few minutes of what became a wedding version of the action on the floor of the stock market . . .

"Cake, I don't give a thud about the cake."

"I'll trade you the cake for the flowers."

"And have rows of funeral wreaths lining the aisles? No thank you. I'm doing the flowers. And I'll take the cake too."

"Listen, lady . . ." Vic jumped from a well-placed nudge under the table, either a nudge from Carmela or a kick from Anthony.

"Photographer and videographer are mine," Delilah snapped those cards out of Carmela's hands. "I already have it booked."

"Well, then unbook it. My cousin Jimmy's gonna do the pictures." Only it came out *pitchers*, which did not escape Delilah's sensitive ears. I flinched on that one a little bit too.

"Cousin *Jimmy* can take his own candids. I have a professional."

"I'm sure you do." Now it was Carmela sneering. This was getting ugly.

"Who wants limousines?"

No takers.

"Nobody wants limousines? Fine, then the kids can go in the minivan . . ."

Anthony was in the game now. He grabbed for the limousines card, and he was now dealt in. "Give me the wedding night accommodations," he pushed his sleeves up. All that was missing was a cigar and a bag of chips on the table.

"Favors?"

"You can do the favors. Just no inscribed wineglasses, please."

"If I'm going to inscribe something, you don't want to read it."

"As long as you spell it right, you can inscribe anything you'd like."

"Inscribe *this!*"

Anthony slapped his hand down on the table to both shut up the bickering parents and claim rights to the bar menu.

"Rentals you can have . . ."

"Table linens is mine."

"I get the band."

"No, I have that one right here . . ."

I found my voice. "That's ceremony musicians on that card, Mother, and you, Carmela, have the reception musicians. It's different."

"I'll take both musicians then, and you can have

the officiant's fee," Delilah wangled. "It *is* the most important part of the day, right?" Carmela accepted the sucker deal and Delilah now held all the good cards.

Or *did* she? Carmela was a smart cookie. She had been doing the equivalent of counting cards, that slick little player. Delilah held a stack of cards in her hand—everything from the flowers to the cake to the musicians, the linens, the crystal, the doves for after the ceremony. Carmela, by contrast, held only a few. Good leverage to get the one she *really* wanted. The reception menu.

"Where is the reception menu?" she asked, lifting up the napkins on the table, pushing silverware out of the way to search for the missing purple card that granted her full domain over the menu for the cocktail hour, the reception, and the dessert table. The food was to be *hers*. Anyone who said otherwise might get cut. That's how fierce she was about it, and Vic would definitely back her up and lie about it in court.

"Here, Mom," Anthony said and handed the card to her, the good son. Delilah and I both rolled our eyes, she more obviously than I. *What a good boy you are, little Anthony.*

Carmela gave him an air kiss across the table, and Vic looked proud. *That's my son.* He had just "beaten" a romance novelist and an advertising executive in a heated game of bridal poker to win the most expensive portion of the entire wedding budget. Good work, Junior.

And in the heat of the fight, no one noticed until after we paid the bill and stood to leave that one card remained on the table: *Write wedding vows.*

* * *

We walked out of there slightly icy toward one another and very icy toward our guests. We never even ordered dinner. It was two drinks, the dealing of the cards, and coffee and espresso. With all the fuss over the food for the wedding, none of us wanted food for that meal.

As we walked back home, I asked Anthony, "So which cards did we wind up with for the wedding of *our* dreams that *we* were supposed to plan with *their* help."

"We got the limos," he said. "And the portable toilets for the outdoor wedding location in the park, if we need them."

"Cars and toilets," I spat. "Perfect."

We were the worst negotiators ever. In the business world, we were aces. Sitting at a table with our parents, we were weenies. Now my part of putting together my dream wedding would consist of going from car lot to car lot to watch Anthony look under the hoods of a dozen Rolls-Royces, Bentleys, stretch Humvees, and probably a classic Camaro or two. And don't forget the highly glamorous job of going shopping for portable toilets. It's my dream come true.

Chapter 12

"The cards are out," I stormed into Delilah's office and gathered up the purple index cards. It wasn't even an hour after the Big Poker Game, and I'd changed my mind and hopped a train to her place.

"What?" Delilah stepped back and I grabbed the index cards and stepped away from her active and humming laptop.

"We changed our minds," I shrugged.

"You can't do that," she snapped. "A deal is a deal."

"Oh, a deal is a deal? Would you like to hear about *my* deal?" I stepped toward her slowly, one step after another, and she joined the dance of intimidation by stepping back, one step after another, her hand guiding her along the top of her desk. "In that little trading card playoffs today, would you like to know which jobs for the wedding that *we* get to do? Huh? *Would you?*"

Delilah could have called the police right then

and been close to right about my being "a menacing stranger."

"We got cars and toilets! Cars and toilets, Mother!" I screamed, my face turning red. I could see myself in the mirror on the credenza, and I was not looking very "radiant bride" right then.

"So, fine," she came back calm and airily, opening her palms out to me. "Take whichever jobs you want. Do you want the cake?"

What I said right then I don't even want to think about now. But you can imagine what I came out with.

Chapter 13

"Em? You asleep?" Anthony's voice came from the darkness on the other side of the bed.

"No," I exhaled and turned my head on the pillow to face him. My pillow smelled like sage, courtesy of Leah's incense fixation.

"Sorry about today," he said quietly.

I said nothing.

"That didn't go well."

The man is a genius.

"So what do you think?" He tried again to get me talking.

"I think we're going to have serious problems when we have kids."

He laughed. A better sign. "No, seriously. How are we going to work this? Your mother has to be involved, my parents . . ."

"*Us* . . ." I reminded him.

"Of course us." He reached for my hand under the covers and I let him take it. His finger rubbed the top of my hand in circles.

"I don't know how to make this work," I confessed, glad for the darkness to keep my one falling tear a complete secret from him.

"Stick with letting them use the cards? Just get a few good ones for ourselves?"

This is ridiculous. This is not Deal a Wedding.

"They hate each other," my voice cracked. "Our parents, they hate each other."

He couldn't argue.

"Maybe I'm the only one looking *past* the wedding to our future, but I can't see them ever getting along. And I don't know why they hate each other so much."

"I know."

"They have no personal conflict, no problem between them."

"It's the classism, Em."

The financial whiz always goes for the money answer. It's because my mother is rich and his parents are not.

"Their bad attitudes have a lot to do with it. Where is that coming from?"

"It's how they are. Nothing we can do about it."

"Hmmmm." It was an answer without agreeing.

"You can't make them like each other, Em."

"I know."

He now rubbed circles up my arm, and I hooked my leg over his.

"Maybe having them work on the wedding plans together would get them to bond?" I tried, and Anthony snorted out a laugh that shook the bed.

"Are you kidding? They'd kill each other!" He should have left it at that, but he took the step too far. "Your mother can be a bitch, but my mother can zing you without you even knowing about it."

Huh?! So his mother is a Stealth Bitch?

He couldn't see my face, but he must have felt it change. "I mean . . ."

"No," I patted his hand, which was a more polite way of getting him to stop touching me in those circles, which were only going to move upward and inward. "I have to figure out a way to make this work. It shouldn't be this difficult." I took a breath and crossed my arms over my stomach. "It shouldn't be this hard. It's a *wedding*."

He didn't say a thing. He didn't have to, because we were both thinking the same thing. It's *us*. We're not leading it right. We're giving in, staying quiet, then exploding later. And our parents are sleeping fine, probably.

"I need to walk," I heard myself say. "By the water, I need to walk."

Anthony propped himself up on his elbows. "Now? Em, it's late."

"It's twelve-thirty. The bars are still open. There will be people everywhere," I patted his chest and threw back the covers.

"Want me to come with you?" he offered, and I stopped where I now stood next to the bed.

He thinks I'm upset with him. "Yeah, I would like that."

Go down to the waterfront at the park at night, and you'll see couples on their first date, extending the hours, not wanting the date to end, walking along the water holding hands or making out by the railing overlooking the city. You'll see drunk kids stumbling through the park to make it to the train station before the last train out, stopping every few feet to straighten their path or throw up into the grass, with their less drunk friends either holding their hair back or pointing and laughing. And you'll see the moon over the city. That's why I go there. And this night, the moon was full, with just a thin layer of cloud slicing through it.

Anthony and I walked silently, identifiable as an established couple by the fact that we were in our sweats and my hair was up in a messy ponytail. We are the sloppy version of an in-love couple. We are the future appearance of that well-dressed couple celebrating the success of their first, or second, date over there on the bench with their faces suction-locked. Glimpse your future, kids.

And then I saw her. At the end of the promenade, leaning over the railing. Looking like she was trying to reach out and touch that abandoned old sailboat that someone left moored out there just off the pier.

Leah.

I just started to run toward her. Dropped Anthony's hand and ran. Five steps into it, I stopped. *What the hell is she doing?*

Leah stood on the bottom railing, leaning out and delivering a mighty and distant toss to something round. It sailed over the dancing slivers of silver on the river's surface and plopped into the water a good distance out. Whatever it was, it didn't make much of a splash.

"Is that Leah over there?" Anthony caught on. "What is she doing? Throwing rocks?"

"I have no idea. Leah!"

Leah stepped back, ran her hands down her jacket to straighten it after that cannon of a throw.

"What did you just throw?" I came right up to face her.

"Nothing," she said, a very bad liar. She looked right down to the ground.

"I saw you throw something, and I've seen it before," I nodded. "Anthony, would you go get us some coffee?" I asked without looking at him, and he knew enough to just go to the park's café without question. Leah would never open up in front of him.

"It was nothing," she tried again, this time kicking a flattened cigarette butt away from her foot.

"Leah, come on."

"All right," she stood taller, defiant. Strange, but taking the strong stance. "I know you're going to think I'm crazy, but it was an orange."

I blinked. *An orange? She came down to the park after midnight to throw an orange into the river.*

"And this is one of your . . . ?" What would be the right word to use? Rituals?

Leah chewed on her bottom lip for a moment, also trying to find the words. "It's a Chinese ritual."

Ritual. I was right.

"On the full moon, you're supposed to throw the biggest, most ripe orange you can find into a large body of water." It made perfect sense to her.

"And this would accomplish . . . what?"

"It's a good luck ritual," she crossed her arms. "Any maiden who tosses the orange into the body of water is supposed to attract her perfect suitor."

Okay, no one talks like that. That's right out of whatever handbook she's studying right now, or from some New Age guru, her acupuncturist, someone else. Leah, pre-meltdown, would never have referred to herself as a "maiden." *Who are you, and what have you done with Leah?*

"Leah . . ."

"Say whatever you want, Em," she shook her head. "Who does it hurt?"

And she turned and walked away. I had a few moments before Anthony returned with the coffee, just enough time to think about how I avoid walking under ladders. Who does it hurt?

"What was she throwing?"

He made me jump.

"Em? What was she throwing?" Anthony asked, and I gave him a you-don't-want-to-know shake of my head.

"The good news is . . ." I did a little drumroll with my hands on my lap for a flourish. "She's stopped with the superstitions that are supposed to make her ex break out in boils and have his penis fall off before birds come to peck his eyes out."

A smirk grew across his lips. "Well, that's a good thing."

"Progress, right?" I nodded, feeling just a bit guilty about my mocking nature. The woman was in pain.

"Definitely progress. So she's throwing out reminders of him? His socks? Movie stubs?"

"She's throwing oranges."

"Oranges?" Anthony wrinkled his forehead. "Was her ex from Florida?"

I burst out in a laugh that spilled coffee on my sweats—no problem, they're sweats—and caused the makeout couple on the other bench to turn around to check if I was laughing at them. *Go about your business, kids.*

Chapter 14

"Mr. Garrity, I assure you that the pitch is on target, and we're doing the boards right now . . ." I drummed my pen on my desk and rolled my eyes. Mr. Garrity is the reason I have this corner office and the 14th Street two-bedroom with the terrace and the fitness center. But he's also the biggest control freak on earth. None of the other chiefs wanted to take his account, simply because he was the type to recross your T's and redot your I's and then tell you that you forgot to do that. He also speaks in jingles and clichés only. Very annoying.

No one could handle him, but I apparently remind him of his daughter. So he adores me, and I adore the $6 million our firm drags out of him each year. I know how to speak to him, usually delivering jingles and clichés right back at him. That package we just sent out is "something special in the air" on its way to him. He loves that. "We work hard so you don't have to." That is the Scrubbing Bubbles motto, but he hears it as a business deal.

Just know your commercials, and you're all set
with him.

"Yes, Mr. Garrity . . . I understand. I'll just do it,"
I said and had to smile at my assistant, Meg, who
poked her head through the door. "Yes, sir. We'll
leave the light on for you."

And with that, I hung up. We could have gone on
for hours, trading jingles that apply to his flight
into New York next week. I shook my head and
whistled a relief sign to Meg.

"There's a Mrs. Cantano here to see you, Emilie." I told her on day one to call me Emilie, which
is better because Meg is five years older than I am.

"Anthony's mother?" I said aloud, scrambling to
slide my feet back into my shoes and stand up to
straighten out my skirt. Also gave myself a shot of
breath spray.

"And she has a . . . guest with her."

"A guest?"

Meg sucked a smile back in and turned around
to go get them. I swiped a pile of Post-its into my
top desk drawer, the usual protocol when your
boss or your future mother-in-law are about to
drop in for a surprise inspection. I rested my hand
on the top of my chair, then tried out the I'm-busy-
at-my-desk seated position, and not satisfied with
the poise of that one, I chose instead to slip my
pen behind my ear and look busy.

"Right this way," I heard Meg say. "Mrs. Cantano
. . . Father . . ."

Father?

And in walked Carmela in a demure black
sweater and black skirt, followed shortly behind by
a very tall and very bony priest with sunken eyes
and a comb-over.

"Carmela." I stood to go hug her, but I didn't

take my eyes off the priest. "Father . . ." I shook his hand. Cold, as expected. And bony, as expected. Firmer handshake than I expected.

"Is there a problem?" I rolled the *pr* in problem.

"No, I'm not here to deliver last rites," Shecky the priest doubled himself over and Carmela laughed in appropriate deference to him. I nervously giggled, and Meg stayed for the show. The girls in the outer office were dying to know why a priest has stopped in to see Ms. Penks. The church is having image problems these days, but hire an ad executive?

"Emilie, I was just talking to Father Justin here . . ."

Father Justin?

"And we'd like to speak with you about how important it is to have your wedding mass in a church." Carmela gave no hint of being nervous. The Lord was with her.

Meg told me later that my jaw was slack and my tongue was visible. Dead eyes, she said.

"Excuse me?" Suddenly my mouth went dry. Must get water.

"Having your marriage sacrament blessed under the eyes of God is simply the most advantageous way to begin a future as a God-loving couple," Father Justin was not going for "funny" anymore. At least not intentionally.

This was sure to go on my permanent record, but I thought that God or St. Peter or whoever keeps the Big Book of Your Screwups would actually applaud me for throwing my future mother-in-law and Father Justin out of my office. I am not an atheist. I am a Christian. But I am a Christian with a job and a big dislike of anyone who brings a scary man of the cloth into my workplace to try to muscle me into having my wedding her way. I could imagine her stirring a pot of bubbling and splattering gravy this morning and coming up with "she can't say no with a priest in the room, right?"

"With all due respect," I began, which is code for I'm about to slap you down. "My fiancé and I would appreciate the respect and the freedom to make decisions about our wedding ceremony on our own."

"Ms. Penks," Father Justin looked down on me. Literally. "I think you're making a grave mistake."

I am going to hell.

"Again, with all due respect, Father, I don't see how 'we'd like to discuss our options as a couple' is making any kind of mistake."

Carmela stiffened and gave me the stern Mom face. That doesn't work on me like it does on Anthony. "Emilie, we came all this way to offer you something to think about. Something that would be important to Anthony."

Nice try, Carmela. Anthony's the one who doesn't want the church wedding. She is slick. She has a future in this business.

"And that is why Anthony and I will discuss it further on our time, not on my company time and in his absence," I smiled sweetly through the verbal slap. "Thank you for stopping by. Nice to meet you. We'll contact you if we decide to go with your offer." How corporate of me, and how damned to hell I am treating a priest like a door-to-door vacuum salesman. How doomed to hell I am for treating *Carmela* like the vacuum salesman's assistant. She glared ice cubes at me and followed Father Justin out the door.

Once Meg had shown them to the elevators, she came back with a crowd of my coworkers to grill

me and to pray for my soul. And someone somewhere up there was opening up my Big Book of
Screwups to record the whole thing.

"Do you know what your mother did?" Why be
miserable, guilty and sinful alone? I dialed Anthony at work after his 4 P.M. market bell and led
him into dishonoring thy mother.

"What did she do?" Anthony was multitasking. I
had a quarter of his attention.

"She showed up at my office with a *priest!*"

Now I had his full attention. "She *what?*"

"Oh yeah . . ." I was pacing, barefoot on my office carpet. My feet were throbbing along with my
head and my hands. Actually throbbing. "She walked
in here unannounced, didn't call first to ask, and
just paraded a priest right here into my office."

Anthony was silent. Probably to hear the sounds
of scribbling in my Big Book.

"They came here to strong-arm me into us having a church wedding! The woman brought a
priest as her *backup!*"

"Father Kevin?"

I looked at the phone like it had just licked me
in the ear. "No, Father Justin."

"Ooooh, he's much scarier."

It took a second, but my voice worked. "Can you
please put Anthony on the phone, whoever you
are? Honey, the woman tried to blackmail me with
a priest. And you don't have a problem with that?"

"Sure I have a problem with that," he was multitasking again, probably cradling the phone in his
neck and caring more about keeping it there than
what he was saying. "I'll talk to her."

"Just do it," I said and hung up, cringing at the Nike slogan Mr. Garrity had in my head. "Meg?" I buzzed my assistant.

"Yes, my child?" Meg was taunting me now, doing a priest voice. She would probably wave crosses over me as I left the office today.

"Very funny, Meg. Can you cancel my five o'-clock?"

"Sure, Emilie, I'll take care of it." She was all business, which was smart of her, but I distinctly heard a group laugh coming from out in the main area. I could only imagine the office pool that was starting right at that moment.

On the way out of the office, Norman Fielding, who didn't get the promotion I did, chose his moment wisely. "Ah, Emilie. Now I understand how you rose up through the company in six years, right out of college, landing the corner office before all of us good ol' boys who've put in our years."

It was a leer disguised as a joke.

"I change my vote. You didn't sleep your way to the top. You made a deal with the devil, and now you're bringing in the clergy to undo the pact. Nice." Norman's words came from an equally ugly face, with its thin lips and slit ratlike eyes.

Adversity reveals character, Emilie. Take the high road.

"Norman?" I stopped my quick-paced walk and held my briefcase at my side, hands loose around the clasp.

Norman weaseled out his version of a smile. "Yes?"

"I hope you don't have plans for the next three

Saturdays," I started, speaking slowly enough so he'd hear all the words above the other voices in his head. "Because I'm having Top send you to sensitivity training next weekend, a sexual harassment seminar the next weekend, and an anger management class the next."

Norman's self-delight turned to steely hatred.

"Say something ignorant like that again, and you'll be looking for another job." I nodded as I was speaking. All that was missing was the *Capeesh?* eye warning that Anthony's father would have glared at him had he been in my shoes at the time.

He muttered something while I walked away, head high and shoulders back. And I looked back at his Weeble self from my spot in the mirrored executive elevator, gave him a pixielike wave and a sarcastic too-wide sugary smile, and enjoyed the doors closing him away from me.

I still got it.

Chapter 15

Can you believe this? Carmela went ahead and placed an order for a cake when it was clearly stated that the cake was my responsibility. Understanding this as a sensitive political matter, I do hope you'll take the appropriate steps to put that vile woman in her place. Classless, tacky, and manipulative. A clear breach of etiquette.

Good morning, Emilie. My e-mail was filled with acid-tongued missives like this one from my mother, and I was glad for the flat absence of any tone that black-and-white e-mail messages provided. The sarcasm was wiped out, as was that tone in her voice that somehow mystified me and overrode my usual sense of self-possession. In print, just words. Annoying words, but just words. And they went on . . .

Emilie, dear. Did you call Sonnanina Bakery and change the cake order? They just called to say that they can't do the chocolate ganache I requested, and I told them that I ordered a lemon cream filling with lemon cake. Then they said we want an eight-tier cake, when I asked for four. Did you make some changes? Come over tonight for dinner and let's have a chat. I'm making lamb stew.

I didn't know Carmela even had e-mail. New revelations every day. But what was shaping up to be an extremely interesting and stomach rumbling turn of events here was the uncanny and consistent bungling of each wedding plan these women had on their plates to take care of. Did the bakery make a mistake? It's possible. Because you know how similar chocolate ganache is to lemon buttercream in both sight and pronunciation. Now I'm not a paranoid person by nature, but this one had red flags all over it.

"Mother, did you call the bakery to change the cake order?"

"No, Emilie, I didn't. Is there a *prah*blem?" She sounded like she was smiling.

"No, Mother, no problem at all." And I hung up the phone to immediately lower my head onto my keyboard, not caring that my nose had signalled the release of a long line of *ddddddddddddd*'s across my in-process e-mail back to Carmela.

I don't understand this, Emilie. The bakery said that I called to change the cake order, when I very clearly did not call. Did you make a change to my plans? You can confess, dear. It's not that big of a deal.

"Hey," Anthony was chuckling when I picked up the phone. I must have groaned my answer, as my face was still dropped and dead against the edged plastic letters on my keyboard. "Are you aware of the Great Cake Battle that's raging right now?"

"Ugh, don't even tell me . . ."

Anthony laughed, amused only by his safe and well-planned distance from the Great Cake Battle of 2005. He would act as war commentator from his safe bunker on the side while the real action raged overhead. "Looks like your mother called the bakery to override my mother's cake order . . ."

"She didn't." It wasn't a defense of her. It was a muttering of defeat.

"Yes, she did." He missed the deflation in my statement. "And she not only changed the size, shape, flavor and filling, she also commissioned sugar paste flowers instead of the fresh flower cascade, which will all catapult the asking price to well outside my parents' planned budget."

I wrinkled my cheeks up and blinked. *Did he just say "catapult the asking price"?* And why does he sound so knowledgeable about cake flavors and fillings?

"Can't they just leave each others' plans alone?"

"Apparently not," Anthony said, and then he sighed. *Such frustration you have from your safe distance away, sweetie.* I vowed to forward him every e-mail I received in 6- to 17-minute increments from the Mothers of the Year. Why suffer alone? And this decision made me feel clever in a no-win situation. Here, during work hours and while I had to come up with a twelve-storyboard presentation for the new fragrance line for Clinique, was the parade of e-mail missives from my cohorts and right-hand women, my partners in wedding planning purgatory:

> Emilie sweetie, something is very wrong with the cake order, and while I hate to jump to conclusions, this is very clearly some sort of game from someone. I ordered the cake, and now it's all different. You can't serve chocolate cake, because some people don't like chocolate. Everyone loves lemon. It's traditional, and I don't know if you're aware of this, but the lemon cake is a traditional Italian custom that signifies the blending of the sweet and sour in marriage, the tender fruit beneath the tougher exterior of the fruit, and an homage to the lemon tree groves in our ancestors' cities, which I don't want to do without . . .

Carmela had expertly played the Ancestors and Traditions card, thereby blocking me from doing anything other than preserving the rituals and traditions of seventeen generations of Cantanos. For God and family and the blood and sweat of those who came to the New World with just the sweaters on their backs and eight cents in their pockets, this cake order must be changed back to the original! Not to mention that the fresh flowers on the cake would signify natural love, as opposed to a contrived and artificial display of the bounty of nature that sugar paste flowers would represent. So speaks Mother Earth. And it wasn't lost on me that Carmela was starting to sound a lot like Leah. Symbolism, ritual. The universe was clearly calling for a lemon cream cake with buttercream icing and a

cascade of fresh flowers. Centuries of departed
Cantano relatives would spin in their graves without this.

Delilah denied her involvement, blaming instead the complete and utter demise of any sense
of work ethic among bakery employees and
teenagers today.

After eight hours and twelve e-mails, the Great
Cake Debate was over. I called Sonnanina's and—
after great pains to convince the bakery owner
that I was indeed the "real" Emilie Penks and not
the two other people who had pretended to be me
with this order—we were set on the lemon buttercream four-tiered cake with fresh flower cascade
and a chocolate ganache groom's cake with red
sugar paste roses on top. Simple. Done. Let me
never hear about cake and filling and frosting
again. Let me not hear anything having to do with
this wedding for just the rest of the day. Just two
more hours.

It was too much to ask for.

"Honey?" Anthony wasn't laughing this time.
And it wasn't like him to call me at the office beyond emergencies. I braced myself for this emergency. What could it be? Certain guests of ours are
allergic to lemons? Or flour? Pesticide warnings
about fresh flowers on cakes? "We have a problem."

How could I not think of Tom Hanks and Bill
Paxton trying to fashion air vents out of milk car-
tons and socks, or whatever they did in *Apollo 13*?
Lost in space with four minutes of breathing air
left? That is a problem. Compromising by having

two cakes instead of one ... trauma. Complete trauma.

"What is it now?" I sighed. "Wait, let me guess ..."

Anthony sighed. Clearly, this was one of those times when he should have saved it for post-wine and post-backrub at home.

"There will only be *two* layers to *each* layer of the cake, instead of the *three* layers that your mother very *clearly* requested. Oh, the horror!"

Anthony was not amused.

"No, wait, wait, wait, I got it!" My voice rose in pitch, my back rod-straight, and I slapped the edge of my desk so that my knuckles tingled with a slight jolt to my nerves. I spun around in my chair to put my stockinged feet up on the desk. "Since lemons are the universal symbol of marital happiness, why don't we build the whole wedding around a lemon theme?"

"Are you done?" Again, not amused.

"Or we could mix the lemon buttercream and chocolate ganache, but if I call now, I'm part of the conspiracy plan to sabotage your mother's will and rights with the wedding plans." I quite amused myself, even though this wasn't my best material. There's not much you can do with lemons and chocolate as your theme to a string-along of bad attitude jokes. Looking back on it, as I did a lot of the events and skirmishes that would come during this planning nightmare, I had to bite the inside of my cheek to keep from crying over the ridiculousness of it all.

"Done yet?" Anthony asked, but didn't give me a chance to answer. "Your mother just called me ... I thought you should know that she's called your father and told him not to come to the wedding."

I felt and heard the air push right out of me. My rib cage was slumped down without my noticing the drop, my shoulders bent inward, my wrist suddenly struggling with the weight of the phone.

"What?" It came out as a whisper.

"Em, she told me not to tell you, but there's no way I'm hiding out with them in this."

"She told Dad *not* to come?" I looked up at the ceiling with this one, shrugging.

He didn't even want to hear himself say it again. "Did she say why?"

It was a question I asked of him, but didn't have to. It was just my brain with the volume turned up. A nonsensical question to a nonsensical decision made by *her*.

Chapter 16

"What in the *hell* are you *doing?*"
I burst through the lace-lined French doors to her office, the swaff of air whisking papers off her French country desk. Even her hair moved a little bit.

Delilah was startled at first, but then assumed her tight-lipped, chin-out snootyville posture. "Emilie Anne, I'll thank you not to use that kind of language with me."

My face soured, my opinion of her plummeting even farther. "Believe me, I censored myself."

I crossed to her side, my hand now pushing down onto the desk, blocking her from getting out of her seat and whisking herself away into escapist busy-ness. I would not follow her like a lapdog into her closet because she just *has* to pick out something new and still tagged for a charity event tonight. I was not going to trail her as she searched for some elusive earring, or straightened her celebrity-studded pictures on the wall. The woman was not . . . getting . . . away.

"You told Daddy not to come to the wedding?" It was and was not a question. It was an accusation with a flip at the end. Before her lined lips could move with some defensive slicktalk, I went on. My face, I knew, was stop sign red. My eyes, I imagined, were serial killer black from center outward. And I can't imagine that my breath was all that great since I was literally breathing anger. "Are you *out* of your *mind*, Mother? How *could* you do something like *that* behind my back! And how could you tell Anthony not to tell me about it? You make *no* sense! You tell my fiancé your big secret and try to recruit him into acting just like you . . . having no ability whatsoever to—"

"Your father said 'fine,'" she purred, and I swore there was a trace of a smile as she said it. The corners of her mouth were not shaped for sadness.

That stopped my rant. I didn't believe her . . . totally.

"Your father said that any wedding of mine was not one he wanted to—"

"Whoa! Any wedding of *yours*?"

She stumbled, stammered, lost the golden polish. "I meant, any wedding I'd be . . . present for."

I blew out a whistle and my knees literally quivered. My hands were in full adrenaline soak as well, trembling enough to make me want to keep them from her sight. I held my hands tightly behind my back now, gripping my engagement ring. She spoke nothing more but kept the most blank look on her face. But she kept her eyes away from me. So I wouldn't see them, not so that I wouldn't gouge them out.

* * *

It's true, my father hated her with a passion. She reinvented herself after fifteen years of marriage and decided he wasn't part of the "After" picture. Her new incarnation had no responsibility to a husband. She broke his heart. He would sit in the dark in his brown leather chair and just stare out the window, drinking Scotch. Wondering what happened to the woman he married. He was no angel. He'd hurt her, too, by making her invisible as a housewife. By coming home with story after story of having to help a friend move for six hours right after work on a Friday night. Or how he ran out of gas, walked six miles to a gas station, forgot his gas can, walked six miles back to the car, then six miles back to the gas station, and then when he got back to the car the battery was dead so he just stayed at a motel and didn't call her because it was "too late." I was a kid, and even I saw right through that. My father was no angel, and I probably would have reinvented myself to rise up from those depths too. Donna Penks was a stereotype in one area of her life, her marriage, but an altogether nonstereotype as a mother. Back then. I guess she missed being a stereotype, so she's chosen Bitchy Mother of the Bride for now.

But to tell my father he can't come to my wedding? Without my knowledge and then make it a party game: "keep this from Emilie . . . you're it!"

How silly of me to expect her to rise above. Just to keep her distance from Daddy and Jenni, his new "midlife wife-iss" as I called her. Peacefully coexist. I actually expected . . . never mind.

"Fix this one, Mother," I commanded, burning with every ounce of anger I had and renewing lots of reserve anger I still carried with me like flower seeds in my mind. Add mention of father-mother feud, and watch it multiply like wild.

"He doesn't want to be there."

"No, he doesn't want to be with *you*. This has nothing to do with me." *Damn it, Emilie. Don't cry. Do NOT cry.* "Daddy would never not come to my wedding!"

"Call him yourself, Emilie. He'll tell you." She gave me her eyes then, looked up to show me that she was . . . sad too.

"No, he's going to walk me down the aisle," I barked, slapping on sharpness like mortar to wall the tears back. "Fix this! I mean it!"

And I slammed the French doors behind me hard enough to crack a pane of glass. If I were four, I'd be running to my room and screaming "I hate you, I hate you" before I slammed my own door. But I don't have a room at Delilah's mansion. And I'm not four. But I did cry and whimper my "I hate you's" while driving home. Road rage? It's dramatic adolescent outbursts with a driver's license. Now I get it.

Chapter 17

3:07 A.M.

I had a date with Ben & Jerry. Chunky Monkey mixed with Cherries Garcia.

In my quiet, darkened living room with one of Leah's serenity candles spiraling a thin waft of smoke to dance in swirls and then disappear into the air, I watched the flame grow larger and more intense and then shrink back down to a pinky nail size. It raged, then calmed, raged then calmed, picking up on some undetected draft in the room, flaring then retreating. The serenity candle was, I decided in my own spiraling mind, not so serene. Spitting out its own anger, then remembering what it's supposed to be and pulling back again.

"Em?" Leah had emerged from her sanctuary, from the red-walled den of romantic safety she'd constructed for herself, wind chimes still, mirrors removed, smooth river stones and geodomes perfectly arranged on her countertops and bedside table.

I lifted my eyes away from the candle flame,

blinked away the brightness and the remaining ghost image glow of the flame in my eyesight. "What are you doing up?" I asked her, unfolding my legs and moving so that she could sit next to me on the couch. We both smacked back the over-stuffed navy blue pillows to lean back more comfortably against our own corners, feet now up in mirror image of one another.

"Just woke up, no reason." Leah smiled, and accepted the pint of Chunky Monkey I held out to her with my spoon. She dug out a spoonful with more chocolate block than ice cream and closed her eyes for a moment in the sinful enjoyment of it. "And you?"

"Can't sleep."

Leah nodded her head. She's no stranger to sleepless nights and agony over other people's false moves and agendas. "Still thinking of eloping?"

"It's looking better and better these days," I sighed in resignation.

Leah dug a few more quick spoonfuls out and quickly took them down before handing me back the pint. We'd move into an effortless flow of back and forth with both flavors soon. Two Ben & Jerry's, two heartbroken women, one spoon.

"Don't do it, Em. Don't rip yourself off," Leah said, and when I looked up from the cherry I was trying to dislodge from its icy hold, I saw my old friend again. Maybe it was the dim lighting or a sugar rush, but Leah didn't have that sunken-cheeked, pale female vampire look going on. The dark circles under her eyes weren't there right now. Her hair was clean and curled. Her socks matched.

"I know," I sighed into a spoonful. "But I'm at the point where whatever we do, it's a lose-lose situation."

"Ah, elope and miss out on the fun, or stay the course and be a stranger at your own wedding." Lost or not, Leah had a handle on the problem. "I know that one very well."

"You do?"

"The wedding I *didn't* have to the man I *didn't* marry?" She shuffled her feet closer to her, rounding more of herself closer and hugging her hands around her shins. "It wasn't my wedding."

I just nodded. *Stay silent. Let her talk.*

"It wasn't my wedding . . ." she repeated and her eyes slid sideways to watch that jumping flame in the serenity candle. It seemed to be on full alert right now, tall and dancing. "My mother, his mother, *him.* They all just grabbed the reins, and everything had more meaning to them than to me. I was shot down and smoothed over, decisions made by council, and I wasn't part of the council."

I know the feeling.

"I started off stronger and got progressively less . . . and less . . ."

Ah, the draining effect of being overruled.

"Any assertiveness trick I had, they had a stronger manipulation trick," she blinked. "How *important* it was to go by the book. What would people think?"

Did we have the same mother?

"I just lost my fight. And resented it. Still resent it . . ."

As I would resent it if I didn't get things on track now.

"Looking back, I'm mad at myself for not having more of a spine . . . not so much mad at them.

They were just overexcited . . . they just got carried away. I felt like I should have been stronger about it."

And before I could even think about applying that statement to myself, she came out with:

"You're strong like that now, Em. I don't think you'd let yourself lose your ability to stand up. And I don't want to see you back down like that, like I did. Because you have more fight than that."

I'll never allow Anthony to call her flaky again.

"It's universal, Em. Everyone has this to some degree. People lose their minds over weddings."

I opened my mouth to tell her how my situation was way worse than anyone else's in the history of the world, but thought better of it. Leah clearly had the winning ticket on that one.

"It's funny that they call it 'the happiest day of your life' when there's so much misery leading up to it . . . if you get there at all."

Go easy on the bitterness, Leah, but continue . . .

"What I'm saying is that the day itself is worth all this . . ." she paused, searched for the right words. "All this craziness . . . it goes away. It's finite. Something you can get through to break through the . . . glass ceiling to where it starts getting good."

I knew what she meant. On the wedding day itself, provided Anthony doesn't run off the night before with a transsexual stripper (not likely), I'm not going to remember any of this. We'll be untouchable.

"It's kind of like having a baby," Leah laughed. "Painful as hell during the production stage but then something inside you blocks out the memory of the pain. And it's all worth it."

We both looked at each other and laughed, "Yeah, right!" We had enough friends who had babies and considered themselves sold a bill of goods about that whole "forgetting the pain" thing. But even they with their reconstructed orifices and railroad tie scars across their stomachs would probably concur; it's going to be worth it afterward. Even if you get split in two in the process.

"Hey, I tried." Leah laughed, her hair shining in the light of the candle flame.

"Yeah, you really reached for that silver lining ending." I gave her a playful push on her shin with my foot. I was glad to have her back.

"That's why they pay me the big bucks," she joked, not actually having a job right now.

After a moment of letting our laughs calm down to a rumble, then a ripple, then a sigh and an occasional cough with a smile as we settled in, the transition was made. "I've missed having you here like this, Leah."

She just smiled and looked down at her feet a moment. "Ah, what can I say?" She blinked a few times, tears always at the ready.

"Take all the time you need." I nudged her again. "It's just good to know you're still in there." And with that, we polished off both containers of ice cream, then winced and each held our heads with the last-bite burn in our sinuses from the cold.

"Hey, Em," Leah called out from around the corner as I prepared to sneak back into bed with Anthony. The ice cream containers would be discovered in the trash tomorrow morning by Anthony, but living with two women he knows not to dare mention it. "The next time the mothers go off like that, overstep their bounds . . ."

"Yeah?"

"That's where you ask yourself, 'How do I want to look back on this moment years from now?'"

Leah winked. "Because that's what stays with you. Each thing in each moment."

Okay, so she got just a little bit Buddha on me there at the end, but I was glad for the transcendence. And glad for the wakeup call.

Chapter 18

"Dad, it's Emilie. Are you there? Pick up."

I hated leaving such a whiny desperation message on his voice mail . . . again. But this was the third time I'd tried to reach him.

"Okay, well . . . please just give me a call when you get back . . . I don't know if you're away for the week . . . or busy . . ."

God, I sound like a stood-up sixteen-year-old trying to track down her errant date. Pathetic, just pathetic.

"I'm trying to reach you . . ."

Really?

"So please just give me a call. Okay? . . . Bye, Dad."

Ugh.

Chapter 19

Delilah was away in Chicago for a book signing or two, so the housekeeper, Tatiana, let me in.

"Hello, Miss Emilie," Tatiana smiled and glistened her light green eyes at me.

"Hi, Tatiana," I said, and surprised her with a hug around her thin shoulders. This poor woman, what she goes through being the personal slave to my mother, I thought . . . without actual proof that my mother mistreats her. It just has to be . . .

"Your mother, she is in Shee-cago." Tatiana shrugged and held out her hands for my coat. I waved her off and took care of it myself. The woman wasn't paid to cater to *my* ego. How did she get here? With only a few vague facts from my mother, I understood that she was once a Russian figure skater back in the old country, trained by the system with hopes of an Olympic appearance. But her partner had killed himself by using his own skate blade to slit his throat. According to the story, Tatiana always thought it was the Russian mob. The story had much of my mother's flair for exaggeration and fantasy, but it was just enticing enough to believe. Tatiana had a slight frame, jet black hair, green catlike eyes, and the legs of a skater. Her every arm movement was graceful and she had the upper body strength of a trained athlete, so it could be true. I tried to imagine her being lifted into the air by a chisel-jawed Russian skater who was two feet taller than her and defended his masculinity by never wearing a ruffled shirt.

"Can I help you with something?" Tatiana snapped me out of my fantasy, squashing the sound of the Olympic theme music and the Russian national anthem with the sound of ice clinking in a glass from the side bar in the foyer. Only my mother would stock a bar and place it within ten feet of the front door.

"Um . . ." *This is perfect.* "I just need to get a few things from my mother's desk . . . wedding planning stuff . . . she knows I'm coming to get some things. For the wedding plans."

Tatiana raised an eyebrow at me, not really needing any spy training to spot that as a stumbling lie. My mother's Yorkshire terrier even whined from the arm of the white couch nearby.

Moments later, I was in my mother's office, riffling through her pathologically organized folder of notes and spreadsheets for my wedding. Within the pastel-colored sheets—all color-coded according to priority—I discovered more than a few interesting tidbits. Delilah was keeping notes for her next novel. Apparently, a figure vaguely resembling Carmela was going to get her comeuppance in the pages of my mother's next book. She would be a minor character, a foil. But she would eventually wind up silent in either a Jamaican bog or a New Orleans cemetery. My mother couldn't quite decide yet. Literary revenge, she called it. Fantastical fictional ends to the one who got in her way. Delilah's books were littered with the renamed bodies of her supposed enemies. She killed off Donna Penks more than a few times, and although I tried, I never quite found myself in any of her romance epics as either top-heavy heroine or mysterious murder victim by a mob lynching, shark tank, or unfortunate proximity to an industrial bread slicer. But then again, I've never had the patience to read through all six hundred pages of Delilah's books. I very well *could* be in there somewhere, the insolent teenage daughter of a diplomat dangling precariously over a cliff because she didn't listen to her all-knowing and very slender and attractive, much sought-after mother. I'm amazed they pay her millions of dollars to basically sketch out her psychoses for a living. But they do say, "write what you know." So Carmela would soon die a bitter death in the pages of Delilah's next blockbuster, with Lainie Kazan playing Carmela in the made-for-TV movie.

And I wonder why I worry about the two mothers getting along.

Delilah's spreadsheet seemed in order. From what my wedding reconnaissance outing here showed me, it didn't seem that Delilah had any further plans to step over Carmela's lines and take over any more of Anthony's family's planning responsibilities. Everything looked in place. I filed everything back into place, knowing to tap the folder down to make all the edges of all the papers line up in an orderly fashion, and I slid the pink folder back into its original upright position next to her computer. I stole a piece of candy from the Tiffany dish on her desk, and exited way more smoothly and calmly than I had entered.

centuries that the reign of all tall medieval
up in an equally tarnished gold, and the pink softer
pinks into an infinite variety. Here I went to the
costumer's, expert, as more clearly from the others
that earlier conclusion-taker was unavoidable that
and lasted their blind sense.

Chapter 20

"Dad? . . . Daddy, are you home? It's Emilie . . ."

Nothing.

"Please don't do this, Dad. I didn't ask Mom to
uninvite you to the wedding. I don't know where
she got this idea, or why she thinks it's . . ."

My father's voice mail recorder hummed, drinking up the desperation in my voice. Allowing me
plenty of time to do my emotional tap dance.

"It wasn't my idea, Dad. I want you at my wedding. And Jenni too, in the front row. I want you
to walk me down the aisle."

Just thinking of that vision, my father in a smart
black tuxedo with his arm bent in offering to my
hand, made me break down suddenly, loudly, awk-
wardly, and probably heartbreakingly to him and
to Jenni.

"Please call me, Dad. Or come to my office. Anything . . ."

And without my knowing it, without it being a planned maneuver, what I said next did the trick:

"Please don't let Mom get away with this."

Chapter 21

Dinner at Carmela and Vic's. And not one bruise upon my arrival. Carmela had suddenly taken to hugging me far less excitedly whenever I stepped into her home, and her coolness was obvious. She didn't look at me when she passed the gravy at the dinner table. She directed all of her questions to Anthony, even those pertaining to me. She wasn't so careful with spearing a meatball and plopping it onto my plate. Shout Wipes were now a staple in my purse, since Carmela always seemed to splash some sort of sauce or marinara or wine onto my shirts and sweaters. Punishment by staining, I imagined.

I was now referred to as *She* and *Her*. My name was verboten, even in the most casual conversations. And Vic had started looking at me like I had accidentally run over his dog with my car.

Anthony had confided in me back at the beginning of this that his mother was planning to give me the handkerchief she used on her wedding day to use as my Something Borrowed. But the offer hadn't yet come. There was, of course, plenty of time for that, but my discomfort at her iciness lately revved up the old paranoia engines I'd inherited from my mother in small sizes, and I convinced myself that I would never get the hankie. And without my understanding it, I was really quite upset about that. About a mothball-smelling, simple white handkerchief with blue edging and a slight yellow mark in the middle. Devastated, actually.

"Carmela," I tried. "Would you like some help in the kitchen?" I gave her my sweetest, warmest smile.

And was met with a forced smile that was more of a leer. "No, thank you. I think I can manage in my own kitchen without help from others."

Well, really.

And with that, the martyr hefted an oversized platter of sausages and braccioli onto one arm, scooped up a wooden bowl of tomato salad, and balanced a basket of garlic bread on the top of her carrying hand to clear the table. Vic poured himself another glass of wine and put the bottle back down on the table with a thud, looking everywhere but directly at me as he drank it down in long, hungry gulps.

Please pass the Advil.

"Are you ready to go?" I leaned in and whispered to Anthony, who just patted me on the leg and launched into a conversation puller with his father. I blinked at him. Was I just dismissed with the old pat-on-the-leg trick? The silencing of the future wife? The Not Now, Honey?

You are so not getting any tonight, mister.

As Anthony and his father launched into a discussion of the Mets, I stood up and approached the kitchen. Carmela was going to get help whether she wanted it or not. There were no other rooms to escape to here downstairs. And I really don't care what kind of season Mike Piazza is having. I am a Yankees fan, a fact which has been fiercely kept secret from Vic in much the same way as if I'd already borne Anthony's bastard child. *Shhhhh, they're going to find out!*

Carmela had already covered and stowed the food platters into her refrigerator and was now sitting at the kitchen table re-smoothing the frosting over the chocolate cake for dessert. She lifted her eyes from the frosting can for only a beat, to show me she knew I had entered the room but was still not worth acknowledging.

"Carmela?"

"Yes?" Smooth, smooth, smooth. Dip and pull to make the wave shapes on top that Anthony likes.

I pulled a chair out, scratching its legs against the floor in a loud drag. Lowering myself carefully across from her, I folded my arms on the table. "Carmela, are you okay?"

She smiled. Something was funny?

"I'm fine. Perfectly fine. *Perfectly.*" Something was sinister about her right then, as she smoothed the frosting way beyond the point at which the cake was actually frosted to completion. Just more smoothing and pulling, smoothing and pulling. "No, I don't need anything. I'll just sit here in the *kitchen* while you all enjoy yourselves and your coffee. Okay?"

I ran a shaking finger over my eyebrow, choosing that motion for my finger instead of another one. "Carmela, why are you being—"

"I said I'm *perfectly* fine." And the frosting knife plunged into the frosting can with deadly accuracy, without her looking. She stabbed the frosting. Stabbed it once and left the knife there to quiver like an arrow once her hand moved to a quick wipe on her apron.

Back away from your future mother-in-law. Just back away.

I slid out of my chair and grabbed my coat from the rack behind the kitchen door, grabbed my fiancé and headed for the safety of home. Unnerved. Annoyed. Slightly frightened for my life and suddenly very concerned about Anthony's DNA and its effects on our future children. But the worst part was, Anthony didn't *see* it. Not the frosting knife finding its smooth and creamy landing mark, but his mother's attitude.

"Oh, please, you're imagining things," he dismissed me with a wave, another strike against him and yet another night of not getting any going right into my mental calendar.

"You didn't think she was being cold with me? You're kidding." I shook my head at my brilliant man's denseness. "The meatball . . . ?"

"It was an accident."

"Has your mother ever dropped anything on me in the last three years? Ever?!"

He looked at me like I was insane. Me. "No, Em," he half-laughed. "But that's not something I keep a log on. So she dropped a meatball on you tonight. It happens."

"And she hasn't said my name. Not once."

Anthony really didn't get it. He looked at me with a mixture of pity and fear. Yes, I am the one to be feared just for questioning his mother's attitude.

"I'm serious, Anthony. Your mother acts totally differently with me now," I said, having less hold

over my emotions than I should. In the darkness
of the car, I could blink away tears of frustration.
As long as I didn't sniffle. He heard it anyway.

"Are you *crying*?" he asked, eyes off the road to
catch a tear's reflection in oncoming headlights.
"Jesus, Em. Take a Midol or something. You're
overreacting."

That's it! You are not getting laid for a month, buddy.
He played the PMS card. He flipped her misbe-
havior onto me, told me to grow up and get over
it? Oh, no, no, no, no, no.

And he actually had the nerve to look surprised
when I tossed him a pillow from the bedroom and
shut the door between us, muttering something
unintelligible about frosting and his mother. Suddenly, I didn't feel so badly about my mother's
planned literary demise for her. In fact, I had a few
suggestions of my own as I lay there on my side of
the bed, steaming and stewing . . . the perfect picture of the radiant bride-to-be three months before her wedding day. Yes, I was an image of
radiance.

Drifting off mercifully to sleep, Carmela's words
haunted me. That look in her eye haunted me too,
but something stood out about the way she
growled *perfectly. Perrrrrfectly.* I shuddered with a little chill, pulled the blankets up tighter around me,
and rolled over to look at Anthony's empty side of
the bed before sleep overtook me. I dreamt I was
surfboarding on waves made out of chocolate.
And of course, the word *perfectly* was written in
chocolate clouds overhead. Maybe I was losing my
mind.

* * *

Sometime in the middle of the night, Anthony had slipped into bed with me. I woke up in the first glow of the morning, the birds outside just starting to chirp, and moved closer against him. He breathed with his mouth open, unconscious to the world, and I snuggled in.

Chapter 22

"**I** am going to kill your mother."

It wasn't me saying it. It was Anthony. And he wasn't dreaming. The doorbell sounded at exactly 6:57 A.M. on a Saturday morning, which is about when Delilah had shown up in the past, buzzed on caffeine and intensely inspired by something Colin Cowie had just shared with her via cell phone from Rome.

"Only if I get to kill yours," was what I said, as I leaned out of the bed and caught myself on bended, wobbly legs, steadied myself and padded across the cold floor to our front door. "What?!" I called out like a hormonal teenager moaning through her bedroom door to make life even harder on everyone around her. I delighted in my immaturity in these early hours. You wake me up, you deal with me.

I threw open the door, ready to give her my best insolent material, and stopped, mouth in word formation but the sound turned off.

"Good morning, Emilie."

I focused my eyes, rubbed the sleep out of them. Then whispered, "Daddy."

He said he hadn't slept all night. That he was just walking for hours, thinking about what I'd said. Anthony came out of the bedroom, as shocked as I was to see him standing there in his jacket, taking off his hat to reveal a more hairless head than I remembered from just a year ago. Having had a past with Delilah will do that to you.

"I know you didn't tell your mother to uninvite me to your wedding, Pumpkin," he said and sat next to me on the couch. Anthony moved immediately to allow him next-seat access to me, and then went into the kitchen to start the coffee machine pre-timer.

A sigh of relief. Then I pulled a throw blanket over my bare legs. Not so much because I was cold, but because I hadn't shaved.

"And don't you worry. I'll be at your wedding. I'm going to walk you down the aisle," he smiled, with larger wrinkles around his eyes, more gray in his beard. He had aged in one year since I saw him last. But his eyes were the same. He patted me on the knee. "I wouldn't cost either of us that moment."

"I don't know where she got the idea to—"

He cut me off when he saw me starting to tear up again, wrinkle my nose to keep the tears back, squeeze my lips together as if facial contortions had anything to do with the release of emotion. Long-waiting emotion. "If I knew *this* woman, I could help explain that, honey."

I nodded. My father knew Donna Penks. And loved her. Despite his admittedly awful and selfish behavior sometimes, he had loved her. Very much. And he grieved for Donna Penks too. Disliked Delilah Winchester too. It all came out over coffee and somewhat stale Entenmann's doughnuts. Anthony and I sat silently as he spoke, as he poured out all of what he knew, all of what I was now deemed old enough to understand.

"Your mother was very unhappy with me," he started. "I wasn't the most perfect husband, but I did my best. We were young, and life was harder than we both expected. I worked a lot, she was cooped up at home and with you, Em." He caught himself and fumbled to recover, "Not that being home with you was—"

I just smiled and waved him onward. *No need to explain, Dad.*

He exhaled hard. "And she just kind of boarded herself away, didn't try to make friends, got really depressed, gained weight. It was a downward spiral. She hated her life, she hated me. She *never* hated you, not for a minute. But this wasn't the life she thought she signed on for."

I nodded. That much I could see. That much I already knew.

"So my . . . bad behavior just set her off. And I don't blame her for being angry, but it was worse to see her . . . kill herself off."

I leaned back into the cushions and grabbed Anthony's hand. *Here it comes . . .*

"Do you remember when your mother decided she wanted to be somebody else?" He lowered his head a little, looked at me from under his furrowed bushy eyebrows, and rubbed the side of his hand over his lips, as if toughening them up a little to get the hard stuff to come out more easily.

I nodded, although I really only remember clips of it.

"She hated her life so much, hated what she had become so much, that she burned everything that was *her*." He shook his head in remembering it, tossed his head to the side to crack his neck muscles, his nervous habit. "Her favorite books, her clothes, pictures, letters . . . anything that was her. Anything."

I remembered. But I remember her smiling over the frying pan, like it was the best game on earth. I even helped collect photos and her oven mitts, her slippers, anything that could burn, regardless of fumes. It was a game.

"I watched my wife die that day. She killed herself symbolically because she was just . . . so . . . miserable." He spoke quietly, as if it still killed him to think about it. "You'll never know what that feels like, to know you've disappointed someone *so* much, hurt someone *so* much, that they destroy who they are to become someone else."

I chewed on my lip, felt Anthony trace small circles on the top of my fingers.

"Her eyes changed that day," he sighed. "She wasn't there anymore."

I wanted to grab him and tell him, "Yes, she's in there! I saw her at Vera Wang!" like we were talking about finding a runaway on the streets of the city years after they'd disappeared. All you could recognize were the eyes. But I held back. He had much more to do here.

"And she had to re-create herself," he shrugged. "She had to start from scratch. Get rid of the . . . frumpy, broken down housewife . . ."

I smarted at that particular wording, trying not

to imagine my father in a diner somewhere back then using that sorry description of his wife to the anonymous woman he sought refuge with in the "my wife doesn't understand me" scene. As much as I disliked my mother, I'd still defend her.

"She had to kill it all off, the bad *and* the good."

The bad and the good. The bad and the good. Yes, that's what it was. She had to kill off what she was, and that would be *maternal, nurturing, caring*. Any small, forbidden part of Donna Penks just wasn't allowed in this shell.

"I'd hurt her so badly." My father now cracked his knuckles, one after the other, but not in a frightening way like Vic does it. My father was wispy, gentle, sort of a lost soul himself. Completely harmless. Whereas Vic had hands like catchers' mitts and a wide, flat face you wouldn't dare disrespect, *my* father was . . . softer. "But she never took it out on you. I'd never allow that. You were old enough not to need the nurturing of your mother. You were almost a teenager, so you were past that. You'd started to rebel, and I was glad to see you had some fight in you. You get that from my side," he joked, and I managed a smile for him. He was trying to lighten the moment.

"It kills me to see her," he confessed. "And it kills her to see me. Probably even to think about me. I hate to see her like this. I mean, I know she's happy and successful and rich and celebrated, living the exciting life she wanted all along. She has all that. But it kills me to see that the light has gone out. You know what I mean?"

The light has gone out. Yes, Daddy, that's exactly right.

"I'm a reminder to her . . . of what she used to be, what she used to have . . ." he said forlornly.

"So, of course, she doesn't want that at the wed-ding."

He said "that." She doesn't want "that" at the wedding.

"She's run from it all her life . . ."

"Because it still hurts her," Anthony ventured, and my father nodded.

"So it's not me she doesn't want at the wedding. It's *her,* the *old* her."

We all sighed at once. We knew this to some de-gree, but we didn't *know* it. I didn't know that she was so raw, that she carried this with her. I thought she'd forgotten Donna Penks, that she was glad to be rid of her. No. Not at all. She fights her back every day.

"But your mother is just going to have to deal with it on the wedding day," he said. A promise. "Because nothing's going to keep me from walk-ing my girl down the aisle." And he looked at An-thony. "I know you're a good man. Knew it the first time I met you. And I know I haven't been around to make a good impression on you, son, but—"

Anthony held up his hand. "No need to apolo-gize, Mr. Penks. You've made a great impression right now."

"Dad . . . you can call me Dad." My father smiled warmly at him, again with the wrinkles and that Irish sparkle in his eye. He was the first of all the parents to invite either of us to use the Dad or Mom title. Everyone else held that intimacy level at arm's length. Or farther.

"Dad, then." Anthony shook my father's hand.

"And I have something for you . . . something I've been saving for you."

My father stood up, went out to our apartment door and picked up a box I didn't notice him leave there when he first arrived. But I was looking at my father then, at his eyes.

He came back and placed a Lord & Taylor box on my lap, a large gift box that whooshed with air when I pulled the top off. Inside I found pictures, a pile of grainy, bad-quality pictures. Before my mind could absorb the meaning of it, my father announced, "They're our wedding pictures . . . of your mother and me."

I flipped through the pictures. *They couldn't be.*

"When she started burning everything in sight, I ran off and took the photo albums . . . the good ones from the top of the closet . . . and I put them in the trunk of my car," he confessed, deflating like a man unloading an ancient burden. He slumped down again into the couch, rounded his shoulders and hollowed his chest. I watched his stomach rise and fall in a deep exhale. There. It was done.

"These aren't your wedding pictures," I breathed. "What are these?"

Anthony looked at me, then looked down at the box of pictures in my hand. I shuffled through, one after the other, inspecting the images, turning each one over as if there was some sort of seal of authenticity on the back of them. Pictures of my mother in her much younger days, pre-plastic surgery with a slightly wider nose, slightly wider hips, flat hair in her natural color. And she wore a simple white dress with layered sleeves, a somewhat ill-fitting dress that cinched at the waist and hung down limply. She held an anemic bouquet of daisies, and they, too, seemed to slump. She smiled in one picture, looked off to the side in another.

Pictures of my father in a suit, and then with his

jacket removed in a short sleeve white dress shirt with the top button opened. He with more hair, longer hair, a wide moustache and no beard. In one picture he held my mother around the waist. In another, he hoisted a beer bottle and had a cigarette poking out the side of his mouth. Relatives I recognized vaguely either sat in tight groups at tables, or leaned over what looked like a picnic table covered with plastic Tupperware bowls of salads. A watermelon sat on a plain dinner plate in the back with a rough, uneven hunk missing from the side.

Then, a picture of an old car, dusty, with white rimmed tires. And my mother and father looking out from the cranked-down window. He was smiling. She was not.

A young girl in pigtails, one of my older cousins, in a flowered dress, crying and holding a naked Barbie doll.

My grandmother, leaning over an ice cream cake, muscling the knife through.

A table of oversized gifts, some wrapped in comics. Most with oversized bows in pink, purple and green.

"What *are* these?" I flipped through them, Anthony's chin now resting on my shoulder as he scanned them too.

"Those are our wedding pictures," my father said with surprise in his voice, the last two words rising in tone, as if he was asking me.

"Impossible," I said, dismissing him and putting the pictures down. "This is a picnic."

My father laughed, with bad timing. "Oh, it was no picnic!" No laugh. Return to subject. "These, Emilie, are the pictures from our wedding, from your mother's and my wedding. At your grandmother's house."

"No." I shook my head. "I heard all about your wedding. You had a five-tiered cake. Aunt Mindy and Aunt Wendy wore ball gowns . . ."

No, they didn't. There. There's Aunt Mindy in a tube top and white shorts, her hair long and straight. There's Aunt Wendy with a bad perm, in a blue sundress, chatting up some young man I assume was her date.

"Emilie, your mother and I didn't have much money then."

"But she *told* me about your wedding," I cried. "I saw the pictures! You were in a tuxedo! This crap . . . this isn't from your wedding. You're lying."

"Em," Anthony tapped his chin on my shoulder. "Come on, give him a break."

"Dad?" I couldn't believe it. Just couldn't believe it.

"Well, I don't know what she showed you," my father said, rubbing his lips again. "Maybe those were pictures from Aunt Wendy's wedding, a real wedding. We were in the bridal party."

"Did my mother wear a beige dress?" I asked quietly, wincing at the forthcoming answer.

"I don't remember what she wore, but yeah, that's possible. It was the 70s. So whatever it was, it probably wasn't . . . I don't know, honey. But that's the only wedding I was around for," he said. Done. Finished.

I was quiet for a long time. I returned to looking at the pictures. Of my sad-faced mother not at all the glowing, radiant, smiling woman she was in the *other* pictures, the ones she pulled out and showed me when I was a little girl. All the stories. She made them up. Her wedding cake . . . it was an ice cream cake, not the five-tiered iced perfection she'd described as "tasting like a cloud from heaven." She carried limp daisies, not roses. Her reception was out in Gram's backyard, not in a hotel ball-room. She'd lied about it all. She'd lied to me about it all.

"I thought I was bringing you something you'd treasure," my father said, stunned, knowing he'd gone just a step too far without knowing it. But it wasn't his fault. He came here with something from his heart, sharing something a mother should share with her daughter before her wedding day . . . if she didn't burn it up in her own self-effigy cere-mony years ago.

Through tears, I thanked him, then walked shak-ily to my room, legs stiffly moving like I'd been sit-ting for days.

Anthony and my father talked for a while longer. I could hear them through the door. My father gave Anthony some money for the wedding, in-sisted that he take it. He was being a good father. Making up for lost time with the first few steps of re-covery. Anthony thanked him, knowing enough not to refuse him this gesture of kindness. And then when my father had gone, his load lightened, his promise made, my future husband came to lie down next to me and hold me as I sobbed.

And we hadn't even had breakfast yet.

"Em," he said through my hair and into my ear. "Now let me tell you why *my* mother is acting so nuts with this wedding too."

Chapter 23

He struggled to explain it the right way, in a way that would get his point across without permanently lodging an everlasting awkwardness from me toward his mother. He knew I had thought so highly of her all these years, and her spooky stranger/slasher persona was a shocker to me. He couldn't stay silent anymore, couldn't play dumb and tell me I was imagining things, he said. She does have a problem. A big one. And like my own mother, it goes back for years.

Here's how I imagined it from his explanation . . .

Carmela's family was second generation immigrants to this country. Poor of cash but rich in the warmth of family. Old World. Traditional. The father ruled the home, the mother stayed silent and nurtured the three generations living in close, cramped quarters with a real struggle for financial survival. Food was often scarce. Schooling came second to work for even the little ones. Third-hand clothes were the norm. They were decent, hardworking people, with little to no frills in their lives, treasuring their closeness as they sat together by the heat of the stove and told stories of ancestors' triumphs, the riches their family had in the old country, romantic triangles between a great-great-grandmother and the baker's son. By candle-light, this family held fast to their traditions, their values, their work ethic, and their religion. It was the precursor to their American Dream, the lean years where their future promises were priming to take hold.

Carmela never knew to be unhappy with that. To wish for better clothes or an extra ten cents to go to a movie. To her, her world was about family and goodness above all other things.

At age nineteen, she married. It was an Old World Italian wedding, shrinkingly modest by today's standards, held in a hollow VFW hall's banquet room, and guest upon guest arrived with platters of pasta, sausage, homemade breads, jugs of homemade wine or wines from Abruzzi. Everyone her family knew, everyone from the avenue, came to the wedding. No invitations were issued; it wasn't a question of who would and wouldn't come. Everyone came to a family celebration. Music came from the spontaneous singing of groups of soused men, as the pudgy-armed women dished out baked ziti in assembly-line style, sweating over the steaming trays. Children ran around in play, inside and out, and deals were made between the men as they smoked their homemade cigarettes and (for the richest among them) cigars. Carmela danced, she greeted her guests, and she stepped into her new life ritual by ritual . . . the first dance, the cutting of the cake (which she helped to serve), the accepting of gifts and well-wishes from those who smiled at her but didn't expect her to smile back.

The beginning of it all happened at St. Agnes' church. The ceremony was appropriately pious, formal, solemn, church-dictated to the letter. What we would call a cookie-cutter ceremony now. *Come in, repeat after me, turn around and go onward into your future, and leave your check at the door.* Carmela kept her head down under her veil and repeated the words uttered to her, crossed herself, and kissed her new husband Victor Anthony Cantano. Vic. Anthony's father.

But he wasn't the man she wanted to marry.

My jaw hung open at that one. "Was it an arranged marriage? A marriage of convenience?" I asked quietly. "Was she expecting?"

Anthony exhaled a small laugh and even I noticed my mother's literary influence on my own expectations. What would make the most dramatic story arc?

What he came out with was better than that. And then I understood. Completely. *Perfectly.*

Carmela's first love was a young man from the wealthy part of town, where the old money lived. The people who were steeped in the spoils of the American Dream, either by hard work or by inheritance. They drove cars, sent their children to schools, dressed properly, made money without working for it. Her first love was the son of a banker, the smooth-haired handsome heir to his father's growing empire. Tall, handsome, refined and educated. Anthony hadn't absorbed the details of this young man's looks, as being a man, that wasn't the part of the story that interested him. But when he heard his mother telling a new family friend this tale, he had to listen. And he remembered the look in her eye, that faraway dreamy wish-look that told him his mother had loved this man very, very deeply. And for a fifteen-year-old boy to catch that message, it had to be blaring from her.

And the young man loved Carmela as well. Deeply. To the point of offering to leave his family and their wealth, give up his golden ticket and take her away to California for a fresh start. And she packed a suitcase.

His family, of course, was not going to accept her as one of their own. She was an Invisible, an unmentionable. Steps below the *servants*. Uneducated to their standards, dirty to their standards. The young man sneaking off to be with her in the evening hours, instead of at society cotillions, was discovered very dramatically, loudly, and with threats from his father and tears from his mother. *How could you forsake your family name?*

And as Carmela packed her worn and faded suitcase with a latch that didn't close without tape, carefully folding few clothes so that there would be plenty of dresses left for her younger sisters to wear, her one bottle of perfume, and a book of poems, across town the young man did not drive to her soon enough. His father came to him and showed him a brighter future if he turned from this great love to a better great love: money, success, welcome into the upper stratosphere of society. A picture painted of a life of comfort and travel, ease, a key that fits in any door. And the sole ownership of his father's vast estate and empire, growing each day by the thousands of dollars' worth without a lifted finger.

What would he have with this *girl* if he left? He'd work. *He'd* be the outcast in a social strata. *She* was used to toiling, to having calluses, sweating, giving all and getting little in return. It was *her* life, not his. What would he do in a broken-down hovel when he had mansions waiting for his name to be inscribed on them? Why would he choose to eat scraps when he had banquets in his future? And his leaving would just kill his mother, just break his mother's heart.

The young man never showed up at midnight to claim Carmela and whisk her away to California. He almost did. He walked to her home to deliver his change of heart, turned the corner and saw her standing there on her front stoop, on the bottom step with one foot innocently dangling off as if to take that next big step. She wore a yellow dress and a yellow child-size ribbon in her hair, something she took from her sleeping baby sister's dresser to remember her by, and she stood there in the moonlight and night air. Stood there in the silence of the night, waiting for her own prince to come take her to their new world. She wasn't running away from her life. She cherished it. She wasn't abandoning her family. She would be back in a few months with success in her own new family, with money of their own, with proof of their love and commitment.

And he just stood two blocks away on that street corner, unseen by her, looked at her there with her suitcase . . . and he shoved his hands in his pockets and walked away. She waited until 4 A.M., and her foot never touched the street level.

Carmela swallowed her sadness and anger. Outwardly, she shrugged it off when her cousins and confidantes asked of that night, shocked as they were to see her there the next morning. She said something to the effect of "it was nice to dream for a while," and went right back to work, head down, working long hours and pocketing her pay for a new future to be hers. Her parents noticed her heartbreak, the entire neighborhood knew of her casting away. It was a hushed rush of words the next day, mumbles and whispers that Carmela had to endure as she walked head-down along the avenue, her coat pulled tightly around her, for weeks. Everyone knew the story of Carmela's broken heart. Her brothers offered to take care of him, but she wouldn't allow it. The Catholic in her would not allow revenge and the changing of someone else's course of life. It was her duty to just accept it. Soon, she was steeled to it. She could tell the story with nothing but a sigh and a resigned smile, and feigned indifference until she herself forgot parts of the story. She was still working on that part. The forgetting.

Carmela was still nineteen when she heard that her rich young man was getting married. Word spread through her neighborhood quickly, and one kind soul came to her directly, so that she didn't hear it at the market. One kindly woman from the avenue came to her and told her. Her young man would marry Kimberly Anderson, a suitable socialite and moneyed heiress this Sunday at St. Patrick's Cathedral. I wished at this point that I was hearing the story from Carmela herself, as I knew she'd have more of the brutal and heartbreaking details that are part of a woman's story to another woman. I was left to my own imagination here as Anthony recounted the story he'd overheard as a child, seconded by his father who was sadly well aware.

The rest of the story had me in tears for Carmela. I could see it all. She made her way not to the church, where she would be seen and probably would be searched for by the young man's family, but to the reception hall. The Biltmore, Anthony thought it was. A grand, flower-filled ballroom with crystal glasses and chandeliers, champagne, strolling violinists, the furthest cry possible from her daily environment. Sneaking through the loading doors in the back of the hotel, she snaked her way undetected by the staff to the kitchen door, rose up on her toes, and peered through the round window of that swinging door to watch her first love take his first dance with Kimberly Anderson. She with her pure pedigree and pristine reputation as a debutante, her upswept hair, her diamond necklace and flowing white gown, graceful arms held out in proper form for a waltz. And he, dashing in his tuxedo. The two of them . . . *perfect*. The thrill of high society and the focus of the society pages. It was like an Audrey Hepburn movie.

And Carmela looked on from the confines of the kitchen. Where she belonged.

"Oh God, how awful!" I wiped a tear of empathy from my hot cheek and shook my head slowly, feeling such a hollowness in my own stomach for her.

"Isn't it?" Anthony whistled, shaking his own head.

"And your father knows all of this?"

"He knows he wasn't her first choice, yes."

"Wow," I exhaled, and then repeated it. "So her dealing with my mother . . . with all this level of . . ." I couldn't say it exactly. It wouldn't be appropriate. "This wedding being so . . . like . . ."

"Exactly," Anthony pulled the message from my stammering. "Our wedding is looking like it's going to be just like that one. Too much of it will be similar."

"And your mother would be—"

"In a way . . . right back at that round window, reliving her nightmare all over again," Anthony finished my sentence. "The outsider looking in at the high society wedding where she is mistaken for the help."

"Ugh." I held my temples, thinking back to my mother's engagement party . . . how the guests were dropping their coats and hats on her arms like she worked there. It must have felt like she was being stabbed.

"So that's her story," Anthony said and rubbed his leg against mine. "You get it now?"

I, unfortunately, got it.

Chapter 24

"I don't understand why the Plaza is out," Delilah followed us, clicking in her heels and tight in her posture, as we toured the Botanical Gardens. Anthony, Vic, Carmela and I were glorying in the gardens themselves, drinking in the colors, the sweet scents and the delicate turns of petals, open to more stimulating scenery than Delilah's current tunnel vision on her own plans for the wedding. She saw nothing around us as we took each turn, crossed footbridges and anticipated the waterfall we heard in the distance ahead of us.

Carmela had been warmer to me that day. She didn't bring any knives along, as far as I could tell, and Vic hugged me like I was already his daughter-in-law.

"I told you, Mother," I sang, just thrilled to be in this warm and lush-scented wonderland and not at all lost on the irony of being followed by a very well-dressed serpent. "Anthony and I prefer the Gardens to the Plaza. Look at this!" I turned to Anthony, pointing to the deep purple irises in clusters around mossy rocks and boulders. "Irises! God, I love irises!"

Anthony told me later that he hadn't seen me light up like that since the night of our engagement.

"Well, then," Delilah sighed. "I guess I'll have to cancel with the Plaza." She waved her hand in front of her face, too warm for comfort in this humid environment. She was immune to the beauty all around her. How very sad.

"Done," Anthony said, causing my mother's head to snap toward him, glaring. "I called them this morning, and we're canceled. You'll get your deposit back."

And I knew he had controlled himself not to say "Don't worry," in the most petulant tone possible before that comment about my mother getting her money back.

Carmela beamed. About the roses, not about the roses. About Delilah not getting her way, about her son telling her she wouldn't be getting her way. It was a good and glorious day for Carmela. She would not have to celebrate our marriage in a hotel ballroom. I leaned down over the irises and inhaled.

Chapter 25

They were at it again.

This time, at the flower market.

"So what would you have happen?" Carmela spat, red in the face and actually physically restrained by Vic's hand gently at her elbow. "You want my Anthony to ride up on a white horse in a suit of armor like in one of your . . . novels."

Thank you for not saying "trashy novels" like you have in my presence, Carmela.

Delilah tutted and raised an eyebrow, clearly enjoying the rise in Carmela's blood pressure. As condescending a tone as possible spilled from her, her voice one part honey, three parts acid. "No, Carmela. That's quite stereotypical . . . which is another word for commonplace."

"Hey!" I shot her a look. "Take a pill, will you?"

"My, my, Emilie, you're starting to sound like them," Delilah said quietly enough for Vic not to hear, which is good because she would have been bleeding from the ears if he had.

"Cut it out, Mother," I hissed. "You're being incredibly rude."

She sighed dramatically, then rejoined us as we picked up stem after stem of white and blush pink roses, camellias, lily of the valley, inspecting each bloom to gather our ideas for the centerpieces. Our floral designer couldn't be bothered to show us photos, but instead encouraged us to go to the flower mart first thing in the morning when the incoming shipment was still fresh and dewy. I was annoyed at him then, but understood the point: *Get this annoying mother of yours away from me and let her wander through the options. She could use the day trip.* Unfortunately, this was a woman who was unmoved by the Botanical Gardens, but it was a nice effort.

"Yes, a nice 'riding up on the white horse' scene with Anthony grabbing Emilie by the hair and pulling her up onto the mighty *steed,* after a sword fight with the maître d'," Delilah taunted. "Good idea, Carmela." But Anthony's mother was out of earshot. Delilah just tagged along like a reluctant four-year-old, angry that she had to go along with others' plans. After all, she already had the flowers chosen for our centerpieces weeks ago. Months ago. All we had to do was ask her.

"Will you get your mother to shut up?" Anthony growled.

"Hey, your mother isn't helping," I said, and then turned away from him. We were not going to have this fight again, because we were coming dangerously close to a "your mom is worse than my mom" level of playground argument tactics. Foot stamping, arm crossing, pouty lips and "nanny nanny boo boo" strictly optional.

"What's this one? Witch's glove? Ah . . . Interesting . . ." came Carmela's voice from another row of flower buckets. I rubbed a fallen eyelash out of my eye and gave Anthony a sour and completely sarcastic smile. He had to look away.

"Do you have any hemlock, any oleander?" Delilah was tickled at her cleverness, but Carmela had read the Oprah's Book Club picks and knew both types of flowers to be poisonous and deadly.

Burly and moustached flower trade workers looked at my mother askance, their thick arms lifting seventy-five-pound buckets without any strain, but still they were creeped out by her eerie references to flowers she knew to be fatal. As she kept on about the hemlock, I wouldn't have been surprised if one of the teamsters actually dialed the police in order to thwart a possible serial poisoner.

"This is impossible," I said to Anthony, whose own blank facial expression told me he had come to the same conclusion. "I don't think we can take them for their walks at the same time anymore."

He chuckled, both of us imagining the mothers as their canine caricature counterparts, with us holding their respective jeweled and rough leather leashes. They fought like bitches, after all, so why not?

"Ranunculus," Delilah pointed. And that's when Carmela shouted out a vast and impressive insult, having misheard the word "ranunculus" for something quite different. Quite the phrase. We ended the shopping trip early and sent the mothers home, with Vic snickering behind my mother's back. I thought I heard him comment about kicking her bony butt, but I'd just prefer not even thinking about that. Oh yes, there was a very good chance of a saloon-type brawl at my wedding. Someone was going to lose teeth. I just knew it.

"What about having two separate receptions?"
Anthony suggested, and I laughed until I realized
he was just not kidding. These women could not
even share the same sidewalk, the same room, the
same flower mart. Two separate receptions? Unfortunately, the safe option was not the best option. We'd put these two Japanese fighting fish
into the same tank on the biggest day of our lives
and watch them go. I had a vision right then of Vic
taking the cash and our guests placing their bets.
Great. A dogfight image for my wedding. Perfect.
Just perfect.

As if we had not had enough for one day, we
took the mothers for another walk. Time was not
on our side with just a few months until the Big
Day, so we had scheduled a meeting with our invitation designer. She was another that Delilah called
darling and had programmed in her speed dial. So,
naturally, espresso, champagne and truffles awaited
us there as well.

The showroom was arranged like a museum, with
each single wedding invitation posing on a waist-
high marble pedestal, surrounded by fresh rose
petals and spotlight from above. Marble shelving
sections held actual celebrity wedding invitations,
complete with signed celebrity wedding photos to
authenticate. The need for authenticity reminded
me of the suspicious nature in the city. Somewhere, shady invitation designers must be printing
out and displaying *fake* celebrity invitations, so this
showroom had to provide the autographed glossies
as proof. *Someone hand me a glass of champagne. I am
cynical today.*

Marge is a woman who doesn't look like her

name. She emerged from what I assume is their
back room, where piles of papers must be strewn
about in complete disarray, pens bleeding on the
table, piles of Post-its attached to computer moni-
tors, and plastic trash bins overflowing. I hoped
for some chaos behind all this perfection.

Marge wore a lemon-colored wrap dress and
high heels, an ankle bracelet, and her ringleted
black hair was held up in a high ponytail. With her
dancer's body and graceful arms—a poised hand
now reaching out to shake my own—I thought: *She
looks like a Claire, not a Marge.* I had heard about
her. My mother had once remarked about her perfect peachy skin, her raven hair in perfect ringlets
that were *natural, can you believe it?* Delilah had created a character for one of her books based on the
beauty of Marge. And, of course, called her Vanessa.

I couldn't stop myself . . . *Marge is what Snow
White has become.* I wondered if she ever put in a
summer or two playing the costumed character
Snow White at Disney World. She could have pulled
it off, to borrow from my mother, *fabulously.*

"I understand we have a wedding coming up,"
Marge squawked, in a voice that didn't sound like
it should be coming from a face that beautiful.
*God, get me a glass of champagne, stat! I am a cynical
bitch today.*

Before I could speak, her nails on chalkboard
voice continued.

"And I hear it will be something of a . . . fusion,"
Marge smiled, eyeing Carmela as if she had heard
all about her. Marge and Delilah were in a silent
duplicity. This should be fun.

*   *   *

"A formal wedding calls for simple, timeless elegance . . ." Marge held up invitation samples as if they were not printed on paper, but on porcelain. She handed each to us with her lips pouted and her hands at ready-to-catch position. Anthony shifted his weight in his chair, and his movement made me look at his face. He had noticed the overprotection too. We smiled at one another. "Is there a problem?" Marge rapped on the table to get our attention. We were caught speaking in class.

"No, ma'am." Anthony folded his hands in front of him, ever the good student.

"As I was saying . . ." Marge went on, and the contenders were laid out before us. All fifty of them. Sometimes there is such a thing as too many choices. We are a group that can't decide between two different colors of napkins. And now you put fifty invitations in front of us, some covering the others? And we weren't allowed to actually *touch* any of them?

"We want color," I dared to speak, as I had not yet raised my hand.

Marge looked like I had slapped her across the face. Her cheeks grew as red as if I had.

"But black on ecru is formal—"

"We want color," I shrugged, putting my hands dangerously close to the edge of a robin's egg blue invitation. That should get her attention.

"Ooookaaaaaaay." Marge cleared away a few dozen of the traditional, formal invitations.

"That's okay, color is in," Delilah assured us, or rather herself by speaking aloud.

Anthony just sat back. He knew what was coming. My posture had straightened, my eyes narrowed just a bit. And I pushed my hair back behind my ears. I had come to play poker.

"We wanted colored print too," I said.

Marge had played poker before. "You mean . . . colored *ink*."

Touché!

"Yes."

"What color?"

I raised an eyebrow as I pretended to think about it. Carmela and Delilah faded into the background. Marge was the only person who, to me, remained in the room. The temperature rose.

Now, do I give her the real answer, or shock her with a fake one?

"Purple," was what came out of my mouth.

"Eggplant or lavender?" *Wow, she's good. She didn't miss a beat.*

"Eggplant," I said quickly, and the protests of the mothers became to my ears just white noise in the background.

"On white paper?"

"Cream."

"You mean ecru?"

"I mean cream."

Marge cleared away another two dozen sample invitations. She should have swiped the tabletop, as none of them were eggplant-on-cream, but for her . . . hope sprang eternal.

"We'll call that Option Number 1," Marge bargained. "How about elegant black print on sage green paper? I just did invitations for Oprah in that design."

Goooooaaaaaaaal! She dropped the O-Bomb. My mother praised and prayed to Oprah Winfrey. She bought everything in *O* magazine's Favorite Things section. According to Delilah, if Oprah wears these pajamas and slippers, so, too, will I. My eggplant-and-cream invitations were history.

Did I not fight for my choice? The eggplant and cream? Did I just roll over and give up my power to my mother, as Leah would say? Nope. Not at all. I am an Oprah addict as well. I own the pajamas and the slippers. I bought white tea hand cream. I once spent $75 on cookies because Oprah loves them. And I was just messing with Marge about the eggplant. So elegant black print on sage green was It.

"And how would you like the wording?"

We were ready for Marge's verbal invitation, ready to avert war. Anthony jumped—literally jumped—off his chair to pull out the printed wording that he and I had created using the formal, traditional wording charts on a bridal Web site.

This was shark-infested water. The message boards on the Web site were littered with the broken hearts of brides whose parents cut them out of the will for listing the groom's parents on the invitations. And these were normal families. Anthony and I read about the invitation wording rules for when you have six sets of parents, after all kinds of divorce and remarriage and sex changes and coming out of closets and life partners and using Doctor and Captain and Emperor, people's formal titles.

We could only leave our parents' names off the invitation if we were planning for and paying for the wedding ourselves, and even then it's proper to still put the parents' names on the invitation somehow. We read about how you can put "The Loving Parents Of . . ." but that would still get us jailed and fined in some intangible way after the wedding. No, we had to follow tradition and put my mother's name first, my father's and Jenni's names second, and Carmela and Vic third. That's tradition. That's how it's done.

Delilah and Carmela would lose their minds.

"*What?!*" the mothers shrieked in unison, one's face turning white, the other lipstick red. MAC lipstick red.

"Your *father* is on it?! He's not a part of this!"

"We're listed *last!*"

"Emilie! You should have *asked me* first!"

Marge must see these scenes play out all the time. And in a better world, she would have come to my defense and explained that our model was the traditional one, according to decades-old decorum, and correct to the letter. But did Snow White whistle a happy tune? No. I had messed with her about the eggplant, so I was on my own.

An hour later, after Carmela and Vic had been moved up a peg, and my father's new wife still included on the invitation (Marge figured out that etiquette breaches on her part could get leaked to the press), we hobbled out of there exhausted. Fonts had been chosen, wording had been set in stone, and sage green would be our packet theme. And my will to live had been severely diminished. I was out of it. So much so that my radar was turned down to level 1. And Delilah knew it.

"Oh my," Delilah patted herself down and looked concerned. "I've left my cell phone inside." She was talking too quickly, and I didn't catch it. "You all proceed down to the Oak Room," for the drinks we all needed after that. "And I'll catch up with you in a minute."

"Delilah, we can wait for you," Anthony's radar was on 5. He picked up a blip. But Delilah was on full throttle.

"Oh, no, you go ahead," she waved us away with

her square manicured fingers, gave us a *Ta Ta* and disappeared back into Marge's letter-perfect paradise.

What I didn't know then, but found out later, was that Delilah and Marge giggled like junior high cheerleaders mocking the fat girl. They changed Carmela's name on the invitation. To Cornelia. And then submitted the order for final printing.

Chapter 26

"What's this?" I blinked the sleep out of my eyes, pulled a lock of hair back behind my ear and focused gradually on the envelopes Anthony dangled in front of my face. He sat cross-legged on the bed next to me, grinning and looking very satisfied with himself. In a moment, my focus grew enough to see the word on both the blue envelopes: *Continental*. My eyes shot to Anthony and he was nodding even while I leapt up to knock him over with a hug.

Four hours later, we were on a plane to Bermuda.

Chapter 27

I tried, like most of the other passengers in business class, to whip out my laptop and multitask in midair, always chasing a deadline or a deal or a deal-breaker. But it just wasn't going to happen. My overtaxed brain wasn't going anywhere near fragrances for Clinique or cliché jingles for Mr. Garrity. In my mind was the tornado from *The Wizard of Oz*, only it wasn't three farmhands in a rowboat, a cow, some chickens and an old lady on a bicycle flying past me out the window. I had Vera Wang gowns, a Sylvia Weinstock five-tiered wedding cake, some strolling violinists, and monogrammed napkins zipping and flipping around in the violent winds. It would have been fitting to have Carmela and Delilah turning into the green-faced witches on a broomstick, but I just couldn't muster that one. Protective instincts. I was blocking them out. Plus, I knew they could never be convinced to share a ride on one broomstick.

I shook my head a little bit as if erasing an Etch-a-Sketch inside my brain, then turned my attention from my own whirring thoughts to an obviously newlywed couple across the aisle from me. They had that glow, a perfect mixture of bliss and bewilderment. The bride batted her eyelashes at the groom, or so I thought until I realized she was trying to dislodge one of those JLo false eyelash segments she'd forgotten to remove the night before. She plucked the tiny hair sprouts from her eye and plunked it into her lunch tray. She had a perfect French manicure with the edges squared. Her hand returned back to high on the groom's thigh and more poked than petted him.

As for the groom, from my vantage point, the back of his neck was perfectly shaved and groomed, which was the only odd evidence I had that he had just taken wedding vows the day before. It wasn't until later that I would see his too obviously waxed and shaped eyebrows. *Please let that trend for guys come to a halt.*

The happy couple snuggled and nuzzled each other's noses. They whispered into each other's ears and the bride threw her ringlet-haired head back in loud laughter. She called him Pookie, and Anthony pretended to fumble for his air sickness bag.

"Were we ever like that?" he whispered to me.

"Absolutely not," came my reply with an unspoken but understood *Thank God.*

Perhaps it was my heightened need for an escape from reality, but I couldn't get enough of watching and listening to the happy couple. In a near-hyperactive state, the bride played with the groom's hair, then went back to poking his thigh. She turned in her chair to drape her legs over him, then twisted again to cross them in front of her. She lowered her seat back and then put it straight up again. He ordered another drink. Ah, connubial bliss. They were thrilled and terrified. They didn't know what to do with themselves, or with each other. There was a distinct smell of "What do we do now?" in the air.

Soon, they were not-so-subtly discussing their strategy for meeting in the bathroom to join the mile-high club. Even I know that you don't plan that for a two-hour flight from Newark to Bermuda. You wait for a red-eye or a trans-Atlantic flight. *Amateurs*.

I nudged Anthony, who looked up from his laptop, and nodded my chin toward the newlyweds, mouthing the word "Listen."

So there we were. Eavesdroppers on the in-flight sexual antic planning meeting of a young couple in love.

"You go first, and then I'll follow in exactly three minutes."

"Why can't we both just go in together?"

"It's too obvious."

"No one will notice."

"Are you *dense*? They'll notice."

"God, you used to be so spontaneous," delivered with a sigh and an eye roll.

Uh-oh, this isn't looking good. Anthony widened his eyes at me, and we both turned to see how the plan turned out. And we weren't being subtle about it either.

"*I* used to be spontaneous?! What about *you*?"

"I'm trying to be romantic here!"

"By criticizing me?"

Ooooooh, good one.

"I'm sorry, sweetie. You're right."

Anthony mouthed the words "good save" and pumped his fist for His Boy. At some point in the eavesdropping, we had taken sides. It was as if we had money on the outcome.

"So you go first, and then I'll fake an asthma attack and have to go to the bathroom to get my inhaler from you." This was from the blushing bride, who clearly had no empathy for asthma sufferers and absolutely no way with sneaking around. She was outmatched in that regard.

"No way, that'll get every stewardess on the plane running to the bathroom door to see if you're okay. They don't want you to die in there."

Anthony raised an eyebrow. His Boy had a point. My Girl pouted. She clearly had thought her idea was brilliant.

"Just go, and I'll be there."

A strange, loaded silence from the bride. Her face changed. Her eyes narrowed. She looked at her groom like he had just told her he was impotent. She wasn't blinking. Her lips were pressed tightly together.

"What?" the groom asked, jerking his head back. We couldn't see his facial expression but could only judge by the tightness in his back and his rising shoulders that things were not going as he planned.

The bride didn't answer. She just glared at him stonily.

"What? What's your problem?"

"You're attracted to the flight attendant, aren't you?" she growled, crossing her arms over her A-cup chest and lifting her chin at the Lucky Groom. "You are! She's blonde and she's thin . . . You are! Just admit it! I saw you looking at her! You're attracted to her!"

"For crying out loud!" The voice made us all jump . . . because it was *Anthony's*. He unbuckled his seat belt with one hand, with the same talent he uses to effortlessly flick open any design of bra clasp I have in my vast arsenal of lingerie, and stood up in the aisle, towering over the young bride and groom who looked up at him in horror.

For an instant, I imagined the six o'clock news reporting the diversion of our flight due to an unruly passenger. But this was more entertaining than frightening. Other passengers around us had become entranced with the scene as well, all probably inwardly thinking of the groom "good luck, buddy!"

To His Boy, Anthony coached: "Here's how it's done." He turned to me, and I suppressed a smirk. "Sweetheart?"

"Yes?" I drew out the word musically, knowing where he was going with it.

"Want to go have sex in the bathroom right now?"

"Sure!" I animatedly unbuckled myself and stepped out into the aisle. "We haven't done it in *this* plane before." I looked around in full overacting mode to the delight of the other passengers who knew from looking at us that we were just playing around with the delicate sensitivities and sheer exposure of the happy couple.

Even the flight attendant was in on the game, having heard every word spoken by the young couple, who now sat stupefied in their seats, white-knuckled stress cases with a great, big unwanted spotlight on them. They were busted.

Straightening her little red-and-white tie, the flight attendant stepped forward to take part in our game and swept her hand in a flourish to show us the way to the restroom. "Take your time. This isn't a crowded flight," the flight attendant winked.

"And I'll have coffee and some chocolates ready for you when you're done."

The formerly histrionic bride now sat with her jaw hanging open, and the groom took in the scene without ever looking directly at the pretty blonde in the blue blazer and red-and-white tie. He did want to get *some* action from his bride this week, after all. And as Anthony took my hand to walk me to the airplane bathroom, the entire cabin smiled and shook their heads. Of course, we didn't rejoin the mile high club during that flight, but Anthony did make sure that we didn't emerge from that tiny little cubicle for at least twenty minutes. We just stood there and giggled like high schoolers, thoroughly amused with ourselves.

Goooooaaaaaal!

And when we returned to our seats, the flight attendant brought us not only coffee and chocolates, but also a pair of hot hand towels from first class.

"And that, my boy, is how it's done." Anthony delivered his line and returned to his laptop without missing a beat. That's *my* boy.

It occurred to me as we stepped off the plane and into the bright, hot welcoming sunlight and deliciously salty air at the airport in Bermuda, that we had just completely traumatized a young couple in love. We were very bad people. But it did feel good to siphon some of that tension onto them. They were being ridiculous and rigid, much like our mothers, so we couldn't resist. Anthony winked at me, and in our co-conspirator status, we walked hand in hand toward baggage claim, our strides matching.

As for the bride and groom from the plane? They walked hand in hand ahead of us, their strides not quite matching. He took longer steps and she was partially skipping to keep up with him. They'd learn in time. He'd shorten his gait, and she'd take longer steps so they'd meet in the middle. They'd learn that without thinking about it, as we had. The groom kissed her temple and whispered something in her ear that thoroughly amused her. As they glowed, we just marveled at the tenacity of young love. He pinched her butt, and she pinched his right back.

We wished them well.

Chapter 28

I just have to call my mother and let her know where I...

I tossed the phone back into its cradle like it had just stung my hand. What was I thinking? We just walked into our beautiful oceanfront suite with billowing white curtains beckoning us to our marble terrace and the never-ending aqua blue ocean beyond. Champagne waited on ice for us, along with chocolate-covered strawberries and vases of white flowers. The room smelled like gardenias.

We passed the mahogany wet bar and came to the French doors leading to the master bedroom. Sweeping open, they introduced a king-sized canopy bed with white-and-gray bedding, sheer white netting cascading from a single point on the ceiling, flower-filled sconces, and a silver tray of truffles by the bedside. The windows were open, and the curtains danced in the bedroom as well. The air had a rhythm. The curtains danced on the scent of gardenias.

In the spa bathroom, a clear-walled shower

with a waterfall showerhead awaited our nightly enjoyment, and a pale sand pink Jacuzzi across the room would not go to waste. The soaps were pink clamshell shapes, and a pink floral arrangement sat on the vanity table. Matching white spa robes and slippers had been laid out over pristine pink slipcovered chairs in the bathroom's third section, and dozens of pale pink candles in frosted white holders surrounded the tub edges, sitting on fresh flower petals.

And my first thought is that I have to check in with my mother? Just one second while I reattach my brain.

We never unpacked so quickly in our lives. This is another way we're alike. We can't just drop our suitcases, strip down and jump into our bathing suits and run to the beach. We both can't relax unless we've unpacked fully, hung up our formal clothes in the closet, arranged our toiletries on our respective sides of the sink, and claimed our own bureau drawers with our folded clothes. We acknowledge that particular pathology and will some-day acknowledge the name for it. We rushed, smiling to one another about how much we needed to jump the divide between the real world and this world. We needed to hear steel drums playing by the pool instead of Muzak in the elevator. We needed cocoa butter scented tropical breezes and not what passes for air in the subway tunnels. We needed to be barely dressed in public. We needed to swim up to a bar rather than fighting through a sweaty happy hour crowd to get a martini and a Heineken. No, hand me a coconut with my drink in it. I need it. Now.

We were wired. We moved in jerky motions, clumsy, tripping over our sandals rather than slid-

ing into them. We slathered SPF onto one another's backs without taking the time to make it
sensual, grabbed our beach bags, slipped our sunglasses on and raced out of the room while the sun
was still at peak. Somewhere on the island, the
happy couple from the plane dropped their bags
and dived into their canopy bed. Of course ...
their wedding stress was over and forever was just
beginning for them. They pushed through the
glass ceiling. The birth was over. And they forgot
all about the pain.

Six minutes later, my lips closed around a green
plastic straw and life moved in slow motion. The
creamy piña colada mix moved up the straw and
over my tongue, and the second that sweet liquid
entered my mouth, every cell in my body relaxed.
Anthony had drained a Corona already, and we
looked at each other with the pure relief of a res-
cued passenger from a capsized boat. Escape.
We'd made our escape. Our bodies may have un-
clenched, but our minds would take a few more
hours to slow down.

We lay in silence on our lounges, closing our
eyes to the sun and listening to the repetitive roll
of the surf, the kids laughing and playing, an older
woman telling her Chihuahua that she has to put
more doggy sunscreen on her little paws. Having
not opened my eyes, I wasn't sure who she was applying the sunscreen to—herself or her dog—but I
had to blink away that train of thought quickly before I was reminded of Anthony applying sunscreen
to Carmela several years ago. Now that I know her
better, that just creeps me out even more. I wondered if that image would ever go away.

Carmela . . .

I drifted in and out of beach consciousness, I think. My drink was drained and I magically had a fresh one. Somehow. A fresh spiky coconut was in my hand now, and I did a half crunch up to take a few safe sips without spilling onto my royal blue bikini, a gift from Anthony, a surprise in my bag.

The steel drum players rolled out a song I recognized but couldn't name. British accents surrounded me, as staff and guests discussed moped rentals and the perfume factory, the botanical gardens and teatime. Their conversations floated into my bubble in midsentence and floated back out again, carried away by the breeze and the sound of the waves. I concentrated on how the dark fabric of my bathing suit was warming up in the sun, that great hot feeling of your first exposure to the sun in months and months. My eyelashes curled in their heating stage, and I dropped my hand down to gently rake the fine pink sand. Years ago, on our first trip here, Anthony and I had bottled up some of this sand and taken it home with us as a commemoration of our first getaway—just two months after we started dating. We keep it on our living room shelf, and only twice had to rescue it back from Leah's ideal love altar. It's just so pretty. Finely crushed salt-sized fragments of pink shells mixed with whites, beiges, grays, tans, even little specks of black and some reds. When you look from far away, it's just a pinkish sand beach. When you bottle up a handful in one of those travel-sized Johnson's baby oil bottles and scrutinize it, you see dozens of colors and shapes in each grain. There was some lesson in that, but I was too blissful with my piña colada and my sunshine to analyze anything else. That part of my brain had blissfully glided to a halt.

But Carmela kept coming back to me . . . there was something there. Something unanswered. The steel drum band played and the surf crashed, slowing down my heart rate to near-human percussion. A cooler breeze tickled my stomach, and my husband-to-be flicked some cold water from his beer bottle onto my chest. I wrinkled my nose and watched as he lay back down on his chaise, those shoulders and that chest soon to be golden bronze. This was heaven.

Did I say *that* was heaven? I was wrong. *This* was heaven. In a strange, subterranean way. Anthony had arranged with the hotel to reserve a cavern underneath the hotel. At first I was puzzled. Why are they locking the big, steel gates behind us? Was this a plan of our mothers? To have us locked away in some cave so they can plan the wedding themselves? I turned to Anthony, who was amused by my imagination and my still-heightened anxiety on the first day of our stay. He took my hand and led me in the darkness down slimy stone steps that—from feeling with our toes—moved in a circular direction downward. I had to silence my inner businesswoman—*Hey, they'd better light these stairs, someone could fall and sue them*—to stay open to the intrigue.

In the distance, a faint purple light glowed, then turned more royal blue . . . then a brighter blue. I felt a brush of something against my shoulder and jumped. Stalactite or stalagmite. I couldn't remember from the fourth grade which limestone formation grew upward in caves and which grew downward.

The lights grew more into a mixture of blues

and purples and pinks. I could now see Anthony's face, and he was smiling. God, he was so handsome.

"Hold tight," he said, squeezing my hand tighter within the crook of his arm.

Don't worry, I will.

"Ready?" he said, and clearly we were about to turn the corner to something spectacular.

And we did.

My mouth opened into an O, and I felt myself exhale with a whoosh. The only sound I heard was a syncopated dripping of water from the stalactites into a pool of crystal clear water that now stood before me. In a crescent shape around it were glistening, limestone cave walls with tiny bits of quartz reflecting the pink, blue and purple spotlights set in the upper reaches of the cave ceiling. The cave sparkled. They might as well have been diamonds embedded in those walls.

A cool, wet metal handrail led us down the last remaining slippery steps to the edge of a private freshwater pool, clear to the bottom where blue and purple rock formations reached up toward us. It reminded me of those Magic Rocks kids play with; those bright, colorful stones you drop into a water-filled fishbowl and watch as they grew into colorful spikes, a watery garden of primary colored arms of all sizes reaching up toward something until they resembled a castle. They must have gotten the idea for that here. The waters were still. We could see the colored castle's arms reaching up to us from below the surface. Beckoning.

I marveled at this underground sanctuary for a moment, taking it all in, and imagined the surprise of the land developers who found it under their hotel. *Should we fill it with cement or keep it in-*

tact and rent it out to couples who want some private naked swim time? Luckily, the developers went with the latter. Without a word, Anthony and I stripped down to nothing and stepped into the freshwater pool. It was cold. No sunlight will do that to a body of water. But a good kind of cold. And the water seemed softer than any other water I'd ever experienced. We floated without effort.

Like dolphins, we swam down to touch the rock formations. We circled one another, touching and holding a thigh, an arm. I ran my hand along the muscular topography of Anthony's back, letting my fingers roll off his neck like I was playing a harp. My hair took on a mermaid quality of dancing around my face and I used that image to my advantage as I then swam demurely away from him, caught from behind and submerged deeper for a passionate kiss. And it's not easy to kiss underwater.

For two hours we swam and made love on the smoother outer rock edges. Anthony had made this *my* day as well. No one could hear us fifty feet below the earth's surface. We had escaped from the world. No one could hear us cry out down here below the surface.

Spent and sponge-toed from three hours in the water, famished and thirsty, we dressed in hormone-soaked silence and climbed the slippery rocky steps back into the remaining daylight sun.

Chapter 29

"Emilie, are you there? Pick up! It's your mother. Pick up the phone."

"Emilie, it's your mother. I know you're there. Pick up."

"Emilie . . . I called your office and they said you were away on a trip. I wasn't aware that you had a business trip scheduled. It would have been nice if you had let me know, as I made an appointment with the most darling shoe designer for those diamond encrusted shoes you wanted."

It was the first I was hearing about diamond encrusted shoes.

"Emilie, this is Carmela. Where are you? Can you have Anthony call me? My pilot light is out again."

"Emilie, this is your mother," A totally different tone. "I'm so worried about you. It isn't like you not to call back." *Yes it is.* "I'm fearing the worst here . . ." *Oh, please.* "So give me a call before I go to the police."

Good manipulation, Mom. I'm not biting. I fell for that one before.

"Emilie . . . I called your office and told them you'd gone missing. They're up in arms and saying something about handing over your account to a Mister Fielder or Fielding or something . . . Call me back." .

"Oh my God, Em, she's going to get you fired," Anthony exhaled when I let him listen to that particular message.

"Nah," I said and rolled over in my fluffy white spa robe so that I would expose just the right amount of my chest and stomach to entice him. "It's a ruse. She's done it before."

Anthony remained wide-eyed.

"The office knows where I am," I shrugged. "She's just bluffing."

"Wow, I'm impressed. She's a real snake."

"That's my mom," I sang out.

"Better send her an e-mail," Anthony said. "Just so she doesn't have a coronary or make Leah's life a living hell."

"Leah went to some conference in Boston, so she's not there either."

"Really?" Anthony's eyebrows raised. Cute little commas that they are. "Wow, I can't believe she took a road trip. She must be feeling better."

"Mmmm-hmmm," I purred, not wanting at all to talk about Leah or any mothers of anyone currently in this bed.

"She probably thinks we eloped," Anthony said, but his tone was almost too worrisome. There was just something off about it. He sounded nervous.

I shook it off, along with my robe, and handed him the coconut-scented massage oil. This was *my* day. And no, *this* was heaven.

Your tan lines always look better when you hit the shower after a day on the beach. With your eyes adjusted, you can appreciate the dark glow of your skin against the pale, pasty white lines of your spaghetti straps. And Anthony could too.

We decided to dress up for afternoon tea, a ritual on this British island and always served in fine bone china from a gleaming silver urn. Scones. Muffins. Petit fours for something a little sweet. A pianist lilted out Rachmaninov. The room smelled of sweet flowers and exotic teas and cinnamon, freshly baked bread. The sun projected long, straight lines of rainbow beams onto the hardwood floors through the bay windows, and the room filled quickly with gentlemen in white jackets and ladies in sundresses. Two small girls wore wide-brimmed white hats with yellow ribbons as they picked the raisins out of their scones and placed them delicately on the side of a saucer. And, of course, a Texan in his bathing trunks and a white undershirt, with a handlebar moustache and a bad sunburn on the back of his neck strolled through the otherwise dignified line of tea enthusiasts, picking up scones and booming "What the hell is this? Where's the shrimp buffet?" *God bless America.*

Anthony and I took our Earl Grey and wandered to the gardens right outside the terrace, stopping to smell the flowers. Anthony gave a playful tug to my ponytail and complimented me on my new white strapless sundress. He snapped a white rose off the trellis by the fountains and tucked it behind my ear.

"Perfect," he said. "You're just perfect."

"As are you, sir," I said, copying the beautiful, lilting British accent of every almost-too-kind doorman and server we've encountered here. They were like angels, all of them. Customer service is alive and well and living on an island just off the East Coast. I'd wondered where it had gone to.

"Let's keep walking . . ." Anthony took my hand and led me across the golf-course-quality green lawn toward a grove of trees with arched trunks and artistically knotted limbs, some branches trained into braids. My high heels had some trouble on the softened earth, but I kept my teacup steady. "Oh, look," he said, pointing from our safe distance through the cooler air beneath the trees so as not to disturb the wedding that was taking place by the ocean's bluff.

"She looks beautiful," I beamed for her, watching the dark-haired petite bride take her new husband's hand and step forward into a kiss to seal their vows. The smiling, super-white-toothed officiant stepped backward, his white robe lined with a pink satin stripe. Only in Bermuda is that the smoothest look ever. A crowd of a half dozen onlookers tossed a shower of white, red and pink rose petals over the new happy couple, and the bride laughed and removed the petals that had sailed into her modest cleavage. Applause broke out from all who happened to be invited or just passing by, including us as we stepped out of the grove. The blissful bride and groom embraced again, he lifting her off her feet as he twirled her around once, then started dancing to the steel drum music echoing from the pool terrace. And the groom could dance, which is always a welcome change.

"Look how happy they are," I said, and even I could hear the envy in my own voice.

"I want to make you that happy," he said, and it didn't sound corny at all in the moment. Anthony is romantic, but never forcedly so, like he had borrowed lines from my mother's books. He always had real words to say. "Right now."

"I am happy."

"No, I mean right now."

I still wasn't getting it. I was still captivated by watching the bride and groom walk off, laughingly trying to tame her veil from the dancing breeze of the oceanside. I laughed and then turned to him, finding him holding a velvet box in his hand.

There are moments in life, important ones, you just really wish you could do over again. Edit yourself. Make yourself not be so vacant-headed. This was one of them . . .

I actually said, "But you already proposed to me."

If I could only go back in time to redo that flub.

And then I got it.

But not before I saw a familiar face walking up the cobblestone path, passing the happy couple going in the opposite direction and also moving in time with the steel drum music. It was Leah. In a light lavender dress, which I knew—from her—was the color of wisdom. She had a light purple flower tucked behind her ear, and she didn't yet have a tan to go with it. She must have just arrived.

"You idiot," Anthony joked, and—at least I'm hoping—probably wanted to do that particular less-than-stellar moment over again as well. "Do you know how hard it was to pull this off?"

A surprise wedding? Once the shock wore off, would I be happy about it?

And here comes another moment in time to wish a cosmic do-over for . . .

"Please tell me our mothers are not here," I begged. My face, he told me later, had turned paper white (or more accurately, *ecru*), which was perhaps a cosmic sign that he had *so* done the right thing by not inviting them.

"No," Anthony said the magic word, which is ironic since this was a wedding moment. "No" shouldn't be part of the script. But it was perfect. *A highlight of my wedding day was when the groom said No.*

"Did you know," Leah started before even hugging me, "that if you marry underneath that circular stone gate over there, called a Moongate, you'll be destined to return to this site again in the future during your eternally happy marriage?"

I hugged my friend, almost knocking the purple flower from her hair. "How did you . . . ?"

She just shrugged and allowed me to hug her again.

"And you . . ." I hugged my groom-to-be. I was quite the hugger today. "What am I going to do with you?"

"Don't you want to see what's in the box?" Anthony made the little velvet box dance in his palm to the rhythm of the music, bouncing it around to make it hard for me to grab. But I did get hold of it.

I bit my lower lip and slowly opened it on its silent hinge. There they were. The platinum wedding bands we picked out. Our wedding bands. Simple, smooth, unadorned platinum. Traditional and elegant. None of those "it opens up into a timepiece" gadgets or Black Hills gold tricolored rings various mall jewelers tried to push on us. No diamond channel-set for me. No birthstones or laser etchings in a lace pattern. No dual-tone metals with a gold edge in case gold jewelry comes back into style. We went simple. Beautiful.

I pulled mine from its slot and held it at an angle. And it was there. The inscription Anthony kept secret from me when he ordered it: *E.—Forever—Love A.*

And that was the first time I had cried in days. The first time I had cried tears of joy in months.

Our wedding took place on a bluff overlooking the aqua blue water's edge, led poetically by the British, bright-toothed officiant in the cool, pink-striped robe. Leah was my maid of honor, holding my teacup instead of a bouquet. My groom was the most handsome and loving man on this earth, and he cried as much as I did as we took our vows . . .

I take you to be my forever partner, perfect in my eyes always no matter what may come. I take you as my best friend in a bond of marriage that no one can put asunder, to grow and climb, to laugh and love, to support and to build our dreams together. I choose you to be with me for all time and even after death. I am yours always and forever.

And with our kiss, we were married. He took my face in his hands just like he did on our very first date, for our very first kiss. I am Mrs. Anthony Cantano. He is my husband. *This* is heaven.

Walking back to the hotel to improvise a reception among the three of us—no floral centerpieces, ice sculptures or Colin Cowie waiting there for us, no one saying the word *fabulous*—my new husband (my husband!) revealed the scheme to me. Anthony had arranged everything. Leah's plane ticket, the suite, the toothy officiant, even somehow encouraging me to pack the new white strapless dress and wear it to tea. He is a genius.

And Leah had taken care of everything back home as well.

"Your mothers are losing their *minds*," she laughed. "I almost feel bad about it."

"Don't," Anthony and I said in unison.

"Notice I said *almost*," she winked. She was back. That was Leah. Shining and fresh-faced, looking happy. I just prayed she didn't ask if the hotel had any big, ripe oranges she could toss into the ocean.

"They're both convinced that you've eloped," Leah reported and I bit my lower lip as she went on. "They're mad as hell. Delilah has called the apartment six, seven times a day looking for you. Colin freakin' Cowie even called and left a message."

"Really?"

Anthony squirmed at my apparent interest.

"I'm surprised she didn't send Vera Wang over to deliver your gown!" Leah laughed.

"Oh my God, the gown!" I stopped walking, one foot in midstep. My gown!

Two arms wrapped around me, one from each side. "Don't worry, baby, you're going to wear your gown." Anthony kissed the top of my head, warm as it was from the sun beating down on us.

I just blinked. Twice. Holding back another comment I'd only want to do over later.

"This wasn't a surprise wedding," he explained. "It was a *secret* wedding. Just for us."

The smile grew across my lips almost involuntarily. It stuck, actually, on my teeth that had just gone suddenly dry from the burst of reality I just tasted.

"Just for us?" I repeated, dumbfounded. He was *really* a genius.

"Just for us."

Leah smiled wickedly as well.

"We're not telling them." It was a statement, not a question. I had just been let in on the secret, which had been planned weeks ago to go something like this: We take off for a stress break weekend in Bermuda. Married? No! We didn't get married! How silly! Would I get married without my Vera Wang gown? Would I get married without a twelve-piece orchestra? Absurd! Would I be so selfish as to run off and get married without thinking about all the time, effort and money my mother has invested into my big day? Oh, *please!* Don't be ridiculous!

Hey, if Leah wasn't concerned about the karmic kickback of starting off our marriage under an elaborate lie, I wasn't either. I think Buddha would have done the same thing.

Chapter 30

"Where *were* you?" Delilah scolded me over her cell phone from Milan. Turns out she needed a stress break too.

"We just took a weekend to chill out," I said innocently, or rather not so innocently as I remembered the chilly water in that underground cavern and the many, many ways Anthony and I enjoyed it.

"I was worried sick!" she exclaimed in her fake voice. She had an audience. Donatella Versace, probably. Just Donatella to her. The designer didn't like it when she tried to called her Dona Darling. It was too Joan Crawford, and I could see her point.

"Well, we're fine, so don't worry. Listen, Mother, I have to—"

"Do you have any idea how *difficult* it was for me to get a reschedule with Colin?"

It was a full beat before I remembered she's on a first-name basis with Colin Cowie. Hopefully, she doesn't try to call him Col Darling. I hear he doesn't like that.

"I know, and I'm sorry," I said, the casual tone in my voice tripping her suspicion radar. She was quiet for too long.

"What's going on?" she said, or rather drawled. *Uh-oh. She's on to me.* I slipped my wedding band off my finger and placed it under my pillow, as if that had some influence on my voice giving away the big secret over an international cell phone call.

"Nothing. We have a lot of work to do for the wedding. There's not a lot of time left until the big day," I said, and even I could hear the insincerity in my tone. I was talking too fast, in too high a pitch. I am not a good liar.

"You sound . . . *odd.*"

Run away, run away! Fake static on the line and hang up! She's on to you!

"I'm just tired. We didn't get much sleep." *That should do it. Delilah can't stand any reference of me and Anthony having sex.*

"Please keep your personal business to yourself." *Got her. Use what works.*

"As a matter of fact," I played along with my newfound mini-manipulation skills. "Anthony and I were just about to—"

"We have a bad connection here." Delilah sounded flustered. "I'll call you on Tuesday when I arrive home. Ta Ta!"

Did she just say Ta Ta to me? Is Ciao out of fashion?

Either way, I now had my answer as to how I was going to keep my mother far away from the truth about my being a married woman. I've just become a raving nymphomaniac and Anthony and I will be *just* about to make love any and every time she calls. That's perfect.

What is wrong with me? I am not a coward.

I hung up the phone absolutely hating myself. Well, not absolutely.

"I've been trying to reach you, honey!"

And now it was time to face Carmela and Vic. I was sure Vic would be able to tell. But he never looked up from the television once the whole time we were there. He even took his meal in the den, something new for him owing to the larger screen television he just won at a Lion's Club raffle. Larger meaning twenty-nine inches.

"We went away for the weekend," Anthony said, and here's where I got nervous. The man can't lie to his mother. She has a deep-seated serious radar on him. A bizarre symbiotic connection. She probably feels relieved when he goes to the bathroom three states away.

"Hmmmm," was all she said, which completely panicked me. She went about cutting the lasagna and digging out a meat-stuffed portion for her darling son. I got a piece from the non-meat side. And I am not a vegetarian. She's just started putting twice the meat on one side of the lasagna so that her son gets more protein.

She doled out salad for me with a flop of the spoon, once again splattering my shirt with oil and vinegar dressing, and then daintily, carefully spooned out salad for Anthony. And tore him three pieces of garlic bread. When he didn't react fast enough to wipe away some sauce on his lip, she reached out with a napkin to try to clean him up. At least now he's been waving her away and wiping his own face.

Isn't she just the most maternal thing alive? So doting! So caring! So generous! So . . .

I stopped cold. I didn't taste anything in my mouth. My lips went numb.

"Oh God," I said quietly, then pushed away from the table to run to the bathroom.

"Em?" Anthony registered concern, tossed his napkin down, and came after me. Had I been in the room, I probably would have seen Carmela make a wicked face and go tell Vic that I'm pretending her food makes me sick. No, something else was threatening to make me sick. "What's wrong, Em?" Anthony pushed open the bathroom door, which had no lock after the unfortunate incident of a young Anthony—at age four—locking himself in the bathroom by accident and screaming bloody murder. They never put a lock back on it again. I just love that story.

"Oh God, oh God, oh God," I just kept mumbling. From the den, I could hear Vic come out with a very Vic-like comment about how I'm probably pregnant. *Nice. And this is the man my children will someday call Grandpa. Tie my tubes now.*

"What? What?" Anthony instinctively and protectively dampened a few tissues with cold water and dabbed at my forehead. "Are you going to be sick?"

"Oh, yeah . . ." But I felt no heaves, had no watering in my mouth, felt no sinking point of no return. I just felt . . . I felt . . . sickeningly *right*.

"Em?"

"I figured it out," I said, then repeated that a few more times to look and sound even more autistic than I actually did. "There was some piece of it that I didn't get, and I get it now . . . why she hates her so much . . ."

"My mother?"

"No, *my* mother." I swallowed hard. "My mother

hates your mother because your mother is everything my mother hates."

Anthony blinked. "Honey, have you started doing drugs?"

Somehow a laugh came out of me, the intended reaction. I punched him in the shin and hurt my hand on bone. "Ow!"

"As you were saying?"

I took a deep breath and exhaled again. "You know how my mother had this . . . other self? Before she became all rich and famous?"

Anthony nodded. The Donna Penks Story. He'd heard it before. Often.

"Well, think about it. If my mother hates what she was when she was a housewife and mother, when she was all nurturing . . . and dependable . . . and loving . . ."

"Oh God." Anthony sat down on the bathroom floor too. "My mother reminds Delilah of the person she used to be . . ."

"The person she *burned* every reminder of to get rid of."

Note to self: Hide all the Bic lighters in my mother's house.

"And Delilah reminds my mother of the worst nightmare of her life." Anthony rubbed his forehead, careful not to detach anything from his swiftly retreating hairline.

"We already had that one, honey." I tried to sound a little bit more on top of it than he was. "So what do we do?"

Anthony didn't answer.

"No solution to this."

He rubbed my knee. "No solution to this."

"We just let them get through the wedding, and

then they don't have to deal with each other again."

"Exactly."

"But it's not that simple," I teared up. "Your mom hates *me* for it."

"Hate is a strong word, honey."

I nodded. "She *resents* me for it. *I* brought it back to her, and to my mother too."

Anthony knows when not to say anything. Especially when I'm right. So the question remains . . . how do I get used to the fact that my marriage has ripped open old wounds for both of our mothers?

"It's actually a good thing," Leah said as we walked through the park. Anthony was off trying to find parking, which was next to impossible in Hoboken these days.

"How is it a good thing?"

"It makes them face their issues, and heal them."

I rolled my eyes. *Shut up, Dr. Phil,* I thought. Neither of them want to ever deal with it again. I made them remember.

"They can't live in pain forever." Leah shrugged, and I straightened up a bit hearing that out of her mouth. And then the downfall: "Twenty, thirty years . . . that's about the right amount of time to run away from it, don't you think?"

"It's not working," I shouted over the band. Anthony held his beer in close to his stomach and guided me by the shoulders to keep the elbowing, pushing flow of bar traffic from knocking me over.

We don't go to bars much, but we had a plan tonight. We were setting Leah up on a date.

Anthony's friend John met us at the bar at five o'clock for happy hour, and I had brought Leah there for the free bar food buffet. She loves egg rolls. I didn't think to ask if they were lucky.

Leah's not dumb. She knew it was a setup, and she knew that Anthony and I did *not* have to go to the bathroom at the same time.

It was painful to watch from across the room.

John tried his best to engage Leah in conversation, and she was giving out every nonverbal "I'm not interested" sign possible, some the body language experts hadn't discovered yet. He bought her a drink, and she refused. He leaned in to talk to her over the volume of the band, and she recoiled. He smiled, she grimaced. He bobbed and weaved to get into her line of vision while she looked all over the room, everywhere and anywhere possible but at him. We felt like we were watching a silent movie, with every blowoff sign magnified and overdramatic. It really was physically painful to watch. Poor John.

"Let's go save him." Anthony shook his head. Normally, I would defend my friend, but John was clearly in need of a rescue.

"Man, someone should check that girl for a pulse," a steely-faced John said, declining our offer to buy him a drink and going straight to get his coat. He couldn't get out of there fast enough. Anthony told me later that John was something of a walking wounded himself; his girlfriend of five years left him for a drummer. He had just bought her engagement ring and came home to a half-empty studio. It wasn't an easy night for him either.

Note to self: Never let Anthony choose the setup guy again.

Anthony and I tried everything to get her to move on. All with good intentions, of course. She simply had to start living again. She had to get out there and try. I deftly pried information out of her to use in our schemes. Her psychic told her she'd meet a man on a train. We recruited one of Anthony's work buddies to track her and follow her onto the train, asking her for directions. What Leah *didn't* tell me was that the psychic also told her this man on the train would be a Lothario and would break her heart. She moved to a different car as if fleeing a mugger.

We went to see the firemen play softball in the park. Anthony got a friend of a friend to make introductions to Nick, one of the cuter, younger guys on the team with soccer legs that *I* found hard to stop staring at. Piercing blue eyes. Buzzed dark hair. The cutest dimple in his chin. But he wasn't in the cards. Leah pretended she didn't speak English. I got his number for one of my other girlfriends, and they're now dating.

I went with her to one of those New Age conferences she's always attending. I figured some likeminded sandalwood incense addict would pique her interest, but she waved off all comers because "the men here are damaged and searching for answers." Oh, really?

Internet dating? No way, and I agreed with her. Too many pedophiles and cheating husbands protecting themselves under the cloak of an old or fake picture and a biographical profile they cut and pasted from someone else's listing. I wouldn't put Leah anywhere near that fishing hole, having been burned myself in the long-ago past. Married men, closeted gay men, and a pedophile. Oh my.

"She's just not interested right now," I sighed as I curled into my own married man who was neither closeted nor into young children.

"So why is she always praying for the love of her life to come, lighting candles in front of an altar that we're on, throwing oranges on the full moon?" Anthony reasonably asked, and the answer is that there's no reason. There's never any reason when you've been hurt beyond belief. Reason stays far away from that scenario.

Well, maybe not that far. Here's what came out of my mouth . . . "Well, if she's always *wishing* for it, then she's never actually at a place where it will actually happen. The wishing protects her."

"I'll never understand you women." Anthony kissed me on the wrist and turned out the lights.

Me neither.

Leah would risk looking foolish to make this belief work for her. She'd risk looking crazy. She didn't care what we thought as long as she was following her heart and what it needed. That, sadly, made her braver than we were. She was hiding for a real reason. We had no such excuse.

Chapter 31

This should be fun.

Delilah had arranged for one of her favorite designers to bring in gowns for her *and* for Carmela. Where did this sudden benevolence come from? And how could I stop it from happening? Trying on designer gowns could push Carmela over the edge. I'd wind up not just with salad dressing on my shirt or a meatball in my lap, but an entire lasagna shoved down my throat and a fork sticking out of my neck. She'd kill me.

Or so I thought. Carmela sounded thrilled that Delilah had arranged a fashion session for her . . . with designer gowns. Something very strange was going on. Delilah did a favor for Carmela, and Carmela was *excited* about it? This has to be a setup. Delilah must be working on a chapter in her novel where the protagonist is choked to death by an haute couture zipper. Delilah must just want to be able to describe the *exact* color of blue a strangled person's lips become.

We arrived at the designer's salon in New York

City, and I was surprised to find it was a designer I'd never heard of. The world had never heard of him. Yves, his name was. Just Yves. His salon was decorated all in white with giant silver Ys everywhere. As in Y would you spend so much money on a simple dress a seventh grader could make with a Butterick pattern? Slap a silver Y on it, and it's priceless. I'm not normally an antifashion snob. I was just dreading this experience.

Delilah was already there when I arrived with Carmela.

Great, Delilah arrived early to set up the plot with Yves.

"Mrs. Can*tah*no!" Yves rushed across the bare white floor on pencil-thin legs, all cheekbones and platinum blond hair. With a little silver Y on the bridge of his eyeglasses. I wondered if people he spoke to went cross-eyed in looking at that Y.

Yves's assistant took our coats and returned in a flash with little flutes of champagne. Y's were inscribed on them, of course.

"How can we possibly improve on such perfection?" Yves gushed, holding Carmela's arms out to the sides and looking at her thick waist.

Now I remembered why I avoid Fashion Week.

"I'm just kidding," Yves's voice changed. He was no longer the flippy gay designer, the swishy swashbuckling fashionista, but rather had a thick Southern accent and now walked with a bit of a lurch. No more prancing. Now that it was gone, I kind of missed it. "No wait, kidding again!" he switched back into swish mode, clapping his hands at how often people fall for that one, and how *darling* the looks on their faces are.

This must be the trick. Delilah has brought us into the Jamie Kennedy Experiment. I looked for signs of a latex wig edge on the guy's forehead. Turns out, he was just crazy. A swishy schizophrenic. *Fab*ulous!

"Okay," Yves clapped. "Today we get to outfit the mothers, because we didn't get the bride."

Great. Start off with a guilt trip. Nice one, Yves.

"Delilah . . ." He clapped, and she scurried to his side, both of them facing the floor-to-ceiling mirror. I'm guessing he did that a lot. This was quite a fashion studio. There were no dresses in sight. "I've dressed you before, you lovely little stick!"

Lovely little stick? Is that what women Delilah's age are asking for when they go to their plastic surgeons? "Doctor, I want to look like a lovely little stick."

Delilah glowed. I reminded myself to call her a lovely little stick myself, and see how she reacts. Ralph Lauren could walk into a room, call her a steaming whore, and she'd blush with flattery. Then she'd call him Ralphie.

"I'm thinking . . . *blue!*"

I'm thinking . . . fraud!

"Baby blue with a beaded bodice, silver trim . . ."

And a great big Y on her butt.

"And a nice dramatic slit to show off those gorgeous legs." Yves was a cheerleader on speed. And Delilah ate it up with a Tiffany silver spoon.

"And *you!*" His sudden turn made Carmela jump. She had been looking at the empty, vast white room and wondering what in the world was going on. She'd faded out of Yves's spotlight and he reeled her right back in. "Baby blue isn't going to do it for you. You're darker . . . an exotic beauty . . ."

Carmela blushed.

"You have the skin of a thirty-year-old, darling. How *do* you do it?" Before Carmela could say the words Mary Kay, which would put my mother into a coma, Yves reliably gushed on. And I mean gushed. "Look at this *hair!* Such beautiful chestnut and caramel colors. Who does your hair? You must give me his card!"

"Yves, darling?" It was Delilah. She wanted her spotlight back.

He twirled to face her.

"My baby blue dress . . . ?" She blinked doe eyes at him, hoping to lure him back to her level. But he was entranced by Carmela.

Watch out, Mom, he's found his new muse. Keep an eye out for the new spring line, Carmela by Yves!

"Just a sec!" He held up a finger to hush Delilah and then went right back to his imaginings for her archenemy. "Gold . . . darling, I see you in gold."

I could see the thought process cooking in Delilah. She was a Rival crockpot of envy. No one has even given Delilah the old "just a sec" finger. I sat back, amazed. Who knew a schizophrenic fashion designer was going to be a catalyst between these two mad women? He could actually get them to bond.

"And the bride!" Yves turned on me next. "I have a few things you might like to try on for your trousseau. Go in the back and Renata will help you."

No way, Y, I'm staying right here.

"Go, go, go, silly little bride," he sang, and I wished I'd brought my mace. Delilah and Carmela motioned for me to go, captivated as they were by their designer. They were All about Yves. I was not needed in the room, so I trailed my way to the back rooms, where Renata had set up espresso and biscotti. Not bad. In a room marked "Emilie" in silver swirly handwriting on a white card, I found a half dozen truly great sexy dresses to try on. Lost in a world of emerald green and fire engine red dresses and high strappy heels, diamond earrings and only one fashion nightmare (a yellow poncho with white puffballs on it—don't ask—there will never be photos as evidence), I forgot about the mothers.

I stepped out into the hallway to listen. No sounds of mortal combat. No name-calling or grammar corrections. All I heard was Yves crying out as if in the throes of passion. No way on earth I was going in there.

Ten minutes later, and it was quiet. Either they killed him, or one of them took out the other two. I stepped out cautiously on stilettos gilded with little silver Ys, of course, (in a slinky black wrap dress that I was *so* going to buy) to find the mothers posing in front of a mirror. Together. Carmela wore a gaudy gold-beaded gown, and Delilah paraded in front of the mirror, trying to convince herself that the silver stretch dress that hugged her body like a glove wasn't too Vegas for her.

"No," I said, cutting the air with my hands. "Absolutely not."

"Honey, you look *fab*ulous!" Yves rushed to me, in a crouched stance that made him look like he had to make a mad dash to the little crazy designer's room.

"I know," I said, owning the room, and then, "Mother, that's not going to work."

"Not for the wedding, but this would be *purrr*-fect for Cannes!" Delilah drawled. Carmela looked miserable. Exhausted.

"The 'Mothers of Invention' here are finding their own style." Yves wrapped his arm around my shoulder, lowered his head and spoke to me from beneath his eyebrows. "Sometimes they have to crawl before they can walk."

Delilah took great offense at that. She was no fashion amateur.

Don't you know who has dressed her, you silly, silly, silly man?

Suddenly, the silver stretch dress had lost its appeal. Delilah strutted, all attitude, toward the dressing room for a wardrobe change. And another glass of champagne. And a Vicodin.

"What about this one?" Carmela picked a dress up off the floor. From Delilah's castoff pile. My mother had tried it on and judged it to be "too Laura Bush at the Inaugural Ball." The red, elegant dress was perfect for Carmela.

"Try it on, sweetie!" Yves clapped. The man loved to clap.

And I saw it coming. The air in the room got thick, everything clicked into slow motion, and all that was missing was that menacing whistle theme music from every western movie right before the big shootout. I saw it like Scorsese would shoot it. The dressing room doors opened simultaneously. A red high heel stepped out. Cut to the blue high heel stepping out. My head moved from side to side, as if I was shouting a big *Noooooo* in silence. Reality was gone.

Carmela appeared first, the lady in red.

Delilah stepped out into the spotlight, in blue and in a mood. "That's my dress you have on."

"I found it on the floor," Carmela sang, clearly in love with the dress.

"It was in my Options pile."

Carmela threw her head back and laughed. Just

diabolical, is the way I saw it. If she didn't already love the red dress, she loved it even more now.

"Take it off!" Delilah shrieked, the veins on her neck matching her blue dress more and more.

"Don't be ridiculous, Delilah. You didn't want it!"

"Uh-oh, catfight!" Yves sang, and inexplicably clapped his hands. This man was clearly insane. I checked again for a telltale line of latex on his forehead. This had to be a *Candid Camera* kind of thing. Delilah Winchester gets Punk'd.

"Take it off!"

"No, forget it!"

"I'll give you my dress!"

"I don't care if you give me your car, I'm not taking off this dress."

"The dress is *mine!*"

"NO!" Carmela thundered, with a look in her eye that made even Delilah step back. "You have it all, and you have to have more! You can't take what I have! You're a classless snob in an elite world, and I wish you permanent incontinence in your old age!"

And she was doing so well!

Permanent incontinence?!

Delilah just started to laugh, and I have to admit, I almost did too. Yves just looked frightened. But he couldn't wait to call the gossip rags with his voice disguised as An Anonymous Source to report that famous romance novelist Delilah Winchester had a catfight with a commoner over his red dress.

"You spoiled, vicious bitch!" Carmela spat. "You think I'm going to just stand here and watch you take what's left over after you're gone?!"

Okay, she's not talking about now. She's talking about thirty-six years ago. She's talking to Kimberly, the socialite, who stole her first love.

Yves went toward her, and I held him back. Delilah stood still in her blue shoes. But she wasn't out of harm's way. Carmela took one step closer to her. Stopped, thought about it. Then another step closer. Stopped, thought about it. And in one sweeping motion before I could unstick my feet from the floor, picked up a beaded yellow dress and threw it at Delilah. Just whipped it at her. The zipper caught her on the wrist, stinging her but not cutting her. Beads clicked to the floor.

"Are you insane?" Delilah stepped back, but Carmela threw another dress at her. A $20,000 dress studded with crystals. Then a lavender dress with a lot of crinoline layers that flew up in the air, opening wildly and parachuting down for a second to pull Delilah's hair out of its chignon. The fabric was caught in her hair. That was my last lucid moment. After that, it was all fabric and taffeta crinoline, an ugly mix of colors and not at all a pretty rainbow of dancing dresses in the air. Navy, lavender, copper, red and hunter green do *not* make for a pretty mix. Beads broke off from gowns and noisily rolled across the floor. Then shoes flying in the air. Sharp stiletto shoes that could definitely put an eye out. One after the other, thudding as they hit the floor and echoing in the near-empty warehouse of a salon.

When they ran out of fabric, or simply bored themselves with the flinging fabric effect, they started throwing their empty coffee cups, gel bra inserts, anything they could get their hands on. Yves was delighted. He just heard a big *ka-ching* sound in his head and kept glancing up toward the ceiling.

You bastard. He was videotaping the whole thing. His security camera had it on tape with a little blinking red light, and that is why I was sent to a back room to try on a dress that I was now so *not* buying.

"Break it up, ladies," Yves said rather meekly when he noticed me noticing the camera. And he was not clapping anymore. Y? Because I had figured out his game.

"Hand it over, Yves." I held out my hand. "Mom! Carmela! He's videotaping you."

That stopped it. Mom knows what an unflattering videotape can do to her. Carmela pulled her straps back up over her shoulders and smoothed her hair back.

"Hand it over, Yves," I commanded. "Mom, Carmela, go get changed. This designer is no longer in business."

I had the tape in my hand ten minutes later, shaking my head at the now-deflated Yves and his assistant Renata, who had definite immigration issues to keep her quiet. "So, will you be taking the red dress?" Yves had the nerve to ask.

Even better, Carmela said Yes.

Chapter 32

It doesn't matter. I'm married.
No matter how many times I said it, it still didn't
make me feel better.

Especially when the Great Frosting War broke
out.

I wish I could say the mothers declared battle in
the spotless baking kitchen of Sylvia Weinstock,
flinging great, glopping handfuls of frosting at
one another until they stood panting, glaring, out
of breath, with dollops of chocolate icing falling
from their hair and chins and noses. That would
have been entertaining, at least. Mortifying to
Sylvia, but definitely something to tell the kids
someday. Definitely a Kodak moment where I
could have something tangible to show those who
would never believe me: "See! I told you they lost
their minds!" I'd shout, shaking an 8x10 of them
for emphasis.

No, the Great Frosting War was waged from the
safety of their homes, through the airwaves, as they
drove poor Sylvia's assistant out of *her* mind.

Ladies and Gentlemen, in the blue corner . . . from Brooklyn, New York . . . Carmela Cantano! Weighing 157 pounds and with a reach of over 50 miles, the "Mother of All Things Traditional"!

I'd been overhearing too many boxing matches while over at Anthony's parents' place, trying to get Vic to warm up to me at least.

And in the red corner . . . from Basking Ridge, New Jersey and New York City and Paris and Milan and Hawaii . . . Delilah Winchester! Weighing 104 pounds and with a reach across the globe, the "Mother of All Things Fabulous"!

I imagined them half-jogging in place, with over-sized mouth guards jutting out their lips, fiercely giving each other the Eye of the Tiger as the referee explained the rules, telling them to keep it clean, no hitting below the belt. Colin Cowie would massage my mother's shoulders and whisper strategy in her ear. Vic would massage Carmela's, reminding her of the illegal brass knuckles he'd sneaked into her gloves.

Somehow I've placed Yves there as the cut man, ready with his needle and thread to sew their split eyelids back up. Hey, it's my reverie.

The fight will last ten rounds, with a three knock-down rule.

And the winner gets this gorgeous Prada belt and the right to decide whether the cake will have buttercream frosting or a rolled fondant!

Fighters ready? They knock gloves. The bell rings. They come out swinging.

These are the scenes that take over my mind when I'm at work. I've put our mothers in *The Karate Kid,* with Mr. Miyagi telling my mother to wax on and wax off. I've had them snapping their fingers and dancing in an alley as part of a strange *West Side Story* scenario with much better shoes. Carmela led the Sharks and Delilah led the Jets. And we all know how that turned out.

Montagues and Capulets. East Coast rap versus West Coast rap. There are no winners. Well, except in *The Karate Kid*, but even then the kid just had to keep on fighting. Wax on always follows wax off.

I was understanding Leah more and more every day. Fantasy is much more amusing than reality.

"Emilie?" Meg appeared at my door. That was never good news these days. Who had Carmela dragged in to see me now? The Pope?

I straightened up and, under my desk, slipped my feet back into my shoes.

"Mr. Garrity is here to see you," she said with wide eyes, a moment before the starched collar and uncharacteristically loosened tie of Mr. Garrity blew right past her, and he flopped down into the leather chair facing my desk. Splayed. Like a frog on his back, waiting for his skin to be pinned back for the dissection.

"Emilie, we need to talk . . ." He did not look happy.

After two hours of hand-holding, after he'd asked me for a Tylenol, and after he pushed his comb-over back into starting position about three dozen times, Mr. Garrity had calmed. Turns out he had reached out and touched someone in his home office, and now he feared they would be suing him for sexual harassment. I borrowed from Pampers, in his native language of commercial jingles to say "Mr. Garrity, we're right behind you.

Every step of the way." And then I threw in a little L'Oréal with "Because you're worth it."

"Really?" Mr. Garrity's cold sweat had turned into a warmer shade of gray. "I guess I should apologize. So that nothing gets out of hand."

That's what happens when you let your fingers do the walking.

"Absolutely, Mr. Garrity." And I couldn't resist speaking Pringles to him: "You know you want to."

"Should I say it with flowers?" he blinked, all wide-eyed terror. He wanted me to jingle him out of a potential lawsuit. There was no jingle on record that said to apologize meekly and then behave yourself. Why couldn't he be obsessed with song lyrics? That would be much easier.

I'm sure there's a rule in the corporate ethics handbook, if not the Bible, that says you shouldn't join in with your assistant's mocking of your $6 million clients when they leave your office. But Meg couldn't help herself. She was on a roll.

"Can you imagine Garrity and his wife in bed?" Meg was always talking with her fingers spread, wiggling like she was typing her words on an invisible keyboard as she spoke them. She even acted out hitting Enter with her index finger to make her best points. I'd learned to ignore it. "Can you imagine what they say to one another while they're *doing* it?"

Now I remembered why I never go out for drinks with Meg after work.

"Ooooh baby, I'm talking your body's language!" Meg amused herself. That was the Always slogan. A few other assistants came running when they heard the Ooooh baby. Watercooler fodder in Ms. Penks's office! Then they all joined in. My office became the henhouse.

"Just a little dab'll do ya'!" That would be Bryl-creem.

"Have it your way, baby!" Burger King, of course.

"Is it in you?" That cracked them up. Gatorade.

I collected some files that I didn't need and smiled in mock solidarity with the girls as I left the room. They got raunchier when I left, though I could clearly hear them through the walls of the copy room. Where my boss was standing. Listening. I just shook my head as the ladies in my office rose to fever pitch:

"Finger lickin' good!" KFC.

"Bite into it!"

I didn't know that one, and even my boss looked a bit confused. Until she said "Ahhh, I got it. That's Minute Maid."

For a split second, I wondered if *my* job would be in jeopardy somehow since I wasn't aware that 'Bite into It' was Minute Maid's slogan. I had clearly confused it with Tropicana's "100% pure squeezed sunshine." I was not on my game.

"Hey, Emilie." My boss filled up a coffee cup and extended it to me. "Think of Nivea and fire your assistant." I took the coffee cup without fully getting it at first, but my boss, Helene, was giving me a message. Nivea's slogan was "it helps protect your skin."

I nodded, agreeing with her.

"Are you hearing me?" Helene's heels clicked her a few feet away, and she looked back over her shoulder at me. "We're all judged by the company we keep."

"Absolutely." I agreed, taking my coffee black. This was not a time to wisecrack "Got milk?"

"If you had stayed in that room." Helene lowered her chin a little and raised an eyebrow. "If you hadn't come in here, if you hadn't walked away from them . . . I'd be firing *you* right now."

I swallowed hard.

"Character counts." Helene winked, then smiled and turned on her stiletto and let the door swing closed behind her.

Chapter 33

I often think about Vic. I see him sitting on the couch, leaning back with his big round stomach sticking out, his legs crossed up on the coffee table, his hands clasped behind his head, watching television without blinking very much. Anthony has said that Vic has been in that same spot for twenty-five years. They had to put a wooden board under the seat cushion, because it was sinking down so low.

A beer always sits on the table in front of him. A wooden bowl of chips or pretzels sits next to it. The *TV Guide*. The newspaper. The remote sitting on the cushion next to him like it's his date.

It can't be easy to be Vic.

It can't be easy to go through most of your life knowing your wife said Yes just to stop people from pitying her heartbreak. It can't be easy knowing you're your wife's second choice. And it can't be easy being reminded, as he has been so clearly now, that she still misses her first choice. That it still hurts her.

Vic pursued her with the chivalry and romance

of a white knight when he saw that lonely figure walking down the avenue. He asked his friends "Who's the girl?" He wanted to know why everyone was whispering about her, jutting their chins in her direction to let others know "there she is."

He said she was like a ghost that just glided through the city. She stopped nowhere. She talked to no one. She bought nothing. She just walked. Every day.

What man can resist the wounded bird?

I'd heard about the Wounded Bird Theory from my male friends, before I found Anthony. In their more brutish, lout days, my male friends referred to the lonely, drunk, sad girl at the end of the bar—clearly drinking her pain away by herself—as the Wounded Bird. She was the first one the ill-intended guys went after. They bought her a drink, complimented her, held the door for her on their way back to her place. And they left a fake number the next morning. That's the Wounded Bird.

In Vic and Carmela's day, it wasn't so sickeningly opportunistic and heartless.

The Wounded Bird, back then, was a target for the white knight, the well-mannered man who saw her pain as poetic tragedy just waiting for the page to turn so that he could ride in on his horse to rescue her and take her to a lighter heart and a brighter life. Those were more genteel days, apparently. Had it been now, Vic would have ridden her once and left a fake number, not seduced himself into a vision of being the hero and spending the rest of his life tap-dancing to please his wounded love. He brought her flowers, which she loved and placed in blue glass bud vases on their kitchen sink. She was delighted, lifted, elated . . . but soon she'd sink back down. He took her to dinner, dancing, to the Poconos. Where she was delighted, lifted, elated . . . but then soon sank back down. He bought her a car. He took her to the Jersey shore. Always the up, and then the down. Some minuscule element of everything he did reminded her of Him. Not Vic. Her first love. The life she should have had. Nothing he could do would ever erase it. He numbed it. It faded eventually. But it never went away. She was with Vic ninety-five percent of the time, and somewhere else the other five percent. He'd never get that five percent. Thirty some-odd years of that can wear a guy down.

When she gave birth to Anthony, Carmela said to her own mother that she was finally full of love. For the second time in her life, she felt love. Vic had been standing just outside the door to her room at the time, holding a full bouquet of flowers. He heard her.

That can't be easy.

Chapter 34

She wasn't kidding about the diamond-encrusted shoes. My feet will have more diamonds on them than will be adorning all the women in the room put together. And you don't know my mother's friends. My conscience has been bound and gagged and stuffed in a car trunk. How could I accept diamond shoes for my wedding day from my mother, when I was clutching the secret that I was already married? Simple. They're Stuart Weitzman shoes. Women would give up their ovaries for these.

Speaking of shoes and secrets . . . what I did not know then, but know now, is that Carmela is quite the demon. She called Stuart Weitzman, pretended to be my mother's assistant, and changed the order for my mother's shoes. Instead of matching lavender shoes, she requested black. Instead of a diamond buckle, she changed it to rubies. My mother wouldn't find out until two days before my "wedding" when she opened the shoebox, gasped, got lightheaded and had to put her head between her knees in a very undignified manner. I think actually fainting would have been better for her reputation. With her lavender gown, it looked at that moment that my mother would be wearing black and red hooker-style platform shoes.

My mother, the great Delilah Winchester, would have to wear shoes *off the rack* to the social event of the year.

Carmela can be a demon. You don't mess with Stuart Weitzman shoes.

Chapter 35

Sunset at Frank Sinatra Park in Hoboken is when the water shimmers like it's made of liquid gold. It's my favorite time to be there. The abandoned sailboat bounces around on the water making squeaking sounds. The kayakers push off from the rocks with their white helmets also reflecting the fading sun. The lights in New York City start to become visible in each skyscraper just at the time most people are leaving their offices for the night.

Leah is off throwing an orange again, hoping for something she doesn't yet want to happen.

Anthony is off getting us coffee and Krispy Kremes. (By the way, I am not one of those brides who starves down to a size 2 for her wedding day. I'm not hiring Radu to train me. I'm not doing Atkins. I am both a bride-to-be and a bride-that's-been who eats Krispy Kremes. And I am staying relatively sane.)

Right now, relatively sane, I am flipping through the old journal I had, the one from many years ago where I sketched out everything I wanted for my wedding. I even stapled swatches of pink fabric to the pages. Folded glossy advertisements from bridal magazines stuck out of the edges. I had a taste for big gowns back then. And big hair. I also had listed the names of friends I had wanted in my bridal party, and this was so long ago that I found myself wondering "whatever happened to her?" for many of those names. I was thinking big. I wanted sixteen bridesmaids. That's how young I was.

So whatever happens to childhood dreams that we forget? Where did that young girl go who wanted pink bridesmaid dresses and sixteen bridesmaids and a horse-drawn carriage? We don't throw out our old journals, but we throw away what's in them more than we even know.

But our mothers never forget.

"I'm glad you're here." Delilah clicked across the room, stepping over a wisp of her office curtains that had blown on the breeze into her line of direction. The windows were open, and we were in the beautiful weather season of my wedding. The days were counting down, and the birds were singing outside. As I followed her direction, I saw Marco the pool boy setting a robotic pool cleaning machine into the surface of her in-ground. Probably waiting for me to leave. And for a split second I wonder why so many pool boys are named Marco.

Delilah returned from her cavernous closet holding a box, balancing it on her palm like a tray of champagne glasses . . . which she would never be serving from her own hand.

"I'm sorry there aren't any diamonds in it," she

said in all seriousness. Donna Penks. I saw it. The way you can recognize a person if you just see their eyes only, like in a burqua or in the face of an old relative you haven't seen in ages or an Oscar-pursuing actress wearing a fat suit. It was my mother. The eyes . . . it was my mother. Donna Penks.

I opened the box and pushed away crisp white tissue paper, which also lofted into the air and danced the breeze down onto the hardwood floor by the French doors.

My mother's wedding veil.

She didn't burn it.

She kept it.

Yellowed at the edges, a bit stiff.

Delilah cleared her throat. "You obviously can't use it as your veil, since Vera is—"

"Thank you, Mom," I said, and put my hand on hers. She was blinking a lot. Looking everywhere but at me.

"But I thought I should . . . I wanted you to have it," she said, then sat down next to me on the oversized ottoman, crossing her legs daintily on automatic. Donna Penks was in the eyes, but Delilah still had possession of her carriage and posture.

"I don't know how we can—"

She didn't let me finish.

"You don't have to use it if—"

I didn't let her finish.

That's what happens when you're strangers to one another for years. Sentences overlap and butt into each other.

"I'd like to use the lace on the handle of my bouquet," I offered, and she nodded. "It will be beautiful."

"It's not much . . ." she said, then trailed off.

"Yes, it is, Mom. Thank you."

In hugging her, I pretended she was rounded, plumper. I smelled for her lilac perfume. I was hugging Donna Penks, the mother I missed for so long.

"She just gave you her veil?" Anthony wasn't reaching for tissues at this sentimental recounting.

"Yes," I said, with tears in my eyes, all but clasping my hands at my heart. "It was wonderful."

Anthony rolled his eyes. "What does she want?"

"Nothing. She was just doing it to be . . . motherly."

Anthony flipped the London broils on our barbecue, and the hiss was louder than I expected.

"Emilie, would you come in here for a minute?" Carmela shouted down the staircase. It creaked with each step I took up to her bedroom. "There's something I want you to have . . . something for the wedding."

Life is just not this ironic.

But it wasn't her veil she was offering, as I'd momentarily feared with a white hot flush. It was her pearl studded satin bag, the traditional pouch for all of those cash-filled gift envelopes her side of the family always gave at weddings. (Speaking of irony, the family in the lower income bracket gives cash for wedding gifts, while the family in the astronomic income bracket gives engraved silver knicknacks and pottery from the Far East.)

"I had it cleaned and freshened," Carmela offered. "It's still not quite perfectly white ... the cousins have all used it at their weddings."

I let my fingers trace over the cool pearls sewn by hand over the entire surface of the oversized string-close pouch. This must have taken weeks if not months to make. Anthony's grandmother had worked as a beading artist. They called them seam-stresses back in her day, and they also paid them pennies. Today, a bead artist with his grandmother's talent would go to Vera Wang and get paid in the six figures to bead Swarovski crystals on celebrity wedding gowns and Olympic figure skating cos-tumes.

"It's beautiful," I breathed. Each pearl reflected a range of pastels, again—like the Bermuda sand—appearing at a distance to be a simple pinkish beige, but with a range of barely there yellows, peaches and the slightest, slightest sage green. They were picking up the colors of the room, and of my shirt. They absorbed everything around them.

"It has to stay in the family," she warned.

"Of course."

"It's very important to us," she warned again, and I looked up to see her blue eyes watery, misty.

"It's very important to me as well, Carmela." I patted her arm. "Thank you."

"Take good care of it," she said, and I knew how hard it was for her to let it go.

"She gave you the pearl bag?" Anthony was im-pressed.

"Lent it to me." I curled up on the couch with him for the start of the Wednesday night lineup.

My legs wrapped naturally over his, and I snuggled my head into his neck. He smelled like cinnamon.

"Hmmm."

"Aren't you going to question her intentions?"

"Nope."

Of course not.

Chapter 36

The train was packed. Riders jammed shoulder to shoulder, everyone with the same expression of blank disinterest, and twenty hands holding on to the same silver pole to steady their balance against the rough rocking of the train back to Hoboken. At one point in the tunnel, it always jerks violently, and you can tell who the novice passengers are by who loses their footing and plants face-forward into the back of the suited man in front of them. During one of these jerks, a novice near me looked up slowly and nervously into the turned face of a six-foot-seven businessman, a portly gentleman with a deep black goatee who growled in a voice reminiscent of Darth Vader: "When those doors open, you *move*."

Shivering, the novice rider just nodded. Such is the *Lord of the Flies* atmosphere of the train home during rush hour. You learn the rules—if you're lucky enough to know them—or you're trampled.

And soon enough, you get used to the hum of the train, the smell that stays on your clothes for hours after you exit the train, and you know when to stiffen and brace yourself against the rough rail switches. You know not to panic when the train stops in the middle of the dark tunnel for no apparent reason, then starts up again with an anguished groan. You know not to panic when the lights blink off for a moment, then turn on again. I see the novices react, because there's nothing else to do on the train but study faces. And feet. The novices always wear thin heels. And if you're a regular, you notice the day when they finally get it and change shoes for the ride home.

Today's ride was uneventful. With the exception of the face-planter, we all seemed to be regulars. Which gave me very little to notice. And very few distractions, so of course my mind wandered . . .

Something old, something new, something borrowed, something blue.

What would mine be?

The something blue was easy. That would be Leah.

The something borrowed would be the pearl purse.

The something old would be the lace of my mother's gown on my bouquet handle.

What would the something new be? The gown doesn't count, since it's a given. It's cheating to call your gown your something new. The diamond shoes could work, but that's a fine line. Shoes are also a given. The rings, too, are not eligible. It has to be non-wardrobe related.

Something new . . . I had to find something new . . . before something new came along to surprise me.

Chapter 37

Today was audition day.

We were quite the auspicious lineup of judges for our own *American Idol*-like competition as we took our seats at a banquet table facing the stage area. Delilah had arranged with the W hotel to let us use one of their largest and most ornate ballrooms to audition bands and musicians for the ceremony and reception. Delilah's handwritten invitations to me, Anthony (she sent separate invitations to us at the same address, by the way), and Carmela said to dress appropriately for this session. So with me in my blue DKNY suit, Anthony in his Armani, and Carmela in black, we passed for an acceptable panel of judges. Delilah clicked her pen on her clipboard and let us in on the rules before the doors opened to what sounded in muffled tones like a *lot* of contenders waiting out in the hall. I imagined the scene beyond those doors as something out of *Fame*, with a lot of young singers belting out their best *mi, mi, mi, mi*'s and Mariah Carey ear-splitting riffs. As it turns out, I couldn't even imagine what was out there. Just couldn't imagine it at all.

Delilah handed us our own clipboards, each of which, of course, contained a silver Cross pen and a thick pile of blush pink (to match *her* suit) assessment papers. She'd been up all night, apparently, preprinting the names of bands, trios, duos, soloists, flutists and cellists, assigning them numbers, and then outlining the many criteria we'd use to judge each one:

Clarity
Vocals
Appearance (Print-worthy?)
Wardrobe
Stage Presence
Ingenuity

And so on. I noticed *Talent* wasn't on there. Wait, were we judging the Miss USA Pageant here?

Delilah was droning on about how we need to mark each performer from a one to a ten, ten being the best and one being absolutely *dreadful,* at which point Anthony sighed and shifted in his chair. Checked his watch. It was going to be a long afternoon. And evening, it turned out.

I would have thought Delilah would have Celine Dion on a plane from Vegas just for our wedding, but Celine apparently had other plans for our wedding day. Same with Sting. And Etta James. So here we sat, at a table draped with a pink tablecloth, an individual mini pitcher of ice water for each of us, an impressive array of spotlights set on the elevated stage before us, and our Cross pens at the ready. Bring in the first contestant . . .

If I ever hear *Up Where We Belong,* again, I'm going to ask Leah to throw *me* into the Hudson River. Same goes for *Wind Beneath My Wings.*

Anthony added a new category to his clipboard checklist: *Cheese Factor.*

I added one to my own: *Wears a Sequined Jacket.*

For every performer, no matter how tone-deaf, no matter how underdressed, undertrained, under-practiced or underblessed, Delilah sat with her hands folded, a polite plastic smile on her lips, and a chipper "Thank you" lopping off their symbolic heads just a few bars into each song. And I was grateful. Not pleasantly surprised at a hint of character in that she didn't critique each hopeful with a "You'll never work in this town" or a "That was bloody awful." No, that attitude had been branded already. I was grateful she's so selfish with her own time that she didn't allow the goatlike bleating to continue.

I have a new level of respect for Paula Abdul.

Mixed among the hopeless cases were some true gems, of course . . . a handsome dark-haired waiter-by-day who sang like Michael Buble and knocked me breathless with his rendition of *Summer Wind.* We heard a pitch-perfect jazz trio that made my Absolute Yes list for the cocktail party, a Carnegie-ready pianist who I would pay to see in concert. The talent column was definitely spotted with big, bold 10s, but I am my mother's daughter and I am auditioning entertainers for my fake, *second* wedding. So allow me to share with you my Hope Springs Eternal list, if only to get the sound of them out of my memory and onto paper so that I can sleep at night and hopefully avoid any post-traumatic stress reactions when I hear the song *Do That to Me One More Time* in the elevator at work. I am scarred for life.

We had a slick-haired boy band in torn jeans and matching white T-shirts, doing *way* too many hand movements. Any word they sang, they had a dramatic hand gesture for it. Their lead singer hit falsetto notes that actually shook the water in our glasses while his background boys did hand gestures for every word *he* sang. It was a strange pop music sign language, and nothing more than a great biceps workout for them.

Next!

We had a nervous Delilah groupie who asked for her autograph rather than singing her song. So we were spared one more rendition of *Wind Beneath My Wings* when she ran off giggling and clutching Delilah's autographed photo in her hands. Yes, Delilah carries her press photo head shots with her for just this kind of situation. Scavullo had taken it. It was a fifteen-year-old picture, and Delilah looked to be about thirty in it. Plastic surgery keeps her adherent to that photo.

Three large black women marched into the room dressed in 1940s army suitdresses, with their hair curled up under little triangular hats that can only mean one thing: The Andrews Sisters. They whooped out a strong-lunged *Don't Sit Under the Apple Tree*, and we all jumped when these women stripped off their army dresses to reveal yellow-sequined miniskirt dresses. They kicked off their staid army platform shoe covers to reveal shiny gold stilettos underneath. They pulled some magic pin in their hair that let loose the tight 1940s curl updo into puffy helmets. The lead singer, Charla, stepped forward with the microphone in her hand, arched backward, thrust her fist into the air and wailed out the unmistakable Diana Ross beginning to *Ain't No Mountain High Enough*. And just when we thought the stripping and belting was over, they tore off their jackets to reveal a strapless look, turned backward and started shaking their very ample bottoms. With visible panty lines. They had become Destiny's Child, and we stopped them before they could get any further into *Bootylicious*. Delilah loved them . . . for someone else's party. She handed them the card for her agent and told them to drop her name.

"Wow, that was nice of you, Mother," I whispered to her as the next act started setting up.

"It's a little game I play with Marvin," she smirked, Marvin being her agent. "I send him these joke acts to make his day."

I recoiled. That's just evil.

"What was that?" Anthony leaned in, talking to me but not taking his eyes off the troupe of Russian acrobats who now climbed up over each other's hips and shoulders to stand on each other's heads.

"Don't even ask," I snarled, taking a sip of water to moisten my dry mouth.

She was decidedly less evil to the others. But I still inched my chair away from hers.

The rest of our afternoon consisted of watching the Russian acrobats contort themselves, jugglers drop flaming sticks and then have to stamp out the beginnings of charring on the dance floor, dueling violinists who were not an act. They were actually *dueling*, breaking a sweat in an intense competition to impress us, cursing at one another in Chinese, displaying a hostile aggression toward one another that hinted at some unspoken infidelity problem in their personal relationship . . . until the one finally let loose in tears and bashed the other over the head with his violin. We called security on them before they tore each other apart.

Yet another boy band, but these were not boys. They introduced themselves as a new group of former Menudo members, all dressed to look like Ricky Martin; all with their shirts open to a smooth-chested, tanned look; all wearing too-tight jeans.

The next act made me want to call child protective services. A four-year-old girl sauntered into the room dragging a fluffy red boa. She wore a red dress, her makeup made her look like she was twenty-three, her lips done up in red gloss, false eyelashes and there was no mistaking it . . . she was wearing a padded bra to make it look like she had breasts. She was *four!* She launched into Faith Hill's *Breathe*, and it was just too creepy for any of us. We glared at the gushing stage mother, done up herself in a red dress but looking decidedly less slutty than her four-year-old daughter. Mom was her pimp. Delilah asked for the child's portfolio, kept the mother's card, and patted my leg under the table. There just might be an investigation after all.

It was just bad timing for the eight-year-old tango champions to follow that act. We had no stomach to watch a brother-sister dance team curl their legs around each other and look into each other's eyes in a flirtatious manner. When the brother started to lift the sister up into a split which he would hold over his head, we all shouted "No!" in unison. Delilah asked the manager to release all child acts from that point on.

After seven hours of belly dancers, ballad singers who actually lit Bic lighters for *themselves* while they were singing, cover bands, and a cellist with a severe case of stage fright, we allowed one more act into the room.

We had already found enough 10s to prevent us from any more desperation acts. We were in agreement on the singing waiter, the Carnegie-ready pianist, the ballet dancers with the lovely pas de deux (provided the male dancer agrees to remove what looked like an avocado from the front of his tights. If he's that well endowed, he can make better money elsewhere, I had joked to my left, so delirious and hungry now that I mistook my directionals and whispered that to my mother rather than to Anthony. Ouch. There's another moment to take back for a do-over). We cheered unanimously for the eight-member band with the repertoire of 50s, 60s, 70s and 80s music plus a costume change into a Zoot-suited swing band, and then another costume change for their percussionists to lead a truly rousing, primal Latin drum line. We gave them 15s instead of 10s. You're hired!

The phone rang. Carmela reported that Anthony's cousin, Jimmy V., would like to sing *Fly Me to the Moon* at the wedding. It was an offer we couldn't refuse. Because we didn't have a choice. What we didn't know at that moment was that Carmela had also paid Jimmy V. $300 to sing Elton John's *The Bitch Is Back* when Delilah enters the room. It would be a musical "hit."

Chapter 38

There she goes again.

We sat on our bench at the park, our bench being the first one, the one that always seems to be available just above the arched curve of white stone steps overlooking the water. In the middle of my audition recap, Leah checked her cell phone to get the time, then excused herself while she grabbed her backpack and jogged down to the railing. Sighing heavily, I stood—giving up the bench to a pair of very tired Rollerbladers who appeared out of nowhere—and joined her.

"Ready? Aim . . ." I joked.

"Knock it off," Leah smiled, producing a very large, very ripe orange from her bag. I noticed she had a banana in there, too, and I hoped that was a snack. From her smile and the way she was shaking her head at herself, she too knew that this was bizarre. Halfheartedly, sidearm, she winged it out over the water.

"Hey!"

It was a man's voice.

Had God had enough of this insanity and was now speaking clearly and loudly to her, not in the rustle of leaves, overheard conversations, music lyrics and slogans on people's T-shirts?

We stepped forward and looked out at the glistening ripples. No one was there.

A duck and her ducklings quick-paddled by, picking up on some animal instinct to avoid the crazy lady and her friend. No, it wasn't a quack that we heard, and I will not make the obvious joke here. I do have something of a heart.

We heard splashing, the cut of a paddle in the water. A red kayak drifted out from nearly under the pier, and the man looked up at us. Helmet on, eyes covered by dark sunglasses.

"Sorry!" I shouted and grabbed her arm to lead her away.

Life is not this ironic either. Leah was not going to meet the man of her dreams by pelting him with citrus fruit.

"Was it bad?" he asked.

"Excuse me?" Leah stepped back to the railing. Or was she?

"The orange you just launched," he smiled. Very toothy, but in a good way. "Was it rotten?"

"No," Leah smiled, all of her relaxed except for her white-knuckled hands, which gripped the wide circular railing top. He couldn't see that from his angle.

"Not hungry?"

Leah just smiled and tilted her head a little bit. A part of her ponytail slipped loose and fell down over her eyes. She pushed the strands back behind her ears.

"Then you must be part of the Homeland Security Task Force, taking out terrorist scuba divers with oranges and grapefruit," he laughed. "Now that's a cash-efficient solution!"

Huh? I blinked. I've been out of the dating game for a long time, but this is what passes for pickup lines?

Leah responded well, giving him the green light.

"Or are you trying to fix the whole seafood-tainted-with-mercury thing by adding extra Vitamin C to the water?"

Who was this guy? Leah's floating flirt eventually pulled his kayak up onto the small rocky jetty and joined us for coffee. I went to buy it in order to give my girl a few moments alone with him.

When I returned, he had removed his helmet and sunglasses and Leah had apparently removed her protective force field. She laughed, she flipped her hair, she doe-eyed him. And he was quite handsome, very George Clooney, with dark buzz-cut hair, big brown eyes, and a gray Long Beach Island sweatshirt hanging loosely over red shorts. And great soccer legs.

"Hello, I'm Ed," he held out his hand to me.

"Emilie," I smiled.

"Oh, that's my dog's name."

Before the words reached my brain to register a Huh? Leah had taken it as *a sign*. "Really?" she squeaked. "Wow, that's really something!"

Yeah, that's really something. Emilie the Dog was a golden retriever, three years old, which made her twenty-one and legal, according to Ed. Any other woman would have walked away on that one, but Leah is not any other woman. I could just about imagine her thought process whirring away in her head: *dog's name is Emilie like the one person I trust in the world, dogs are loyal, he's wearing red shorts and red is the color of the life chakra and also of passion, the dog is a golden retriever and gold is the color of* . . . blah, blah, blah.

She was doing the touching thing. Touching his arm while she talked to him. Always a good sign. He was now showing her the scar on his knee from his college football days, and that was enough for me. Once you get into trading scar stories, you're good for at least two dates. According to my calculations. But then again, things have changed a lot since I was in the dating pool.

"Leah, I have to run," I announced, breaking them out of their mutual attraction bubble and seeming to remind them that I was indeed still there. "Ed, nice to meet you."

"Bye girl," he said and patted my head. I stepped back, eyebrow raised. "It's a joke . . . you know . . . like, my dog is named Emilie, so I was saying 'bye girl' . . . um . . ."

Yeah, keep talking, Ed.

"I guess it sounded funnier in my head than out loud," he confessed, shrugging.

Oh, yeah, these two were going to get along just great. They both have no social skills. But then again, it *was* me muttering to myself as I walked home, sending a concerned mother with her kids crossing the street to avoid me: "My *dog* is named Emilie . . . you remind me of my *dog* . . . bye *girl* . . . Who does he think he is, talking to me like that? What kind of first impression was that?"

I was a slumped-shouldered model of self-righteous indignation, high and mighty judgment and one or two of the seven deadly sins. God, I sounded just like my mother.

* * *

"And . . . ?"

Leah closed the door, giggled, and said, "If it's not too late, I *would* like to have an *And Guest* on my wedding invitation."

We squealed, jumped around like idiots, and cracked open the Ben & Jerry's. I wanted to hear *every* detail.

Chapter 39

Salami slices on a wooden board. Mozzarella balls peppered with basil. Warm cracked wheat rolls. Shining red steaming meatballs and sausages, string-wrapped braccioli. Garlic. Hot red pepper flakes. Parsley, fresh chopped from the garden.

But no Vic.

Anthony and I sat at the table, hands clasped in our laps, listening to the kitchen clock tick and watching Carmela try to fill up the time. They're Old World. She wouldn't dare serve dinner without her husband in place at the head of the table.

"Ma," Anthony tried, but was swiftly shut up by Carmela opening the hot water tap full-force and soaking the meat pans. She gave the wine bottle a quarter-turn on the counter, but did not uncork it.

Vic was never late for dinner. Vic never left home on Sundays to be anywhere that could make him late for dinner.

"Ma?" Anthony tried again, but she shushed him in Italian.

And then . . .

A SLAM!

Papers blew into the kitchen from the living room. Had someone driven their car into the front of their house?

Vic stamped in, jaw set, eyes narrowed, lip jutting out. His sloped forehead seemed even more sloped than usual—if that was possible—and his barrel of a chest stuck out. The man had the walk of a tiger about to pounce. Carmela stepped back against the counter, her hands clasping on to the counter's edge and the diamond in her ring caught the sunlight for an instant, a flicker of radiance.

Vic marched right up to her, almost nose to nose, glaring. All that was missing was the ring through the bull's nose.

She lifted her chin a little bit. The international sign for *I'm not afraid of you.*

He took a big breath, then blew out the air through his teeth.

Anthony stood, his own eyes narrowing as he assessed the situation.

And lightning-fast, Vic slammed his hand on the countertop. We all jumped. "Here!" he shouted, red-faced, neck veins forking in bright purple lines. Under his hand, flat on the counter right next to Carmela's arm, was a small white piece of paper. "Here! Here, Carmela! Here's his name! And here's his number! You happy?! Call him! Go on . . . call him! This is what you want so much, you go call him!"

"Vic—"

"NO!" he thundered, pushing her arms away from him. "No more!"

Carmela's lip trembled. She brought her hands to her chin, as if in prayer. And I had to wonder if it was a Thank God kind of prayer, or a Help Me,

God, This Can't Be Happening kind of prayer. Her eyes gave away nothing. Which was something Vic had had his very last moment of.

"This is not a life! This is not a life for a man whose wife always, ALWAYS wanted someone else!" Vic shouted, shaking his fists in the air. I shrank in my chair. Was he drunk? Dangerous? He paced now like a caged animal, never for one second taking his eyes from Carmela. She couldn't look him in the face. He spoke the truth, perhaps the first full truth ever in their thirty-five years of marriage. "I have spent my whole life as your second choice, your second place, your confirmation prize!"

He meant *consolation prize*, and I silently prayed Carmela was not so without survival instincts that she would dare to correct him on his vocabulary.

"You looked past me, always PAST me!" He waved his hand back over his shoulder. "Like the ghost of HIM was standing there. And I stayed. I took care of you. I loved you. And I was not a man, keeping quiet, saying 'this is fine, she's here.'"

You go, Vic. Anthony thought the same. He sat down, hand rubbing his chin.

"So here you go . . . he's divorced. For the third time. He's a doctor, a heart doctor!"

Perfect. Maybe the Doc can fix Vic's.

"Here you go, Carm! Here he is . . . the man you wanted first! So go get him!"

He stopped for a second, caught his breath. Maybe bit his tongue to keep himself from crying. Sadness in a bull like Vic has to come out angry, irate, frightening.

And then quietly . . . "I'm sorry I gave so much of my life to you."

Vic turned, patted his son's shoulder, avoided my eyes, and left.

We were silent.

Anthony exhaled and looked down into his lap.

I knew that doing nothing and saying nothing was the only right move. Carmela didn't look like she needed a hug. She didn't cry.

She just picked up the white paper.

Read it.

Folded it.

Put it in her apron pocket.

Then turned around and blasted hot water into the meat pans.

On the way home, Anthony's grip on the steering wheel was loose. He nodded his head along with the music on the radio, laughed at something the shock jock said.

I looked at him, my eyes watering.

"What?" he said.

"What do you mean, 'what?'" *Am I marrying an emotional corpse?*

"You want me to cry?" *Or a juvenile?*

"Something would be nice."

"Wait 'til we get home," Anthony said, then looked to his left . . . for a long time.

"Leah, do you need these?" He held up a big bag of oranges from the refrigerator.

Behind him, I shook my head No in a silent warning to her.

"No, they're all yours," Leah said quietly, tentatively.

"Good!" Anthony stormed out of our place with us on his heels. He shifted his weight from heel to heel during the elevator ride down, and we braced ourselves against the brown mahogany elevator walls. He recoiled at my touch, which was fine. Understandable.

Leah questioned me silently as we hurried after him. Reaching the railing at the end of the pier, surrounded by yachts moored in place, and with New York City sparkling in the distance before us, Anthony ripped open the bag of oranges, spilling several to the ground.

With a primal grunt, he launched an orange out into the water.

And then another one.

And another, each with a grunt that was turning more and more into a cry of pain.

"How COULD she?!" he finally yelled.

I mouthed the word *Carmela* to Leah, who had already heard the saga of unrequited love and elitist erasure.

With each orange launch, Anthony cursed his mother for treating his father like second best. "She acted like *he* was the second-class citizen! He was always a few steps below!" Launch! "Like he could never do anything good enough for her!" Launch! "And I watched my dad tap-dance for her!" Launch! "Jump through hoops!" Launch! "Panting like a freakin' puppy trying to get her approval!"

Launch! Launch! Launch!

"She loved holding it just out of reach!"

Launch!

"And HIM!"

Launch!

"He STAYED!"

Launch!

"Put his tail between his legs, did everything but bow to her! He stayed and let her treat him like crap! Just parked his ass in front of the television

like a good boy while she gave him his freakin'
beer and chips!"

Launch!

"You don't stay when you're treated like nothing! That's betraying yourself, too!"

He raised his arm to throw another orange, but
stopped. Put his arm down. He turned to me with
wet eyes. I stepped forward, expecting him to fall
into my arms in tears.

"Em, have I ever . . . *ever* . . . made you feel second best?" His eyes were wide. He was raw.

"No, baby," I stepped into his chest. He was not
the falling-into-my-arms type. "I have *never* felt like
second best. You've never made me feel like that."

I could feel him nodding above my head. "I love
you, Em."

"I know," I whispered. "I love you too, A."

For good measure, Leah threw the last remaining oranges into the water, and hooked arms with
me as the three of us walked back home. For the
rest of the night, we did the *real* planning. We
talked about *marriage*, not the color of napkins,
the perfect shade of peach for the centerpieces,
buttercream or rolled fondant. That's not the real
planning. What's real is talking about love and
commitment, what happens when things get rough,
when life bangs on the windows and doors and the
winds blow unwanted issues into the room. We
talked about strength and courage and communi-
cation and valuing another's happiness above your
own, loving each other enough to tell the truth, and
loving each other enough to protect each other's
truths to others.

I learned more about him that night than I ever
thought possible. Now how does anyone plan a

wedding without this kind of soul-searching? Vic and Carmela each married a stranger. My father didn't really know my mother's truths when they got married. It's all about integrity, marriage is. It's all about truth.

Chapter 40

*I*t's all about truth.
And here I stand for my final fitting in my Vera
Wang gown, fashionettes pinning and tucking
here and there, letting a little bit of fabric out at
the waist because I am a bride who does eat Ben &
Jerry's.

And it's all a lie.

I look at my mother's face, searching for that
Donna Penks flicker in her eyes, but she is on her
cell phone right now, and I'm stuck with the false
face in the mirror.

I can't do this . . .

My breathing got shallow. I gulped for air. Felt
tingling in my hands.

Fashionette Number 1 stepped up on my platform to affix my headpiece and veil, then smoothed
the ends over my shoulders, smiling, hugging me.
And my face was blank.

I can't do this . . .

"Emilie, is something wrong?"

There! Donna Penks! In my mother's face, not

just her eyes. She was concerned, and her empathy brought out her other self. She stood and came toward me, picked up my hand and put two fingers on my wrist to take my pulse. *Mom* . . .

"Get it off!" I whispered, not a reaction they often get in the Vera Wang dressing rooms. I acted like it was made of a rare fabric form of acid.

The fashionettes laughed. "Calm down . . . every bride has a panic attack when she first sees herself in her gown." They rolled their eyes and laughed. They probably have Xanax stocked in the back room for the faint of heart like me.

"Emilie?" my mother put her hand against my cheek. Her palm felt like ice against the hot flush of my skin.

I took a breath. "Mother . . . there's something I have to tell you."

Chapter 41

"**Y**ou *told* her?"

Anthony was furious. He rubbed his forehead back and forth, always careful of the hairline.

"She was going to find out anyway," I reasoned, bringing the General Tso's chicken takeout to the couch with two forks. "When your father wasn't around anymore."

I had chickened out. I swallowed my own truth and gave her Carmela's. I told her Vic was gone.

"She probably loved that," Anthony dug in.

"No, actually, she didn't."

He rolled his eyes, as if saying *you poor naive little girl.*

"I'm serious. She was actually quite sympathetic. She asked how your mother was doing."

"Sniffing out the injured prey to go for the kill."

I clicked the channel. We'd been watching way too much Discovery channel.

"No, she asked if she could do anything to help your mother." I told him the truth. "She asked if your mother would like to stay at the Plaza for the weekend, to get out of the house."

Anthony raised an eyebrow. "Seriously?"

"Seriously."

"Wow, I'm surprised."

"I'm only half-surprised," I shrugged. "She does have a heart in there . . . somewhere."

Exactly ten minutes later (we eat quickly), I opened a large box that had come in the mail that day. Our wedding invitations. Three weeks late. And Anthony's mother's name was printed as *Cornelia.*

"You were saying . . . ?" Anthony grumbled as we loaded reams of sage green card paper into a shopping cart at Office Max. With only three weeks until our wedding, there was not enough time to order new invitations. I was steely silent as we loaded the paper, envelopes, calligraphy pens, color ink cartridges and gold foil labels onto the checkout cashier's counter. I whipped out my credit card and unconsciously tapped my foot as the charge went through.

Anthony, Leah and I spent most of that night designing our new invitations on our own home computer, and we changed the wording. Wiping out the four separate lines of parents' names now that most of them were single, we chose to open our invitations with

The loving parents of
Emilie Anne Winchester
and
Mr. Anthony John Cantano
Cordially invite you to . . .

And we used the term *loving* after a long discussion. Because you can't put *The petty, selfish and insecure parents of* . . . on a wedding invitation. It would be true, but it wouldn't be right.

As the printer whirred and spit out our invitations—hunter green ink on sage green paper with swirled hunter green borders at the top and bottom, our monogram *ECA* at center top (actually, far more lovely and simple and classic than the ones we had ordered), the phone didn't stop ringing. Delilah was dancing as fast as she could, apologizing for a momentary lapse in judgment. *Momentary?* Regretting the timing. Apologizing for her bad behavior.

Too little, too late.

I would have turned off the ringer, but it was day three and Leah was expecting Ed to phone. In the middle of this maelstrom, true love might be trying to call. Leah grew to hate my mother too, as every nerve-jangling sound of the phone ringing raised her hopes, then dashed them down and ground them out. It's a form of seasickness that hopeful romantics know only too well, that up and down.

While I manned the printer, handling the square cards with as much delicate care as possible, paranoid about smudging the ink, I heard Anthony on the phone in the other room, whispering. Here is what I heard . . .

"Oh man, Ma . . . you *didn't* . . . Well, what did he say? . . . Did he remember you?"

Oh no, she went to see the doctor, her first love. I looked at the wall where his voice was coming from, as if I could see through it. I imagined him pacing, his hand on his hip. *Please* . . . I irrationally thought, somehow hoping for a violin strings moment where the doctor would throw down his scalpel and embrace Carmela, confessing that she was always on his mind. She was the one that got away.

"Well, what did you expect?" It has been thirty-six years, after all.

My stomach sank. He didn't remember her.

"Not even a little bit?"

He didn't even remember her a *little* bit. Now my heart sank too.

"Ma . . . stop crying . . ."

Poor Carmela.

"Ma . . ."

Then I heard Leah whispering something about advising Carmela to incant to Mary Magdalene, the saint of broken hearts and losses. My imaginary X-ray vision through the wall saw Anthony wave off Leah like a gnat.

"Ma . . . stop crying . . ."

My dear husband wasn't aware that thirty-six years of walled-up pain can't be turned off with a flick of a switch. She'd likely cry for months over this one. He said "Ma, stop crying" about thirty-six times before he hung up and came back into our home office, slumped into the desk chair, and shook his head. It's the man version of empathy: part pity, part well, that's what she deserved.

"He didn't remember her?" I ventured, stopping myself from kneeling in front of him, clawing at his thighs like a thirsty nomad and begging for every detail. What did she wear? Did she make an appointment with him, or did she use the element of surprise? What did he say? How did he look?

Anthony just shook his head no. I'd get no details. It was left to my imagination, a tragic fairy-tale ending that was more Shakespeare than Delilah

Winchester. If this were a novel, my mother would
have had the dashing, gray-templed doctor gather
her up in his arms, whisper "at last, at last" and
bend her over his desk. But that was Delilah's world.
Carmela's was a very dark, quiet place where she
wobbled on her heels with a dazed look on her
face, more dazed than those who just got their pos-
itive biopsy reports back, having only the inch-
wide green line down the center of the hospital
floor to guide her back outside.

"Ma, you *didn't!*" Anthony's voice came through
the wall again, hours later as we hand-addressed
our wedding invitations. I am humbled that his
handwriting is better than mine. My husband has a
secret talent for calligraphy. I'd keep that to myself.

What did Carmela do now? Fling herself on the
doctor's Mercedes, begging for the life she should
have had? Wailing, crying, mascara streaming
down her cheeks? The doctor calmly hitting his
OnStar to report a maniacal hood ornament?

It was worse.

She had called Vic. To beg him to come home.
Vic hung up on her.

My flair for fantasy was confused. Who do I
pump my fist for? I wanted a happy ending for
Carmela, but truth be told, she didn't deserve
one. Where's the happy ending? Is it a happy ending for Vic that he stepped on her when she came
crawling back? I found myself proud of Vic. I
wouldn't have respected him if he just grabbed his
suitcase and ran back to second place, to his saggy
seat on the living room couch, his cold Bud and
his pretzels in place of wifely warmth. He wouldn't

be her confirmation prize, as he said. And I was proud of that. Doing the right thing for yourself sometimes doesn't fit into the happy ending musical swell-type of fantasy.

Did I enjoy thinking of Carmela sobbing on her kitchen floor? No. Was it justice? Don't ask me that question, or I'll have to answer it.

Chapter 42

Leah called it the *Anti-Delilah Bridal Shower*. Not in print, of course, but it was clear to anyone in on the scene that Leah had very brazenly and very intentionally planned a shower for me that was everything my mother would hate. So much for being a spiritual person. Leah had an edge too. As she said to me upon revealing her devilish revenge plot, "Hey, I'm not in the will. I don't care if your mother hates me."

Leah will almost certainly be killed off in my mother's next novel.

With my mother off in Australia for a book tour and Carmela heavily sedated, Leah had plenty of time to swipe the bridal shower right out from under them. Colin Cowie had been informed to scrap the pink tulle and the petit fours, as his services would not be needed. The Plaza's Tea Room was now open for regular business on that Sunday afternoon, as our private party had been canceled.

When my mother was told that I'd very much like my maid of honor to plan the party, since it's tradition, Delilah scoffed. "The bitter bridesmaid planning the shower?" she sniffed.

"It's important to her," I explained. "And it's important to me." Of course those two reasons didn't even register, so I went for the part of her brain that *does* register something: her ego. "Leah couldn't possibly pull off something of your caliber, so imagine the contrast between *her* party and *yours*." I had to stop myself before I said *your wedding*. A little too much truth there.

The wheels were turning.

"It's just going to be a modest little party," I explained according to script. "Consider it the intermezzo."

Had Delilah's face been able to, she would have raised an eyebrow in interest with that one. Leah's party would be a palate cleanser for the guests so they could *really* appreciate the rehearsal dinner and the wedding, both in Colin's hands and in Delilah's credit. She relented.

To hammer it home, I appealed to her other magnet: her status. "Besides, you have a book tour. People understand that you're just so busy, so in demand, right now that it's *generous* of you to share the fun."

Busy. In demand. Generous.

Each one was like a dart hitting the bull's-eye. We were in business.

We further assured our safety in this scam by telling Delilah the bridal shower would be one day, when it would actually be another. Tatiana, her assistant, was in on the plan, penciling in a meeting for the real day of the shower so that Delilah would show up where she needed to be at the right time. She would be the one to walk in to a surprise. It was a delightful irony. Normally, it's the bride who is surprised at her shower, but for our purposes, giving Delilah the shock was a wedding gift unto itself. We had peace, we had quiet, we had time to plan.

The only request Delilah made was that the guests be instructed to bring their gifts *unwrapped*, so as to avoid the lengthy unwrapping, *oooh*ing and *aaahh*ing session that is paramount at all bridal showers much to guests' groaning dismay. We hate sitting there while it takes three hours for the bride to open and unwrap every saltshaker, champagne flute and microwave while we drink lukewarm coffee and shift in our seats, but it's a requirement. It's tradition. So Delilah's request was a slip of the mind, our oops. And Leah promised to box up her gift set in as many different wrapped packages as possible. That, we so maturely clinked glasses, would show her.

For the location, we chose a rooftop restaurant in Hoboken, one that overlooked the marina and the harbor and the city skyscape. Divine providence gave us a gorgeous day, warm sun and a slight breeze to twirl the cheesiest white crepe paper bells and pink and white streamers you've ever seen. Huge bunches of white and pink balloons anchored to guest tables by silver-wrapped mini sandbags danced and bounced in a mild rhythm. Leah and I had needed three carts at Party City to laughingly collect the tackiest décor, pink paper plates, pink cups, pink plastic utensils, pink *paper* tablecloths, pink party favor bags (paper bags, of course), and for good measure . . . a pink-and-white piñata.

For the bridal shower favors, we selected hot

pink panties with the word *Angel* dotted in rhinestones over the backside.

We rented folding chairs to replace the restaurant's good chairs, and we ordered an enormous pink-and-white banner that said Happy Shower, Emilie. We thought about putting Cornelia, but that was a step too far.

After helping us set up, all of us laughing like the drunk kids on the train at 3 A.M., Anthony made a "for his own safety" exit before his testosterone dried up to go and do something more masculine, like skin a rabbit. "Make sure you get this *all* on video!" he exclaimed, kissing me before he departed. He is probably the only straight groom ever to utter those words about a bridal shower.

Leah and I hurried to catch our bus—a bus!—to the meeting place for the start of the shower. We met our mothers, my friends, Tatiana, and thirty-two of my mother's closest friends and colleagues for a deceptively lovely Phase One of the bridal shower at the Museum of Natural History. We would tour the butterfly exhibit, walking through a circular glass biosphere filled with lush green plants, waterfalls, a stone walkway and cut-open fruit on pedestals to attract the hundreds of butterfly species who lived in that warm, tropical-inspired safety bubble.

It was like walking through Eden.

Delicate, magical butterflies flitted from tree to tree: yellow and black monarchs, orange julias, red tiger-stripes. They circled our heads, checking out what strange and beautifully colored creatures *we* were, landing on our shoulders and gracefully lowering their wings. They chased one another play-

fully, tumbling through the air in either play or a
mating ritual. They skimmed across the surface of
a small water pond, then rested on rocks for a
quick butterfly chat and a "gotta fly!" departure.

The guests, my friends, were delighted. Delilah's
friends took pictures with their hideously expensive digital cameras, some of which were presenter
gifts from the goodie bags at the Golden Globes,
we were told . . . often and loudly.

Just as I posed for a shot with Leah, a Monarch
arched into the frame and hovered. I slowly lifted
my hand as a cup for it to sit on, and it lighted gently on my fingers. That photo is now one of my fa-
vorites. Leah and I have this look of wonder on
our faces. We look like young girls, eyes wide, inspired and awed. The Monarch smiled for the
camera.

With our keepsake butterfly keychains in hand,
Leah surprised our guests by whistling for Phase
Two. A bus pulled up in front of us, and half of our
guests noisily climbed aboard without a second
thought. The other half, the half wearing Manolos
and $10,000 designer suit dresses, stopped at the
curb. I could hear them thinking, a *bus*? That's
right ladies, a bus.

One of the braver heiresses threw caution to the
hot pretzel-scented wind and stepped aboard,
looking as disoriented as if she'd just stepped onto
a submarine. She looked down her nose at the worn
seats with torn covers, the red cord you push to
make the bus stop, the tired expression of the bus
driver, and—deciding this would be like a *safari*—
waved the rest of the Junior League Golden Brigade

aboard. Clutching their Vuittons, the women followed. Lemmings.

Delilah's sour face glared death rays at Leah and me as she took a front seat, and we whispered about how many of them would burst into puddles when they realized we were taking them to the *tunnel*. In a *bus*.

"We're going to . . ." it was too difficult to get the word off the tongue for one of them. "New *Jersey*?"

Purses opened, and several of them popped some kind of tranquilizers, we guessed from our obstructed views. Distress calls couldn't be made on cell phones from under the river in the Holland Tunnel. We had kidnapped them.

"Emilie," Delilah's voice was high-pitched, almost too chipper. "Perhaps it's best if you tell our guests our destination . . . ?"

Yes, she said *our* guests.

I toyed with the idea of playing with them, announcing "you'll see" with a diabolical laugh and the twist of an imaginary handlebar moustache, but thought better of it. There's a fine line, after all. These women all had lawyers on their speed dials, as well as their shrinks. "We're going to my favorite restaurant . . ." I said, then added a pulse-calming qualifier. "It's a rooftop garden overlooking the city."

A collective sigh. As long as they could still *see* New York City, these hothouse flowers would be able to breathe. My friends at the back of the bus lounged, feet up on the seats, gossiping gaily and straining to see over their seats the dramatic fanning going on in the front half of the bus. The wide-brimmed ladies-who-lunch hats twitched nervously with every shake of their heads, and gloved hands gripped at the hand-rests whenever the bus hit a big pothole . . . which was often. Bottles of Purell hand sanitizers were being passed around up front, and at least one of them was trying to speed dial her shrink over and over again.

Daylight came at last, the ladies relaxed, and my smile only grew as we headed up Main Street toward 14th where the party of the year was waiting for us. And the piñata.

Leah and I practically ran up the stairs to get in place with the video camera, an older model that was most definitely *not* part of any celebrity goodie bag at any award show. They initially walked in happy, all in pastel suits and hats, my friends in city-chic black pants and miniskirts and black or white shirts. We couldn't have divided the group better if we actually gave them a dress code.

We caught every facial expression.

The lilies of the group dropped their jaws and looked from side to side in sweeping glances, taking it all in. *Is this a joke? Has Colin Cowie lost his mind?*

My friends whooped with joy, being stylish enough to know that going full throttle for ultra-cheesy actually means you've reached the other pinnacle: sensational. It was over-the-top, and they loved it. Our puffy Pepto shower was a hit with my friends, the magazine editors, the fashion assistants, the ad executives with an eye for making an impact. They rushed to their tables to find their names written in pink glitter pen on their place cards. Priceless. Daphne, a friend of mine who works as an editor at *InStyle*, asked if she could pocket the place card for use in their upcoming Weddings issue. Delilah overheard that *that* would be the icon of my wedding that would make it into print for all the world to see. She reached for a glass of lemon-wedge ice water as quickly as she could.

To our disappointment, none of Delilah's friends swayed on their feet, fanning themselves, dramatically dreading an oncoming faint. But we did get a wide range of pursed lips, blinkless stares, and almost careful steps forward. One by one, they looked to Delilah who had only a second to save face. Her horror clicked instantly into her stage voice.

"Isn't this *darling?*" she said, media-savvy enough to sound normal through her clenched jaw. "Didn't the girls do something *wonderful* here! How *delightful!*"

She would have said the same if we'd taken them all to the dog races.

The ripple worked its way through the crowd, and the ladies who lunch decided that *this* lunch would be fine, given Delilah's approval. So their dismay that turned to horror that turned to shock that turned to disgust, now spun on its heel to amusement that turned to giddiness that turned to abject approval. *Ah, this tackiness was PLANNED! How brilliant! How ingenious! It's a PARODY!*

Pretty soon, we'd have a let them eat cake moment, and it would be a photo airbrush-topped cake from Carvel with a side of Krispy Kremes. I couldn't wait.

We knew enough to get the good champagne. Cristal. Half of my party would fling themselves off the roof if we served them anything less.

Their snobby instincts now bypassed by the queen bee's social okay, they dug into the enchiladas, and picked at the nacho platters with their manicured fingers. *Is this Arborio rice?* Some shocked their tongues with a fiery jalapeño circle, having assumed it was an olive circle, then handed the plate of jalapeños to their friends as if it was a new discovery, a party game. *What a curious olive! Taste this, Penelope!* They inspected the tapas like they'd find a diamond inside. And at least one pigeon courageously dive-bombed to grab a garlic bread braid from the table. The ladies who lunch applauded, as if we had trained the pigeon to do so.

My friends drained their margaritas, laughed uproariously at our inventiveness, at the pink candy cane circles as napkin rings, even better because they were *fake*. Across the great divide, the ladies who lunch had turned from their champagne to margaritas—bright red, blush pink, neon blue, with colored salt around the rims. They had been converted. And they were loud.

Delilah sat with a stone-silent, almost catatonic Carmela, who I really hadn't even noticed was with us until now. She just sat slumped in her chair, a glass held up stuck to her lip, but not drinking. She faded out like that, lost in thought. Then something caught her attention, something shiny probably, and she was back in the game.

All glasses raised in clinks—that was probably what did it—and the guests yelled out "To Emilie!" for the tenth time. Leah, knowing our guests were sufficiently toasted, took that as her cue to stand.

"May I have your attention, please?" Leah noiselessly tapped a plastic fork against a plastic margarita glass, and our guests took a few moments to simmer down. "We're here today to wish Emilie well . . ."

Cheers, whistles, even some woofing . . . mostly from the ladies who lunch.

"She has found something wonderful in life . . . a love you can count on."

A whimper from Carmela. *Oh God.* How do you make a true love toast when the mother of the groom was a wreck over the topic of love you *couldn't* count on? And that she was the one who made it not count?

"Emilie is like a sister to me," Leah said, holding her glass high. "She's seen me through a lot, and I will be forever grateful. Friends are like family, and family should be like friends." She was looking right at Delilah on that one. Carmela even straightened in her chair. Okay, so her head lolled a little bit, but she was more lucid than usual. "Here's to everlasting joy."

Cheers!

Delilah took her turn to stand.

Uh-oh.

She did not look happy.

"Thank you, Leah," she said, as if Leah were understood as her opening act, and she was the keynoter. "I think we can all agree that this party is . . . *something.*"

I heard a very, very quiet comment from behind me: "Oh, get the broom out of your ass, Delilah." Wow. I didn't even think it was one of my friends.

"And our very . . . *creative* hostess does touch upon a fundamental truth." Delilah walked as she spoke, holding her hands out in demonstration as she does at her speaking engagements. What a shame we didn't pay a cover to see her appear. "Love is like a waterfall . . . so powerful, so constant, so inspiring . . ."

These were novel lines she was trying out on us. The woman breathes in cliché. Her daily life is her first draft. So inspired was she by her own powerful, constant, and inspiring speech that she didn't notice the eye-rolling, the finger drumming on the paper tablecloths, the people checking their watches.

Somewhere around the twentieth cliché, her speech stopped. Because the restaurant staff had brought in the piñata. Taking the candy-colored, ribbon-wrapped stick, I rose, smoothed my skirt, and walked to my mother. Leah jumped up, fearing that I was about to make a human piñata out of her, beating the literary crap out of her, but I handed *her* the stick.

"Mother," I proclaimed. "You may have the first whack at it."

This is a woman who has never used the word *whack* in her life.

Delilah took the piñata stick between thumb and forefinger like I'd handed her a dead bird. "You want me to . . . *hit* it."

"Oh, Delilah, will you just lighten up?!" It was Rose, her editor, the woman beneath the slightly lopsided pink hat, with the big pink lipstick stain on the edge of her fourth margarita glass. "This is a *party*! For your daughter! So drop the novelist bravado and just *whack* it."

The chant started softly, Leah egging on my friends, then grew to our entire guest list. "De-liii-LAH! De-liii-LAH!"

I would have preferred Whaaack IT! Whaaack IT! as the soundtrack to my mother's first swings at a condom-filled piñata, but you can't have everything you want, now, can you?

* * *

Well, the night wasn't over yet. Delilah let down her guard, caught up to everyone's margarita count, and loosened up almost to the point of fitting in with the commoners. She didn't even mind that I took my time unwrapping all the gifts, which of course came wrapped, against her wishes. And we hadn't even gotten to Phase Three yet.

Phase Three began as we said good-bye to the majority of the shower guests, shipping them out on a bus to take on the tunnel and find their own way back to Park Avenue. I imagined that after the sheer number of margaritas these women put down, it was going to be a much more festive ride home for them. They were *adventurers*. They had partied in New Jersey. They had taken the tunnel, and wore as much pride for that accomplishment as if they had just macheted their way through the Amazon jungles. They had eaten jalapeños, and they had beaten on a piñata. Our work here, in corrupting the blue bloods, was done.

Our ride pulled up right on time. With three handsome men standing up out of the sunroof. Did I mention they were three, *shirtless*, handsome men? I wasn't quite sure how male dancers were going to do any actual dancing in the back of a limousine, and it was with that intriguing logistical question in mind that Leah, my mother, Carmela, Tatiana and a few of my friends climbed right in to introduce ourselves to Shawn, Hawk, and Gregorio (not their real names, of course), our quote-unquote escorts for the next hour. Not surprisingly, a pink-cheeked Carmela came back to join the living.

* * *

I've always known that Carmela was a competitive woman. Surprisingly competitive, and not just in planning the wedding. The woman cheats at Scrabble. She sits on the X and the Q, keeping them out of the little red tile pouch, then deftly slides them onto her wooden tray when no one is looking. Then she goes to church to pray.

So I should not have been surprised that she battled my mother for the attentions of Hawk. Or rather *Da Hawk* in his South Boston accent. Leah and I watched in horror mixed with amusement as the two premenopausal mothers, one sleepy-eyed from antidepressants and the other shockingly girlish and unrefined after too many margaritas, pulled at the man's giant biceps, pawed him, and—I'll need therapy for the rest of my life after this—licked tequila from his chest. One licked, the other scowled. The other licked the other pectoral, while the other scowled. I stopped it when *Da Hawk* offered to fill his belly button with tequila and let them fight over it.

With a screech, the limousine pulled to the curb, and our three shirtless dancers were unceremoniously dropped off at 5th Street. To find their shirtless way home. To be fair, we did drop them off in front of one of the most teeming, wild college bars, so we had no doubt that Gregorio, Shawn and *Da Hawk* would find themselves very sticky with tequila and rolling in cash by the end of the night. Carmela and Delilah knelt like puppies on the backseat of the limo, waving out the tinted back window to them as we drove away. I was told I am no fun. By the mothers, not my friends.

* * *

I am not so different from my husband. And, believe me, I was keeping my alcohol intake low that night so that my notoriously loose liquor-lips wouldn't have me saying something incredibly damning, like "Hey, wanna hear something funny?" as I elbow my mother in the ribs. "I'm *married!*" Only I'd be in very little control of my tongue, so it would come out as '*maui'd*'. "Isn't that just *hysTERical?*"

I'd keep the shots to a minimum.

As I was saying, I am not so different from my husband. If you call me a coward, I'm going to prove you wrong by going bungee jumping. If you say I'm irresponsible with money, I'm paying not only my credit card balances in full that very minute, but setting up another savings account to pay myself an extra ten percent of my gross income for a rainy day fund. And I had just been called no fun.

Look out. It was time to clear my name.

I just needed a plan. After a quick consult with Leah, who picked up the sleek black phone on the wall to whisper to the driver up front, we swung around to go back through the tunnel into New York City.

Twenty minutes later, we were on the sign-up sheet. At a karaoke bar. I am not only fun, I am *retro*. And it turns out I am a genius. I found the one thing that could ever bond my mother and Carmela . . . mutual disdain at others' singing abilities. We had revisited the musician auditions for the wedding. We were now uncredited judges with shining neon martinis in front of us. We crowded into a way-too-small round booth on a rise overlooking the stage and the dance floor while a man in a cowboy hat and tight jeans sang *Desperado*.

Our bracelets jangled as we clinked glasses to toast everything we could free-associate. We toasted our hot bartender Chad. We toasted the fact that it was not raining and that my friend's curly hair had not frizzed. We toasted Tatiana's birthday, which was four months away. We toasted my unborn child, which was according to our schedule about three years away from being conceived. We toasted Delilah's upcoming novel launch and Carmela's ten-pound weight loss. Lip gloss that really does last for four hours. The electric charge of a great first kiss. The personal shopper service at Bloomingdale's. Ben & Jerry, not necessarily in that order. Fathers who make time for their children. Whoever invented clear plastic dress straps. Really good guacamole. Life that exists on other planets (one guess who came up with that one).

Having chipped a martini glass on that last one, we called it a night on the toasts. It had been half an hour, and we had been so busy lifting our glasses, we hadn't had time to drink from them. We were losing our buzz. The mothers were starting to crash. Their shameless dismissal of each singer as "amateurish," "spine-hurting," and "someone should slap his mother" was starting to dwindle. They were slumping and had resorted to silent thumbs up or thumbs down reviews. Then something very interesting happened. Delilah said, "Carm, let's go check out the ladies' room."

Fearing my mother's unpredictable timing for reprisals (I remembered that in one of her novels, the villainness got her rival drunk, lured her out to the parking lot under the pretense of finding the coat closet, and stabbed her to death with an S&M stiletto heel through the eye and into the brain), I followed them. As a tiny-waisted singer belted out *I*

Will Survive I stalked my mother and mother-in-law, unnoticed by them, which is how stalkers usually do it. I'd read enough of my mother's novels to know the cagey steps to take.

They joined hands like young English schoolgirls, wobbled on their high heels, and threw their heads back laughing at some shared joke. Who were these women? Moments later, I found out they were women who had decided to be best girlfriends for the night, standing guard for each other while one used the unisex bathroom stall and the other body-blocked the door with the broken lock. I couldn't peek around the corner any further or I would be spotted. But I was satisfied that no one was going to be killed tonight and headed back to the table. Moments later, the mothers tumbled back into the booth, sliding on the leather seat, bumping clumsily into one another and Tatiana, laughing hysterically.

"Your mother . . ." Carmela was laughing, then snorting, fluttering her hand in front of her mouth. "How do you kids say it? She got digits!"

Delilah smiled in a Cheshire way, folding a business card and stuffing it into her blouse. She had a purse with her. She just liked the effect of being someone who stuffs a business card into her bra.

"One of your fans?" Tatiana winked.

"He will be on Saturday night!" my mother howled and drained her Neon. She lifted her glass for the hot waiter to refill. Our table cheered and drummed our hands on the table, somehow turning into a tribe of frat boys. The woman on stage with too much dark eyeliner ringing her heavy-lidded eyes, choking out *All By Myself* didn't appreciate our interruption. The rest of the crowd, cringing at her bare naked misery and screeching sour

notes, took our outburst as a cue and applauded
the broken, sad shell of a woman off the stage.

To the heavy bass of the beat box back music
he'd turned up high to get the crowd's pulse back
up from near-hypothermia after that woman's soul-
sucking rendition, the karaoke announcer shouted
in what could only be described as a really fake
British accent: "Are you ready to *party*?! Are you
ready to get *hot*?!" The crowd cheered. Testosterone
was now surging back into the systems of most of
the bar patrons. He had revived them from near
slack-jawed comas. "Then let's bring up the *hottest*
women in the room!"

Cheers, whistles and chest-thumping surrounded
us as a spotlight we hadn't noticed before swung
circles around the room and landed on us. We
were the hottest women in the room. Two im-
paired women in their 50s, me, Leah, my mother's
thick-accented Russian personal assistant and
three of my friends who really should have been
sent home in a cab hours ago. This was not going
to be pretty.

It didn't take him long to recognize her.

"Everyone, we have a *celebrity* in the house!"

Of course, I assumed he was talking about my
mother. She did too, slapping on her camera face
and waving to her ogling admirers, many of whom
were probably too drunk to discern that we were
in fact women.

"Say hello to Kelly Ripa!"

Our spotlight zipped away from us and to Kelly
Ripa's table of blondes. Kelly politely waved and
toasted the room with her pink martini, that rock
of a ring from her husband catching the perfect
ray of light to shower rainbows all around her. I in-

stinctively brought my left hand behind my back, but then stopped. *Hey, I have three carats here!*

Luckily for us, all eyes were on Kelly Ripa, drinks were being sent to her table, and men were puffing out their chests as they imagined she might actually check them out. We would, it seemed, get through *Lady Marmalade* (not my choice, but I did manage to veto *Funkytown*) relatively unnoticed.

That is, until my mother whispered to the announcer.

"It's celebrity night here! Ladies and gentlemen, please welcome Delilah Winchester!"

She asked for it. Just a smattering of applause by the six people in the room who made the connection. Hey, if Stephen King were bagging my groceries at the Stop and Shop, I wouldn't notice him because I'd never expect him to be there in the first place. Luckily, the music started up, and Delilah took the first part . . . and the second . . . and the chorus. We were her backup singers, following her lead with the dance steps. Until Carmela burst out of her Celexa fog and stepped forward to *unbutton her shirt* to the waist, showing off a red bra, and then shocked us all. She could *sing*! And *dance*! And she was a showstopper, strutting back and forth, bending down to brush the cheek of a very impressed and very handsome corporate type in his suit and loosened tie. That did it. Carmela took hold of the tie and led the model-handsome junior vice president onto the stage with us.

It was as if Carmela was the equivalent of a Hollywood fat suit that unzipped from the back, and out stepped Bette Midler to the roar of the crowd.

I had to steal a glance at Delilah's face. She was fine. Impressed. She had a business card in her

bra, so she was set. She'd allow Carmela to slide
her back up and down against the junior VP. And
he loved it. His girlfriend, it must be said, did not.
Belting out my *voulez-vous couchez avec moi*'s in the
background with Leah and Tatiana (the other girls
had abandoned us), I watched with puzzled mirth
as the VP's *gorgeous* leggy girlfriend in the tight red
top, size 0 black pants and diamond teardrop earrings glared a flamethrower jealous-rage hatred
stare at *Carmela*, the paunchy middle-aged mother
of my husband.

The junior VP danced with Carmela, spun her
around, dipped her, then came back and joined
our marginally talented and marginally coordinated
background singers line. The guy loved the ladies.
At second glance, Size 0 was no longer at his table.
Well, I guess that's one way for a guy to blow off a
high-maintenance blind date. Get on stage and
grind with a drunk, matronly lady on prescription
drugs.

The last part of the song was coming up, and
Delilah stepped forward. Not to steal the spotlight
from Carmela, but to *share* it. Somehow these two
archrivals managed not only to deliver the song's
dramatic big closer, they did so in an amazing war-
ble of harmony. Carmela took the high end, and
Delilah smoothed it with her pitch-perfect lower
notes. They even fluttered their voices in unison,
each note perfect to the last closing punch of their
hands into the air. Even Kelly Ripa was on her feet,
applauding. The mothers owned the room. We—
Leah, Tatiana and I—were honored to stand in
their shadows.

"I think it can be said," I shouted above the
standing ovation to Leah as we were virtually pulled
from the stage to give Carmela and Delilah their

by-audience-demand encore. "Even though I was just a background singer no one noticed or heard . . . I am *fun*."

"Yes, you are," Leah turned us both around to stand in the front row where Size 0 used to be, next to the smiling Junior VP who didn't bother to chase after her, to watch my mother and Carmela deliver a five-star, five octave version of Aretha Franklin's *Respect*.

By the end of the night, just after last call, both Carmela's and Delilah's bras were stuffed with business cards. Leah headed home, and the mothers joined me for waffles at the diner. They had the munchies.

"Wow, I thought I'd come home, find you on the couch, and have to explain."

Anthony stood at the kitchen counter in his boxer shorts and white socks. It was 4:30 A.M. I had beaten him home from *his* bachelor party. Thankfully, it didn't look like he'd done too much damage or needed much recovery. But he was making coffee and eating cold delivery pizza right out of the box.

"Oh, you still have to explain," I smiled, hugged him from behind, and grabbed a cold slice from the box for myself. I stepped out of my heels and kissed him between the shoulder blades. "How many?"

"Strippers?"

No, states in the U.S.

He answered anyway. "Just two."

Hm.

"And they were just . . . skanky."

Go on.

"Really disgusting, you wouldn't believe it."

You're making this way too easy for me.

"We got bait-and-switched, apparently."

Did you really?

"You know, the guys ordered hot strippers, and they sent over the bottom of the barrel."

I didn't realize there was a top of the barrel when it came to strippers.

"So they did their whole thing . . . made out with each other, and they looked really bored."

All in a day's work.

"It was like kiss, kiss, then some incredibly cheesy dirty talk. 'Where's our groom?' and they just shook it around in front of me for a while, until they saw I was watching SportsCenter on TV . . ."

I know the feeling.

"They got kind of offended that we weren't really into it. And then, let's put it this way . . . I'm never drinking from a beer bottle again."

I just sighed. Nothing to work with here. His mother got more action that night than he did.

"What?" he stanced defensively.

"Nothing." I shrugged, tugging at some cold pizza crust with my teeth.

"I was good!"

"I know it. You're a married man."

"That's right. I am." He nodded, calmed.

"And you love me."

"That's right. I do." He gave me a kiss on the shoulder. "How was your night?"

I smiled. "Let's just say . . . better than expected."

"How many?" he asked.

"Three."

"Three male strippers?"

"Well, yeah, but we threw them out of the limo. It was an episode of *When Mothers Attack*." I gave him the Don't Ask shudder. "But it's the *three* en-cores our *mothers* got at the karaoke bar I was talk-ing about."

"Karaoke?" he blinked. That was probably the last thing he ever expected to hear. "How did you get from the puffy pink Anti-Delilah bridal shower to a limo with strippers to a karaoke bar where our mothers got three . . . encores?"

"We have it all on videotape, babe."

Anthony shook his head. "You amaze me."

"I amaze myself."

I took a final bite of pizza and filled our coffee cups. *Uh-oh.* We were apparently a little loud. Leah shuffled into the room, looking displeased.

"Oh my God, sorry Leah!" I cringed. "We woke you up."

Leah silently adjusted her pajama top, which was buttoned off-kilter, opened the refrigerator, grabbed *two* sport bottles of water, gave me a wink, and disappeared back into her room. *Two* sport bottles.

"Trust me, you didn't wake her up." Anthony rolled his eyes and nodded his head toward the black leather jacket and backpack on the couch. "I have way too many disturbing sounds and images in my head for tonight."

Should I tell him his mother unbuttoned her shirt to reveal a red lacy bra while she was singing onstage tonight? Nah. "Well, then let's replace them with *bet-ter* sounds and images." Not having his shirt to pull on, I tugged at his waistband, pulling him against me. The kitchen table would hold us.

Chapter 43

I knew the Love Fest wouldn't last long. And I'm not talking about Leah's late-night rendezvous with Ed. His talents and cardiovascular fitness are quite apparently intact, as we heard through our very thin walls that night.

I'm talking about the mothers, who just the night before held hands like sisters, talked about going on a Mediterranean singles cruise together, and all but braided each other's hair that night. True bonding was too much to hope for. No doubt they woke the next morning with throbbing headaches, vague recollections of the night before, and a big dose of *What did I do?* Margaritas and karaoke can only do so much. Rivals in their DNA, it can't be overcome.

Delilah had risen back to her cloud. Carmela had remembered the mess her life was in, that Vic was not in her bed the next morning, and that the cardiologist had never carved her into his Life's Greatest Regrets list. They had forgotten who they were for a moment, and now it all came rushing back on them. *That's right. I HATE her. I almost forgot.*

This morning's melodrama was about the invitations, of course. "The loving parents of" gave no one top billing. No ego boost. No social status. They had been lumped together as something as heinous as just mere *loving parents*. Oh, the horror!

"Do you realize that our guests will *notice?*" Delilah growled into the phone. "Do you realize that the people on *our* side are proper?"

"There's nothing wrong with the wording, Mom. That's how you're supposed to do it when there are too many parents." I held myself back from saying *divorced, separated and bitter parents.*

"Well, that's not *our* fault. Your father and I have been divorced for *eons*, and he and that Jenni girl are not a part of our wedding!" Yes, once again, she said *our*. "Just because that Carmela *trashed* her life"—emphasis on the *trash*—"right before the wedding doesn't mean that *I* have to suffer."

I sighed and rubbed my eyebrow. "That's besides the point. This is just how it's done."

"No, it's not proper to—"

"I'll send you the link to the etiquette article so you can see for yourself."

Delilah hung up on me. I had made the grave mistake of making a point, rebuking her with reason, logic and proof. She had been proven wrong, and there was no rescue for her ego.

"It's supposed to say *Son of Mr. Victor Cantano and Mrs. Carmela Cantano*," Carmela sobbed. "He's my only son! I will never be on a wedding invitation, ever!"

"Carmela—" I started, but the wailing continued.

"Your mother did this!"

No, actually, she changed your name to Cornelia on the original version.

"Carmela, listen to me . . ."

And she hung up on me before I could refer her to the link.

And then . . . the Mother of All Motherly Wedding Threats came to me in the form of an e-mail:

Emilie:
Since we cannot agree on the most fundamental issues of proper style and honor, I will not be in attendance at your wedding. Your Mother

Now she'll call it *my* wedding.

"Man, Em, maybe we should tell her," Anthony rubbed his forehead and swiveled back and forth in his chair when I showed him the missive. Or dismissive, as it were.

I stared at the words long enough to be sure I'd see them even when my eyes were closed. Certain things have a way of showing up on the back of your eyelids when they're horrendous enough.

"All this because her name is not on the invitation?" Anthony was talking to himself as much as to me.

I found myself embarrassed to be her daughter. Regardless of the *many* opportunities in my life I had to be embarrassed to share half her genes, this was the first time I ever really truly was. I worried that Anthony would, in some small degree, wonder if I'd turn into my mother someday. If I was capable of such treachery. If some seed lurked inside me that would spring out in the future to reveal that I am also small and petty and heartless and vindictive.

"It's not the invitation," I whispered, still staring at the screen, at the dark red print (like blood) and the scrolly font.

He didn't hear me. "Maybe she was drunk."

"She wasn't drunk."

"She can't actually *mean* that, right? It's just a bluff . . ."

No, it's not a bluff. She would do it.

With one tap, I deleted the message. As if that could erase it.

"She can't be that psychotic," Anthony shook his head, and I closed my eyes. "It has to be a bluff, Em."

"Well, then she's made her last bluff to me," I stood up, the back of my knees shooting the rolling office chair across the floor, skidding it on two wheels with the other side of the chair lifted off the ground, then crashing it into our bookcase.

The first rule of marketing is that you can't make someone change his or her mind. Once it's set, it's set, and any effort you put into changing it is just wasted time. They're going to grasp onto what they know. For the second time, and with the same woman, I had lost my mother. Donna Penks was surely dead now, choked off by the bitter weeds that had grown in tight spirals around her inside Delilah Winchester's shell. She couldn't have made that threat—no, that *promise*—if any part of Donna Penks was still living and breathing in there, sending tiny bubbles of messages into Delilah's conscience. Donna Penks is gone.

This is how my father must have felt when he watched his wife burn every trace of herself on the kitchen stove.

"She's sick, Emilie," he had said to me. "She has an illness that makes her not recognize herself, want to erase herself."

"No, Daddy, it's YOU! You made her sad, and you never did anything to make her happy like she used to be," I had screamed at him, throwing a handful of my scrambled eggs at his chest. I must have broken his heart that day. He, just like Vic, hadn't left soon enough. And I defended her. I didn't speak to my father for years. I must have broken his heart that day. Again.

"Em?" Anthony's voice trailed in like an echo as I stood in front of the coffeemaker, waiting for the coffee to be ready. But I hadn't clicked it on.

And I heard myself say, "Yeah?"

"What do you want me to do?" He meant, *cancel the wedding?*

That would only inflate her sense of power. That would be her victory dance over the corpse of Donna Penks, mangled, unrecognizable, with a trail of blood trickling down the driveway and into the gutter, curling into scrolls that looked like computer font letters.

The phone rang, and I jumped. I felt cold.

Anthony ran to answer it, and Leah came out of her bedroom, unaware of the somber turn my wedding had just taken. She waved her hands in front of herself, gesturing *I'm not here.*

"No, Ed, she's not here," Anthony shrugged at Leah. *What are you doing?* "Sure, I'll give her the message."

Looking relieved, Leah went back into her room and closed the door.

I just shook my head in disgust. *The first rule of*

marketing is: You can't make anyone change his or her mind.

It astounds me the way a theme clicks into color in your mind. *I am surrounded by people who will do anything to avoid being happy.*

"Leah?" I knocked on her door, and smelled the faint scent of incense through the door. She didn't answer. I heard CD harp music coming from inside, so I turned the doorknob. Locked. "Leah, what's going on?"

No answer.

For two days, Ed called. He sent her flowers. He called some more.

Leah was heartlessly avoiding him. Anthony took offense. "See that right there?" he paced. "*That's* why guys have a hard time of it. We're the heartless bastards? We don't own the market on that."

"Shhh, she'll hear you."

"Do you know what it takes for a guy to open up like that, to really fall for a woman, and then get the telephonic stiff-arm?"

The telephonic stiff-arm?

"It's harder for us guys to be really attached, without the net under us."

Delilah would tell him to stop mixing his metaphors. I just listened. My insane circle of friends and family were serving only one benefit: a deeper look into the mind of my husband.

"And when we do . . . we fall hard. Once we let down our guard, which by the way we only do when we really feel you want that, we're just naked. Completely naked."

Okay, so he's not very eloquent about it. Men don't sit around and discuss the intricacies of vulnerability. We women have had near-constant practice since we were twelve. We have magazines and television shows, talk shows, books, CD-ROM, daily e-mails from our friends, e-mail affirmations, comic strips, specials on *E!* and *20/20*, conferences, seminars, board games, card packs, and journals with quotes on them, tearaway calendars, bookmarks with "The only true thing in life is to love and be loved" on them, music videos, compilation tapes our ex-boyfriends made us back in high school, our journals, our yearbooks, and thongs with Angel written on them.

"The guy is in *pain*, Em. Leah just ripped his heart out. Playing the avoidance game is just torture."

I know.

"She's just passing along what her ex did to her," Anthony concluded. "She couldn't hurt her ex, so she's taken Ed and is making *him* pay."

No she's not. She's scared.

"I never thought that she could do a thing like that, never thought she had it in her. Em, are you listening?"

To every word.

Chapter 44

Do I take Leah by the shoulders and shake her? Do I slap her across the face and tell her to snap out of it? That didn't work for Cher in *Moonstruck*, so it's not going to happen here.

How do you tell someone who's been through an unimaginable hurt and humiliation 'Don't be afraid, it's not going to happen to you again?'

You don't.

You can't.

You can't guarantee that.

How do you tell her to be strong, and be brave, when every day she gets out of her bed to face another day is already taking all the strength and bravery she has?

How do you tell her to just have faith, when her faith was taken from her by her groom who ran off with a transsexual the night before her wedding, in front of all her friends and family? Especially when her father told her it was *her* fault. (I'd have no problem slapping *him*, by the way.)

I had no pep talk for Leah. Not with what I had on my plate already.

Go ahead, Leah. Run away. Ruin it.

I used to believe that it was the right thing to do to stay, to fight for what you loved. But all this . . . all this I'm seeing around me . . . is making me wonder if running away is sometimes the best thing to do when you're just too scared. Otherwise you'll just destroy the person who loves you.

Who am I kidding?

I've *never* believed in the weasel's way out.

And that's what it is when you run away without a word of explanation, or some honest culpability. How hard is it to say, "I'm scared to death, so I can't be here with you right now?" How cowardly do you have to be to just take off and leave the other person with nothing but questions, no answers? Vic, at least, didn't leave Carmela guessing. He was direct and honest and open. Never in a million years would I have guessed that *Vic* would be the model of integrity for all of us.

I pounded on her door. "Leah! Open the goddamn door!"

"And *you!*" I stalked into my mother's office, the French doors smacking against the walls behind them, Tatiana pretending to run interference for her boss, but knowing enough from the look on my face that she'd better just keep a safe distance. She scurried behind me shouting a halfhearted *Wait, stop.* She didn't want me to stop. She wanted me to get in there and fight. Finally.

Delilah didn't look up from her pink legal pad. She lounged in a white silk robe on her Victorian couch, pillows behind her, her legs curled with marabou slippers on her dainty pedicured feet, her hair in a French braid. She looked freshly scrubbed and the room smelled of gardenias from her recent essential oil bath. She floated gardenias in her bath water, as befitting the goddess she thought she was.

I stood with my legs at hip-distance, hands clenched at my sides to keep me from grabbing her by the throat, leaning slightly forward and clenching my teeth together so hard they hurt. But she was a picture of serenity. *Oh, yeah, Daddy, she's ill.*

"Tatiana," she breathed. "Would you please close the doors? If they haven't been broken."

You bitch.

Tatiana closed the doors silently, looking down at the floor, presumably for broken glass shards but probably for fear of her employment and possible deportment.

"Are you *kidding* me?" I railed. "Threatening to not come to the *wedding!* That's low," and I said it: "even for you."

Delilah still did not look up. She just pursed her little pink lips into an O, as if whistling but not with sound.

"You think you're really something." I took a step closer, and she just kept scribbling.

Another step closer.

"Don't you?"

Another step closer.

Her writing grew quicker, the only sign that she had a quickening pulse.

"Well, let me tell you something, lady." That's right. I called her Lady. Which was an insult to true ladies everywhere. "I . . . know . . . who . . . you . . . *are.*"

My hand was now on the smooth back of her couch. She could probably feel my breath on her. I may have spit a little bit on her face. But she wouldn't lower herself to wipe it away. She just remained in her bubble. I was just a character to her right now, feeding her lines for her next novel.

She sighed, bored with me.

"Better yet." I leaned in even closer. "I will never let *you* forget who you are."

That got her. Her pen stopped midswirl.

"Nothing to say?" I stood straight again, satisfied that she wouldn't elevate herself by tearing into me. "Not protected by a computer screen right now? You're pretty brave typing that in an *e-mail*, aren't you?"

Delilah looked up at me with tears in her eyes.

No dice, lady. The waterworks are a ploy. You taught me how to bite on the inside of my cheek to make the tears start back when I was in high school and trying to get out of detention. I learned a lot from you about playing people and playing the system.

"Proper and honor?" I used her e-mail words against her. "What's proper, what's honorable about playing hardball with your own daughter? What's proper and honorable about taking the *low* road and threatening to not come to the wedding? Does that make you a proper and honorable *mother*?" I hadn't had any of this planned. It wasn't part of my rehearsed speech in the car. I was just flying along on my own, without a net as Anthony would say. That's okay. I wouldn't need one. I came in here with nothing to lose.

I was wearing my wedding ring.

"Still nothing to say?"

Delilah sensed her tears weren't going to accomplish anything, so she tried posture. She straightened up a little, squared her shoulders, and pulled the silk ties of her robe belt across to the other hip, for no reason. The pen was quivering in her hand. I saw that much. Time to let *her* see something.

I slapped my hand flat on her pink legal pad. My left hand. The ring hand.

Delilah jumped, first at the unexpected press of my hand against her stomach through the writing pad. Pressing on the exact place where she once carried me. Notice I didn't press my hand against her heart.

Then she noticed my wedding ring. Nestled against my engagement ring. All cozied up together like they'd been living together for years. She blinked, unsticking her mascaraed eyelashes to really focus on it in a *what's wrong with this picture* game she played as the reality slowly and foggily sank in. A silent *ding!* registered, and she looked up at me. With different eyes. Not Donna Penks eyes, but shocked, stunned and hurt eyes.

"That's right," I announced, wishing better words for myself, as this part of the confrontation wasn't planned nor practiced either. I was quite comfortable without the net below me. Do you know how slowly you chew each bite of really wonderful, butter-soft chateaubriand or filet mignon with béarnaise sauce, something that just melts over your tongue and sends you into another realm of taste? You take each bite, each chew more slowly because it just feels *so* good? That's how each word felt in my mouth. "Anthony and I *had* our wedding already. We've been married for *two months.*"

She swallowed. I waited for the rage to switch on in her eyes. But it didn't. Those were real tears.

"It was a beautiful wedding." I exhaled the word *beautiful,* not doing it enough justice. "On the beach. In Bermuda. Just the two of us. And Leah was my maid of honor."

Delilah closed her eyes. I didn't know if she was trying to picture it, or block the picture from her mind. In truth, it really didn't matter.

"And it was . . . *perfect.*" *Because you weren't there.*

I left her with the sound of my heels clicking away from her, which was usually her method of departure. And I felt lighter. Softer. My anger sifted away, and as I waved a friendly good-bye to Tatiana (who knew if I'd ever see her again?), I walked out of my mother's house ready to never walk back in again. That character in there, that actress lounging on her white Victorian couch, was not my mother.

I remembered what Leah said at my shower. Friends are like family and family should be like friends. If she were not technically my mother, would Delilah be my friend? No. Would I choose to have her in my life? No. I'd never choose to have someone so selfish and so cowardly as my friend.

Which is why I couldn't bear the idea, as announced when I got home, that Leah had bought herself a plane ticket to Paris. One-way. She would leave in three weeks.

The wedding, my mother's wedding, was called off.

We sent out announcements to all 350 guests. Colin Cowie had been informed, and seemed oddly relieved. The doves would not fly on June 24th for me.

And I was *very* happy about it. Finally, the charade was over.

We didn't hear from the mothers for a week. No apologies. No "let's make this right." No "I was wrong." Just phone silence.

Were they angry? Absolutely. But not about the wedding being called off. They were just angry women in general.

And they needed to think about that.

Chapter 45

Now we had another war on our hands. The *Who's Going to Break Down and Call* war. And we were all victorious so far.

In this quiet time, which I should have been appreciating for the absence of drama, I filled the void with a kind of dreamlike fantasizing. Like "wonder what they're doing right now?" "Wonder if they're miserable?" I was thinking about them more than I did before.

I imagined Delilah suffering from a miserable case of writer's block, curled into the fetal position on her Victorian lounge, unwashed, unkempt, her French manicure in dire need of a re-do. Tatiana would bring her a silver tray of champagne and orange juice, blinis with caviar and strawberries, and with a whimpering moan Delilah would just wave her away. Even Marco the pool boy's tanned bare chest and blatant offer for a visit to the poolhouse wouldn't break through her cocoon of regrets. She wouldn't take her calls, not even from Ralph or Donatella.

I imagined Carmela standing at her kitchen counter staring out the window at her apple tree, forgetting that the lasagna strips were on a high boil, and them turning to mush in the foamy water while she remained in her zone-out. She wore a blue-and-white checked dress and a white apron, and her hands hung limply over the edge of the kitchen sink. The oven buzzer was blaring the pasta's fate, but she did not hear it.

I wondered what they were doing, if they were sad at all.

It was a great way to keep me from thinking about the fact that I was sad and almost worthless at work. I had an ad to work on, a mother-daughter moment ad for an herbal tea company. The brand message was, "for the love that never ends." You can't swing for the fences, push the envelope or get the least bit genius on that when all you're thinking is *Yeah, right.*

In a daze, looking very much like the novice on the train, I stumbled out of the car and herded with the others up the crowded stairs, careful not to touch the banister with my bare hands. It's just something you learn.

Making my way up 14th Street, I passed noisy sidewalk cafés, tattooed biker guys with their muscle shirts adjusted to show off nipple rings, frowning young professionals undoubtedly reliving the horror of their own office politics in silently recollected conversations of the day, heads down, briefcases swinging angrily.

Nannies taking their screaming charges to the park, the little cherubs in designer overalls ignoring their caretakers' calls to not run ahead, not cross the street, and *listen to me*. A long line at the Ice Hut, where similar cherubs screamed bloody murder because *I said Stwaaaaawbewwy, not Banilla!* Resigned to a life of servitude, the caretakers, parents and older sisters busily yakking into their cell phones just handed over another $5 to get the angel what he or she demands this time.

Uptown, the bistros cranked out music that almost succeeded in lifting my mood. How could music from the 1980s not do that? Brightly colored frozen margaritas peppered the tables, crowds of sixteen people crammed around tables for eight, and the air smelled like really great Mexican food: refried beans, jalapeño spice so strong it filled an entire block with a taste that sizzled on my tongue. The faint whiff of tequila. Three steps later, the scent of roses from the bodega, bucket after bucket lined up in splashes of red, pink, yellow, orange, camellias pushing against the lilies, the roses standing tall, Gerbera daisies yelling out "Will everyone please just smile and be happy?" Glistening red apples slept next to bright, round Australian oranges, wet grapes dripped onto the lipstick red strawberries, and fuzzy brown kiwi ovals held their emerald green sweetness inside as a surprise.

I looked up at the clear blue sky. Spotless. Cloudless. The sun was shining warm and constant. It was a gorgeous day. And it had taken me a twenty-minute commute and fourteen blocks of walking to notice that. To look *up* and around instead of *in*. The young, muttering professionals with the death grip on their briefcases? They probably didn't see it either.

* * *

I heard voices when I walked in my front door. Not "time to call the doctor" voices. Worse. My mother's voice and Carmela's voice. They were in my home. I closed the door quietly, silently. I stayed in our partially hidden foyer, hoping my entrance had been secret, that they didn't notice I was home. So I could either (a) slip back out and go for a burrito and a tequila and one of those Gerbera daisies or (b) eavesdrop on them. You know me pretty well by now. What do you think I'd do?

"I really don't care."

It was Leah. Talking to them, with their combined voices protesting about luring them there under false pretenses. What had Leah told them to get them to drop everything—including a *very* important meeting with ABC producers and a session of holding the crack-addicted preemies at the hospital (and you know *them* well enough to guess whose story was whose)?

"Aren't you the least bit *ashamed?*" *You get 'em, Leah.* I sat crouched in my own entryway, hiding in the shadows, miming out my responses to everything they said. If Anthony came home right now and opened the door, I'd go flying into the living room like I was sliding face-first into third base.

"*Ashamed? Ashamed?!*" That was Delilah, trying to grab back Alpha Female status from Leah. No kooky, New Age, candle-burner was going to tell her what to do. *Please, Leah, tell her we have video of her licking Da Hawk's chest!* "Funny that *you* should be calling us ashamed, when you *knew* they were married this whole time. That bridal shower was a charade, a ruse, a hoax and a deception!"

Wow, we'd gotten all four. Job well done.

"How could you *doooo* that to us?" Carmela

whined. "After all that we've been through, all the time, all the effort—"

"All the money?" Delilah must have spat that one at Carmela, because she said it in the form of a question. *Leah, really. Please tell her we have that video.*

"You're both very concerned about what *you've* been through with this wedding, aren't you?" Leah said flatly, and I imagined her standing, with her arms crossed on her chest. She had the Alpha Female crown firmly in place.

Silence from the two of them. I imagined eyes rolling on one face, and a sour, lips-turned-down expression on the other.

"Do I really need to say it?" Leah had the Condescension crown on too, apparently, and wore it like a master. *What about what Emilie has been through?* "Now I want you to tell me what *you* think Emilie has been feeling for the last six months."

All those self-help books have served her well.

"No answer?" Leah hadn't given them time. "Well, let me give you an easier question."

Take it easy, Leah. They could turn on you with claws out.

"How do you think an engaged woman should feel while she's planning her wedding and getting ready to marry the love of her life?" *Excellent, Leah.* "Frustrated? Angry? Sad? Upset? Pissed off enough to actually be *happy* about running away to have a secret wedding, secret from all of her friends and family? Relieved—"

Say it, Leah.

"—that you both weren't there?"

Silence.

So Leah went on. "I was there. Emilie was the happiest I've seen her since the night of her engagement. She didn't look worn and haggard and dark-eyed and old."

Hey!

"She looked radiant, and joyful, and elated, and thoroughly peaceful."

That's better.

"Was it because you weren't there?" Leah said, her voice rising a little. "No."

Even I was confused at that one.

"It was because your *dramas* weren't there."

Absolutely.

"She could finally focus on her and Anthony, who by the way *loves* her. And my heart bleeds because she shouldn't have only one source of that. She should be getting all that unconditional joyful love from the two of you. More than anyone."

Tears came to my eyes, as much as I wondered if tears came to theirs.

"I hate it that Emilie had to run away and not have the wedding she planned," Leah said, emotion welling in her voice. "But she had the wedding she *wanted*. And Anthony set it all up."

"Anthony?! *My* Anthony?!" Carmela had thought it was my idea to steal her baby boy to a British island where I'd claim him as my own, ripping him from her.

"Okay, right there, Carmela. He's not *your* Anthony."

Brava!

"And it was his idea, he surprised Emilie, he bought the plane tickets, he called the wedding officiant in Bermuda, he brought the rings, he did it all. And he included me, because Emilie is my best friend and I love her like a sister. So she had one happy relative with her that day."

I imagined the looks on their faces, which I

hoped was a heart-tugging sadness, a realization, the lights turning on.

"He *loves* her, and he had his priorities in place. For him, it was about the two of them getting married and being together forever, and that their ceremony was simple and pure and just about them," Leah was out of breath. "Not a dog-and-pony show with celebrity designers and tens of thousands of roses flown in from Chile."

"Argentina," Delilah corrected her, but quietly. The realization pulsed in her voice.

"And have you noticed . . ." Leah went on, wisely ignoring the interruption. "That after all this you put them through with your whining and bitching and moaning and self-pity and controlling and sniping and criticizing—"

Okay, we get it. Get to the point.

"Emilie and Anthony never fought."

Silence.

"They never turned against one another. They never took out all their frustration on each other. They never had that sick, sinking moment that a lot of couples have, where one says they shouldn't get married. That's what *scared* couples do. They turn against each other. They fight. They argue over little things like the font on the invitation, the wording on the invitation."

That's bringing your point home. Excellent.

"And Emilie and Anthony never did that. They just loved each other and supported each other all the way through. There wasn't a moment where you turned them against each other or against the idea of getting married . . . which is what you were trying to do."

Huh?

"Because look what marriage did to the two of *you*."

Okaaaaay. I reached up, turned the door handle silently, opened it while praying for no squeaks, crawled out of my own home, shut the door with barely a click and practically ran down the street for a burrito, a tequila and a Gerbera daisy.

Wow.

So I was the sad girl at the end of the bar, downing a tequila shot and following it up with a Corona. My mother would not approve. I fended off the lurking male predators wearing black tight T-shirts and gold chains with purely the look in my eye. *Don't even think about it.* Happy hour was in full throttle. Quite ironic, isn't it?

I thought it was all just about the mothers hating each other, because they were symbolic of something they hated in their own lives. That was the first peel of the onion. A few layers down, underneath fear of aging, jealousy of the attention, the danger of the cord being cut, and another layer of fear of aging . . . the mothers were trying to prevent me from getting married? Could that be true? Or was that just how Leah saw it, being deathly afraid of marriage herself? Whatever it was, it wasn't good.

I ordered another Corona and waited for my burrito, giving yet another gold-chained predator the turned-back brush-off.

Chapter 46

"So..." I settled into the couch, or rather spread out onto the couch, having eaten about five pounds' worth of beans and rice and tortilla on top of two Coronas. After all, I didn't have to diet my way into a wedding gown anymore, so why not?

Leah sat innocently, legs up over the arm of the couch, flipping through a copy of *In Style*.

"Did you have a good day?" I tried.

Leah just shrugged. "It was all right."

Hmmm. Crafty.

"Anything interesting happen today?"

Leah just shrugged again. "Nope."

Hmmm. Liar.

The door flew open, and there was my husband with a bouquet in his arms. Gerbera daisies. Hot pink. My favorite. When I ran to kiss him, he told me I had bean breath, and I didn't care. "So how is my beautiful wife?" he winked, after accepting a full-on bean-and-beer-scented kiss. The man loves me.

"Full," I laughed.

"So I guess you don't want me to poke you in the stomach like this." He poked me in the stomach.

"It would be a bad idea . . . for you."

Leah looked up over the edge of her magazine and smiled.

"So what did she say?" Waiting until bedtime is never a smart move when you're trying to get the dirt from your husband. He had told me his mother called him at work.

"Dinner's at five on Sunday," he shrugged. We were back on schedule, having missed a Sunday dinner at Carmela's house during the great telephonic stiff-arm standoff.

"That's it?"

"That's it."

"She didn't say anything else?"

He wrinkled his nose at me. "Go brush your teeth, Bean Woman."

Through a mouthful of foamy Crest, I continued my hunt for inside information. "The mothers were here. Leah met with them, and I heard a little bit of it."

"What did you hear?" He was in the other room, so I couldn't search his face for hidden signs of knowing. Not that I would recognize them, he has such a great poker face.

"Leah just gave them hell and told them to think about how I feel."

"Good advice."

"And then." I ran back into the bedroom, leapt and landed on my knees on the bed. "She told them they were just out to bust up our marriage."

"What?!" Anthony laughed. "That's ridiculous."

"I'm serious."

"So am I. The two of them just hate each other. It doesn't get much deeper than that." Anthony sighed, rolling onto his side to set the alarm clock: 5:45 A.M.

"So you think that's just Leah's assumption?" I pulled the covers up over my chest, settling in against him in our automatic position.

Anthony just patted me on the thigh. "Good night, Em."

"Good night, A. I love you."

"I love you too, Bean."

I had gained a new nickname. Bean. The Little Bean. Beanie. Beanie Face. Bean Martin. Where You Bean. Over time, there was no end to his variations on a bean theme, and for Christmas, he even bought me a kidney bean-shaped silver pendant. I had branded myself that night. And it would last forever.

As Leah said, good thing I didn't go out to gorge on cheese that night.

Chapter 47

Dear Emily:
I owe you an apology. And lest you think I'm "hiding behind my computer" again, let me assure you I plan to deliver my apology in person when I return from Sydney on Thursday. But I couldn't let another day go by without telling you I'm sorry. It was unfair of me to treat you with such disregard, and I do hope you can see into my heart right now. I am thinking of you every day.

   If I could turn back the clock and do it all differently, I would.
Love,
Mother

I closed my eyes. The words did stay on the back of my eyelids.

I wrote her back immediately . . .

Dear Mom:
I miss Donna Penks. Please bring her back to me.

Please share who you are now with who you were
then. That is the only wedding gift I want.
Love, Emilie

And then I cried.

Chapter 48

Carmela was like one of those plastic windup mouse toys. You wind her up, wind her up, wind her up, and then set her on the floor and watch her race right into a wall. Then she bounces off and races across the room into the other wall.

That's what she reminded me of as she put the finishing touches on Sunday dinner. She made me tired just watching her. She zipped over to pull the lasagna out of the oven. (Hers never spills over out of the pan to make a black lava mess on the oven floor.) Then she raced over to stir the sauce. Then she raced over to mix the salad (always iceberg, torn, not cut, and always with a very generous shaking of salt with the oil and vinegar dressing she makes with an eye-measurement that's always perfect).

"Ma, can we help out?" Anthony took his place at a side chair (no one would dare sit in Vic's seat, even though he wouldn't be using it ever again).

"No, thank you, Anthony," she said very politely, then pulled out a truckload of sausages, oversized meatballs stuffed with gorgonzola and basil, a veal round with a pesto sauce, a crown roast with little paper booties on the top of each bone (these had browned), a tray of manicotti, a platter of buffalo mozzarella and roasted red peppers cut into perfect inch-wide slices, an antipasto with rolled ham, salami, pepperoni, pepper-edged ham, hand-broken chunks of provolone, hard-boiled egg slices, and more roasted red pepper strips. Freshly made wheat rolls were followed by grissini sticks, garlic toast squares with parsley and extra chunks of garlic on top, a broiled garlic head that ooozed like molten butter, the good virgin olive oil poured into little ceramic plates imprinted with purple grapes and grape leaves. And four bottles of an amazing wine. And there were just three of us.

I didn't quite know what Anthony meant when he said, "Just pray that the New York Jets are also coming too." I thought he meant we'd need big, hulking linemen to protect us. Or a placekicker to kick Carmela's butt to Queens. But what he meant was *There's going to be enough food to feed a professional football team.* And there was.

Carmela apologizes with fat grams. She cooks, bakes, boils and broils her apology and serves it to you on the good china. With a side of garlic.

"To your marriage. *A la famiglia!*" She raised her red wineglass high, then pulled me over by the shoulders to give me a kiss on the forehead. I never heard her call Anthony *My Anthony* again. And that was the best lasagna I'd ever had in my life. My piece had meat in it, and I rose from the dinner table with no sauce or dressing on my clothes.

Later, as Anthony worked on the garage door

opener for her, Carmela and I did the dishes side by side.

"Would you like to call me Mom or Carmela?" she finally asked after some way-too-intensive scrubbing. I just blinked, my arms red from the scalding hot water that Carmela can withstand like her arms were made of Teflon. "You can just go on calling me Carmela. Never mind."

She offered it, then took it back.

Our hands were buried in suds, feeling for forks, spoons, serving spoons, serving forks, and slippery dishes.

"I think I can get used to calling you Mom," I finally said. "But if it's okay with you, I'd like to call you Ma, like Anthony does."

The true test. Would she allow me that familiarity? Or would she scowl and twitch because I've placed myself at Anthony's level in her world?

She smiled immediately, automatically, warmly. "I'd like that," she said. "Ma. That works."

"All right then, Ma, can you turn up some cold water here? I'm boiling alive!" I laughed, and she jumped to twist the cloudy plastic handle with the C on it.

"Laughter? Laughter in my kitchen?" Anthony walked in, greasy-handed from the garage door opener chains.

Carmela flicked a palmful of suds onto his face. "It's *my* kitchen."

"Right you are, Ma." It probably sounded better coming from him, but it sounded fine to me. "Everything was delicious."

Carmela raised her eyebrows like she was saying *Of course it was*, and Anthony kissed her on the forehead. They do that a lot in this family. She turned to him, wiped her hands on her apron and her eyelashes were wet. Not from the dishwater. "I am so sorry for how I acted."

"I know, Ma." She was talking to him, but I answered. Anthony was taken aback by both occurrences, the first he'd heard of both.

"I know, Ma," he said. "All is forgiven."

"All?" she said. *She's talking about Vic and their long, torturous hollow marriage, and the way it caused her to latch on to her son.*

"All."

"Good," she said, blinking the wetness in her eyes away. "Now go sit down. I have espresso, cappuccino, banana cream pie, chocolate mousse and peaches on pound cake."

Peaches on pound cake? I stepped back, a little lightheaded, but not noticeable to them. My mother, back in the Donna Penks era, would always make me peaches on pound cake when I got home from school. She'd have it sitting on the kitchen table with an empty glass and a cow-shaped gravy boat she knew I liked to pour my milk from to fill my own glass.

"Sounds great." Anthony broke me from my zip back to the past, and I followed him into the living room. Carmela had gotten a new couch.

Chapter 49

I recognized the voice.
It was Ed.

At 2:15 in the morning, their hushed voices still slipped under my door. Anthony slept through it all.

"I am so sorry," Leah said to him, her voice muffled as if she was pressed into his chest and speaking into his shirt. "I didn't mean to make you feel that badly."

"I'm not going to say that's okay." His voice was soft. "But I want to make sure *you're* okay."

Leah sighed. "You know . . . I will be." Silence. "I will be okay. I just have to get out of this town."

"Running away never solved anything. 'Wherever you go, there you are,' you know?"

"Yeah, but everything here reminds me of *then*, you know what I mean? It's impossible to heal and get past it when every time I pass a restaurant on Main Street, I'm thinking 'we went there' or 'is he in there?' I just can't get away from it."

"You're really suffering." He wasn't sarcastic. He

was empathetic. At that moment, I thought she'd be talking about him years from now once she clicked into her right mind again, wondering how she ever let him go. He was a terrific guy. One of a kind.

"Yes. I am."

"And you really think that running off to Paris is going to help?"

Please, buddy, don't beg her to stay.

"It's my Do-Over," Leah explained, and I heard the creak of the couch. They were sitting down now. "I don't know how to explain this so you'll understand . . . But . . . I feel like I have to go back and . . ."

She struggled.

"Okay, here's how it went. When I met my ex, I was all set to go off to Paris and go to a culinary academy. I'd won a spot with a prestigious school, I had my plane ticket, I was packed, I was learning French . . . and then I met *him.* I just got swept off my feet, and it was fiery and passionate and all-consuming. He said all the right things, did all the right things, bought me flowers and when he found out I liked pears, he had a case of pears sent to my office."

Okay Leah, get to the point. He's male. He doesn't want the flowery details. I'm female and even I'm losing focus here.

"I fell in love. He didn't want me to go away to Paris when we had just met each other, so I canceled. I canceled my spot at the culinary academy, I canceled my plane ticket, I unpacked. And I stayed. And it was wonderful for a year. Just wonderful. I'd never been that happy."

She wasn't crying, I noticed. A good sign.

"We got engaged and started planning the wedding, and—well, you know what happened the night before."

Mr. Wonderful ran off with a man in a miniskirt.

"I was just a cover," Leah whimpered. I knew the tears were coming. But she cleared her throat, collected herself and went on. "Do you know how disgusting I felt? Like I couldn't take enough showers."

Ed said nothing. I imagined he was rubbing her leg, trying to take her hand to comfort her, but she stayed stiff. She wouldn't give him her hand to hold.

"So anyway . . ." she cleared her throat again. "I decided that I would go back to that moment in time when I had my bags packed, and my airline ticket and my priorities in line. I'd give myself a Do-Over now."

"And the culinary academy?" he asked.

"I applied four months ago . . ." And her voice came formed through a smile. "And they accepted me."

You didn't tell me that!

"So I get a Do-Over. I'd been praying for one. So that I could go back to that crossroads where I turned left instead of right, him over Paris, and now . . . now I'm turning right."

I imagined Ed nodding, proud of her. "It's something you have to do for yourself."

"Absolutely."

I was proud of her too.

They spent hours talking about the best places in Paris, the places to avoid, the time that Ed's car blew up in the French countryside and how hard it was to find a towing service when everyone in the cobblestone-streeted village he wandered, knocking on doors and sputtering flawed French, kept

calling him an American *cochon*. The old farmer
who gave him a ride into town had told him that
cochon was a compliment, another word for "re-
spectful visitor," and he encouraged Ed to go into
the town hall and introduce himself as the American *Cochon*, which he did. Only *cochon* means "pig."
The folks at town hall laughed hysterically at Ed's
being the butt of a cultural joke, and the old
farmer man had taken off in his pickup truck to
tell his other farmer buddies the riotous story. At
least the old man brought him into town.

Ed and Leah became close friends. And they remained so for years, even after he met his girlfriend and brought her to Paris two years later.
Leah met them there and served as the creative
force behind Ed's romantic proposal at the top of
the Eiffel Tower. Leah had gone to the flower market at sunrise and gathered a bouquet of lilies, gardenias and lily of the valley, which was the
girlfriend's birth month flower. She added orange
blossoms to symbolize the purity of the first-time
bride, and she studded the rose blooms with pearl
pushpins to symbolize wealth. She packed a picnic
basket with her own chocolate truffle delicacies, orange cream chocolates to make use of that whole
orange-throwing blessing, white meringues, strawberries, and a bottle of fine French champagne.
She had had the napkins monogrammed in red,
for passion, and lined the basket with red velvet
for effect. She handed off the basket to Ed, kissed
him on the cheek and sent him off to seal his destiny with his bride-to-be, Daphne. Before leaving,
Ed told Leah that he was proud of her.

When I received her e-mail, together with digital graphics of Ed's proposal (she'd supplied him
with her camera as well), I was proud of her too.

I never expected her to meet the man of her dreams in Paris. That wasn't what she was looking for. What she was looking for was a way to find out what the path would have held for her if she'd taken it years ago, instead of getting engaged and getting her heart broken. But she didn't find that either. She found a new path. And getting engaged, getting abandoned, and getting her heart broken was the most important part of it.

It helped make her the success she is today. Without that heartbreak and humiliation, that wrenching healing process, she never would have immersed herself into all that symbolism, the myths and rituals, the goddesses, the outer edges of faith and spirituality. She would never have known the flowers of the gods, the fruits of the mythical lovers, the orange-throwing ritual, the meanings of crystals and each color of candle as an incantation of health, prosperity, wisdom, passion, pure love, and serenity. She never would have taken that subterranean flashlight tour of her heart's greatest wishes from every angle, so that she could answer the question of "what is the love that everyone is looking for?"

She never would have opened L'Orange, named by *Newsweek*, *Newsday*, and every other kind of news in the city as "*the* premiere hotspot for marriage proposals in all of New York City." Leah framed and hung the following review on the wall of her new 14th Street penthouse apartment, with terrace and garden and an unobstructed view of the river and the city and the yachts in the marina and the moon, just above our place:

With its lush red walls and couches, romantic dimly lit corners and nooks, velvet curtains to set off roomy private booths, endless bouquets of fresh, bursting flowers chosen specifically for their romantic messages and symbolism, candles on pillars and pedestals and picture shelves, glowing French sconces, and a crystal chandelier to take your breath away, *L'Orange*—for all its name—is a surprise. A delightful and decadent surprise that this city didn't even know it had been awaiting, much like the level of true love this dessert and champagne only club describes in thought-provoking printed cards outlining the history of romantic myth and legend. Each room is named after a goddess of love: Venus for passion, Oshun for sensuality, Freya for magnetism, Persephone for the elimination of past relationship debris, Gauri for a long and happy, satisfying marriage, Isis for rejuvenating stalled romantic relationships. The Sophia Room attracts the happily single as the goddess of compassion, and owner/ dessert virtuoso Leah Vestania welcomes the bliss of self-contentedness into her "home" as well as the bliss of romantic love. "You can't have one without the other," says Leah Vestania, hailed as Entrepreneur of the Year and profiled across the country as The Woman Who Brought Back Romance.

Her menu is simply divine: white chocolate truffles that even chocolatiers can't reproduce, chocolate raspberry fondues, triple layer chocolate ganache cake, dark chocolate mousse served in dark chocolate swans, hand molded by the chef and one of the top choices for the presentation of engagement rings, edible flowers on heavenly petit fours, and a twist on tiramisu that you just have to experience for yourself. Words cannot do it justice.

Situated ideally right on the river, French doors

open to a long, flowering tree-lined promenade overlooking the water, enclosed by low stone walls and arched Moongates, and guests are encouraged to take their Moet with them for strolls under the moonlight. High-powered telescopes line the promenade, with attached astronomy charts for the easy location of constellations of the season. Waterfalls flow like a magic wall down the side of the building, and—most enchantingly—Leah Vestania provides a large woven basket filled with ripe oranges. Oranges? A brass plaque on the wall, read through the clear mirror of the waterfall, tells the story of an ancient Chinese ritual in which young maidens would throw full, ripe oranges into a body of water on the night of the full moon to bring about the arrival of her True Love. Guests are encouraged to throw an orange either for their own true love wishes, or for those of a friend. Leah Vestania admits that she spent many months throwing oranges for her true love to come along, and it did. L'Orange came into fruition, and Ms. Vestania lives a blissful, romantic dream every day and night since the full-mooned midnight when L'Orange's doors opened.

Magical, ethereal, and enchanting in appearance and ambience, plus the flawless and heavenly menu of desserts, champagnes and Ms. Vestania's radiance, we don't just add L'Orange to our Must-Do list in New York City. We've placed it at the *top* of our list.

In just six months, L'Orange has been the setting for over 2,000 marriage proposals—most by men, some by women, all "Yes!" answers—including many celebrity and royal proposals, plus that of the city's social elite. Top hats off to Leah Vestania, a magnificently talented woman of vision and a symbol of everlasting belief in the magic of true love.

And *that's* what Leah's Do-Over brought into her life.

Chapter 50

We were to meet at the Plaza for tea.

You would think it's impossible to feel anything other than elation when you walk into the Plaza and turn the marble-floored corner leading to the Palm Court, with its majestic Italian marble columns, potted trees with their graceful frond arches, Versailles chairs, and classical harp music announcing "this is the good life." Tuxedoed waiters with uniformly neat short hairdos and suave Italian accents present three-tiered platters of pastries, scones and petit fours to the discerning eyes of the Ladies Who Lunch, the Ladies of Leisure in their feather-accented yellow and pink hats. Hands weighed down with diamonds and rubies and emeralds pointed out their chosen scones, and the waiter's deft tongwork delivered the order to a delicate pink floral china plate without so much as a single crumb dropped onto the pristine white tablecloth. Earl Grey refills kept the women's tiny china teacups at an acceptable level of warm temperature, probably laboratory tested not to scald the tongue or melt the lipstick.

In the past, I had felt at home here, like I'd flown to London just for the ritual of high tea.

Today, surrounded by elegance and opulence and mirrors that cost more than my annual salary, I felt very, very small. I straightened the silverware, refolded my white linen napkin on my lap. I suddenly felt very self-conscious that I wasn't wearing a hat with feathers on it. Thinking *you have arrived*, I swallowed hard and watched the condensation droplets race one another down the side of my water glass. And I must have been concentrating very hard on the one larger droplet I'd silently placed my bet on to be the winner, because I didn't see her sweep into the room, wave a finger, tinkling hello *darling* to her society friends, and stand demurely next to the table, waiting for the nearest suave Italian waiter to pull out her chair for her.

Heart thumpingly nervous, I had to speed-search my inner database of charm school lessons: was I supposed to stand? No, wait, that's for the men to do. I was *that* out of it. It was as if I was in a courtroom, not the Palm Court, and she was the judge presiding. All rise.

"Have you been waiting long?" she spoke at last, cool and calm and casual as if the last few weeks had never happened. As if she had never said what she said.

"Not long," I answered coolly, refolding my napkin in my lap. Again.

A smiling, handsome waiter appeared out of nowhere to pour Delilah's tea and refill the quarter-inch of my own that I'd had time to sip. He presented us with the tray of scones and petit fours, and knew without asking which my mother preferred. She was a regular. They all knew it was to be the pink petit four with the white icing rose on top. I gave away my station in life by asking for the tiny square slice of banana nut bread. It was still warm.

"So . . ." Delilah began, folding her hands primly against the table's edge in front of her. "We have a lot to talk about, don't we?"

I blinked, posture perfect. "Yes, we do."

I searched her face for signs of *let's get this over with,* a cynical, sarcastic going-through-the-motions, put-out-the-fire absence of heart. But there was something softer there. Her eyes were a softer blue, and I noticed the tiny lines around them, the curl of her eyelashes. Her jaw was relaxed, not contracted in a purist kind of way. Her lips, brushed with pink pearlized gloss, held in a hopeful place that was just ahead of a smile.

"Emilie, it was never my intention to hurt you," were the tender words those pink pearlized lips said to me.

Hmmmmm. She didn't come out with an attitude or spiked verbal jabs. She wasn't on the attack, on the defensive, on the hunt. Cautious still, I let her go on.

She reached across the table to lay her warm hand on mine. "You know that, don't you?"

"I do now," I heard myself say. Inside my head, I was still warning *be careful.*

My mother registered that with a slow blink and a nod of her head. "I don't blame you for how you feel . . . how you felt. What I said . . ." It was difficult for her to get out the words, a rarity for her. "What I said was just awful, and I can't tell you how much I regret doing that." Not even she could fake that true regret that dulled her eyes. She really meant it. I saw it. I felt it. It was real. One hundred percent real. My mother is not that good a performer, and if she is, then she needs to act in her own made-for-TV movie. If this was a fraud, then polish up that Oscar.

I nodded, willing myself not to cry. Tears would stop the flow of what she needed to say. Tears would slow her down, censor her, and stop me from getting what I needed.

"And I'm not just saying that," she winked.

She knows I would be likely to question her sincerity. The fact that she knows makes it legitimate. I haven't just been imagining things.

"I don't blame you . . ." She shook her head, humbled, her eyelashes doing a quick flutter as if even she couldn't believe what she thought back upon, her own words that haunt her. "I really don't blame you . . ."

For which part?

"I probably would have run off to Bermuda to escape me too," she said with an awkward, crooked smile. *She's nervous.*

I found my voice, unlocked it. "We didn't run off to escape you."

My mother interrupted me with a quick shake of her head. "In part, yes you did."

Don't argue with her to make her feel better. She's right.

"And I don't blame you at all. I acted like a complete *witch* . . . just deplorable," she confessed, patting my hand and then returning it to clasp her own in front of her again. With her fingers intertwined, it looked almost as if she was praying. Her blue eyes widened. "Looking back on it, I can't believe I was so self-righteous . . . with *you* of all people."

She was hitting all the right keywords on the checklist of her indiscretions. Just a few dozen more to go. *Continue . . .*

"Your friend . . . Leah . . ."

"Yes?"

My mother laughed and looked down briefly into her lap, then returned her eyes to mine. "All I can say is that you have a very loyal and wise friend there."

I smiled, and broke off a corner of my banana nut bread to taste. Magnificent, as expected. My mother sipped her tea and brought the cup soundlessly back to rest in the saucer, smiling to herself over some memory I had not shared with them, something brilliant Leah said or did after I ran for the nearest burrito that day.

"You might not be aware of it, but she gave us a good talking to." She shook her head again, more impressed than insulted. Actually, very impressed. "It was what I call a 'morals slap.'"

I laughed, liking that description, making a silent mental note to use that one in my own business vernacular. "I know," I said.

"She told you?" my mother cocked her head and wrinkled her eyebrows. No Botox treatment this week, I guessed. Her face had expression.

"No . . ." I hesitated with my confession, anxious that my saying "I was hiding in the hallway" would close down our mother-daughter summit, that she would redefine once again that defining moment and turn on her heel, feeling set up and outsmarted.

But she progressed, releasing that loaded moment into the ether. "It's amazing how the most basic things can get buried under self-interest, how you're blinded by—"

"Mother." It was my turn to put my hand on hers. She stopped midsentence. "Speak to me. Don't write."

I had never told her to can the flowery prose and clichés before, and she twitched, like an electric current started at the base of her spine and zapped up to her jaw. I was afraid I had taken a step too far, that I had just stun-gunned a sleeping Bengal tiger and then still expected it to let me pet him nicely.

"I'm sorry," she said, her voice a bit wavery. "It's automatic." She shrugged in an almost childlike confession, her hand now with a slight tremor as she brought the tea to her lips. I hated the part of me that still thought *if this is an act, I'm going to kill you.* I softened my face when I realized I was staring at her with my eyebrows pulled down, the unwanted, automatic thought showing outwardly, betraying my self-promised open mind.

"I got carried away." My mother shrugged, then uncharacteristically slapped both hands on the edges of the table and slumped back into her chair. The big-hat, big-diamond women at the tables surrounding us leapt a bit in their Versailles chairs, flustered and wiping spilled tea from their chins. My mother was immune to their reactions, never went near the almost manic awareness of *what will other people think,* and never adjusted her posture in response to their mutterings. "That's it," she continued. "I lost my mind, I lost my focus, I lost my *priorities.*"

Her confession came rapid-fire, the *bam bam bam bam* of a machine gun.

"I didn't think of you and what you wanted, I didn't think of what the wedding meant to you, I didn't treat you well, I talked to you like you *worked* for me . . ."

Okay, there's a mirror to her character as a good boss, but we won't focus on that right now.

My mother exhaled. "I was just thinking of myself."

And there we have it. The center of the onion.

I nodded. She tilted her head again, this time the other way, hoping I'd respond in some way, just waiting for me to tell her *no, you weren't that bad.* But I had changed my game plan. I was here to listen. And she *was* that bad.

"So *any*way . . ." Delilah bit into her petit four, slicing it into a perfect half, with not a smudge to her lipstick, not a smear of icing on the corner of her mouth. Once chewed and swallowed, she continued. "I need to hear that you forgive me."

"For what?"

She grinned, all but clapped her hands in front of her, thinking that my response was the classic erasure of insult, the international sign for *it never happened.* But I was being literal. *For which things do you want me to forgive you? You only confessed to one.*

"No, seriously. You have more than one offense to confess to."

I watched her take note of my *egregious* grammar, but let that pass too. "Well." She scuffed her chair closer against the table and returned her hands to prayer. "For saying I wouldn't come to the wedding . . ."

"And?"

"For treating you unkindly . . ."

"And . . ."

She looked annoyed. "Seriously, Emilie, are we going to play this game?"

I never broke eye contact. "*And?*"

She sighed, knowing when she had the diamond chips stacked against her. "For being controlling about the wedding . . ."

"And . . ."

"For making a few . . . *changes* to your plans . . ."

"And . . ."

"For being . . . *cranky* . . ."

I smiled. That was a Donna Penks word. She never cursed, Donna Penks. If someone was being bitchy in line at the bank or the grocery store, she'd call that person *cranky*. "And . . ."

"Why are you smiling?" She switched to distraction, trying to stop the *And?* game.

"Nothing," I shook my head, my curls bouncing on my shoulders. (When you get a new haircut, you notice these things.) "You just reminded me of the way you used to talk."

That did it. She shut down. Her smile tightened into a sour pulled purse string, and her praying hands came apart, lowered to her lap. "We need to talk about that."

I swallowed hard. I felt small again, feeling very much like I was standing at the ocean's edge, my feet stuck up to the ankles in the suction of the sand retreating with the tide, and an enormous wave with an angry curled white top was coming . . . right . . . at . . . me. I knew my eyes were wide, announcing my terror, and I couldn't fake adjusting them.

"I know you want me to be like I used to be," Delilah breathed, and I was angry at her for being so calm, so assured, not a wreck like me. *This should be hard for you! You should collapse into tears, apologizing for the mistake of your re-creation! You should want to go back! You should promise to . . .* "But that is *not* going to happen." She said it slowly, head down, eyes up, delivering each word right into my eyes and hopefully, finally, into my brain.

My exhale came in jerks, stuttering.

"I promise you . . ." she was being real, as real as I have ever seen her. "That is not going to happen."

A single tear was the jail-breaker, leaping out of my eye and onto my cheek. *Traitor,* I cursed it, wiping it away with the back of my hand.

"Oh, honey." She placed her hand on top of mine again, wrapping her slim fingers around it. Her hand was smaller than mine, I noticed. It looked younger than mine too. Paraffin dips, probably. "I know what you miss about the way I used to be . . ."

No, you don't.

"Yes, I do," she answered, as if she could read my mind. Well, actually, in that instant, she had. "I know. But let me tell you something . . ."

Please don't let her be right in what she's going to say.

"Don't you think there are days . . . many days . . . when I wish *you* could be more like you were back then, too? Tiny and helpless and clinging to me, looking at me like I'm . . ." She had a similar watery jail-breaker dragging a trail of her mascara with it as a tracer down her cheek. "The most . . . amazing person in the world?"

Oh, hell, just open the jail gates. We were a mess.

My mother sobbed, not caring at all that we were being watched in the Palm Court by *everyone.* "You were my little girl, and you adored me. I could do no wrong. Don't you think I ache for how it was when you were just a little girl?"

The sniffling was too much for our nearest neighbors, who loudly asked to be moved to a more *ap-*

propriate table. Our waiter came over to fill our tea and implore us with his eyes to keep it down. We didn't even look at him.

"I have no right, no expectation to even think about asking you to be the person *you grew out of.*"

And my worst expectation came true.

Was true.

She was right.

I felt my head drop. Not into unconsciousness. More like the opposite.

"Honey, I *grew out* of being that person. It didn't fit me. It wasn't who I was deep down inside," she explained, squeezing my hand. She was strong. "I was miserable pretending that was the life I wanted."

I understand.

"Having dinner on the table at six, never going out to dinner where they had real silverware, food shopping on Monday, Wednesday and Friday, not having enough money to ever get my hair done, not having any *friends*," she explained. "Waiting . . . waiting for your father to come home so that I could feel like I was . . ."

She didn't finish. She didn't need to. I remembered those nights, praying to God *please make my daddy come home tonight so Mommy doesn't cry.*

"I loved you, with all my heart, and I still do," my mother explained. "Never doubt that."

"I never have." *Well, almost never.*

"I was never unhappy because I was your mother." She squeezed again with one hand, wiped off the last of her tears with the other. "I was unhappy because—please try to understand this—I felt like I was nothing more than a mother."

I nodded. "I do understand that."

She smiled, relieved. "And when I decided to change . . ."

That would be when she loaded up the frying pan with everything that was *her*.

"It was the best thing I ever did. I'm proud of that moment. I hated myself for taking so long to get to that moment, taking so long, swallowing so much, pushing away what I wanted because I was afraid of what would happen next. And now . . . now I can make my life anything I want it to be. I have earned for myself anything and everything I ever wanted, and I *like* this life. I may not always be the happiest person in the world, and I know I can get overly stressed and act pretty awful sometimes . . . but trust me, Emilie . . . this is the life I've always wanted."

I squeezed her hand back. "I get it now."

"Do you?" She searched me.

"Yes." I truly did.

She sighed. The truth shall set you free. Free at last, she popped the other half of the petit four into her mouth and smiled as she chewed. *We're good. Happy ending. Let's go shopping at Bloomingdale's together.*

"If you want Donna Penks back, if you ever thought she was gone," my mother leaned in. "She's not. She's right here. She's just wearing much better shoes."

That is what I've wanted to hear for all of my adult life.

With another wink, my mother became human again. At least to me. The cartoonish romance novelist character, the overly dramatic actress splayed on a white Victorian couch in a silk robe, the label worshipper, the style maven, the toast of every major city across the world, an Oprah friend, jet-setter, A-list partygoer (not bad for a woman in her 50s,) and soon-to-be *Forbes* wealthiest list member was Donna Penks all grown up. What she was now, that I could see better once I took off my "you killed my mother" glasses, was a kick-ass woman in her 50s, owning the age and selling the age, breaking the rules and looking great in the morning. She dated men half her age. She'd been proposed to by kings and men twice her age. She'd stood on a movie set while George Clooney and Gwyneth Paltrow acted out the scenes she had created in her mind, spoke her words, entwined themselves exactly as Delilah Winchester had imagined they would. She met Princess Diana months before the crash. She attended Oscar parties. She established a foundation for single mothers who wanted to be writers, and established a scholarship for an arts college. Harry Winston lent her cognac-colored diamond earrings for her induction into the Romance Writers of America Hall of Fame.

These were her dreams, the far-off ridiculous reveries she imagined while she was making waffles for me and my father all those long years ago.

She changed her name, took the leap of faith, and her dreams came true.

In that way, I thought comfortingly, as the warm tea slid down my throat, we had a lot in common.

"I'm sorry," I heard myself say. "I feel kind of ridiculous . . ."

"Why?"

I exhaled, and held my hand up to stop the overly solicitous waiter from topping off my Earl Grey. "It occurs to me that I've had the wrong idea for so long, and I . . . I'm sorry, but I didn't like you very much for changing."

"I know. That was the hardest part. Putting what I needed above what you so obviously wanted. You wanted your mommy back."

Well, I wouldn't put it exactly that way. She read my expression and actually looked rather cute when she wrinkled her nose in apology.

"I wanted something back. But I didn't understand it all."

She nodded, understanding me clearly. "Well . . . now that you understand where I'm coming from, maybe you'll . . . be open to . . ."

"Getting to know you better, as you are," I answered, sitting taller, both my mother's hands in mine. My mother beamed. "You know, I am very proud of all that you've accomplished, Mom. You amaze me."

"I amaze myself," came her quick response, and I realized that we weren't going to be starting from scratch as we both got to know one another better. We'd both grown up together, essentially.

"So do you still need to hear that I forgive you?" I ventured.

She gave my hands a squeeze. "No, you already told me that."

"Do you forgive me?"

My mother nodded slowly, with the exact loving look in her eye that I missed so much to the point of anger and insolence for a long time. My dream came true.

"And do you forgive Carmela?" I laughed, capping the moment.

My mother bit her lip, raised an eyebrow and looked to the ceiling as if in deep consideration. "Ah, Carmela. Let's leave it at 'one healed relationship at a time.' There's plenty of time for that. A lifetime, I'd imagine, with how much you and Anthony love one another. Speaking of which . . ."

Uh-oh.

"Do you know that the two of you make it impossible for anyone around you to *not* believe in lasting love?" She tilted her head. I didn't know she had such faith in us, or that we inspired her. Or that she even liked Anthony. I beamed and admired my own engagement and wedding bands, both with diamonds that glittered in the light of the Palm Court's chandeliers. "So . . ." My mother tapped a finger on the Asscher cut of my diamond. "I want to hear *all* about your wedding. Don't leave out a single detail . . ."

Epilogue

INSTYLE WEDDINGS—Spring Issue

Celebrated romance novelist **Delilah Winchester** *is world-renowned for her surprise endings that bring a flutter of hope and inspiration to the hearts of her legions of fans. But this time it was her daughter* **Emilie Penks,** *a 27-year-old advertising phenom who opened her own agency in New York City this year, who delivered the romantic surprise ending to her mother. Not even Delilah Winchester could dream up a plot twist this enchanting: Emilie and her fiancé, financier* **Anthony Cantano** *were not actually engaged but had eloped to Bermuda months earlier. And that wedding was a surprise to Emilie herself, all planned by her handsome fiancé.*

Delilah Winchester tells us that her daughter "absolutely beamed when she gave me every detail, from the white strapless dress Anthony had persuaded her to pack, how he had flown in her best friend, now culinary student Leah Vestania, and arranged for the ceremony to take place at the ocean's edge, under a lucky stone

Moongate that legend holds as a portent for a long and
everlasting marriage. The maid of honor held a china
teacup instead of a bouquet, and the bride wore a white
flower in her hair.

Love is often best defined in elegant simplicity, and
love can take you by surprise.

"It was torture hiding the truth from our mothers,"
admits Emilie. "But we wanted to find the perfect moment. The unveiling, so to speak, was quite dramatic,
and it brought us all much closer together as a family. So
we decided to celebrate together as a family, surrounded
by the 200 close friends, family and colleagues who
would have been invited to our traditional wedding, if
we had one."

Emilie Penks glows when she looks at her mother, and
the two women recount the details of the day they
planned, together with the groom's mother, student nurse
Carmela Cantano. "We called it a 'Celebration of Our
Marriage,'" says Emilie. "And we invited all of our
loved ones near and far, including my mother's most
well-known friends, for a garden party at Tavern on the
Green. I wore my Vera Wang gown, Harry Winston lent
me a necklace to die for, my bridesmaids wore pink, and
Anthony and I arrived by horse-drawn carriage."

Delilah Winchester takes over like an enthusiastic sister with her description of the five-tiered wedding cake de-
signed by Sylvia Weinstock, the Moongate-shaped groom's
cake, the bride's bursting gardenia and pink rose bouquet, and the menu made up only of dessert and champagne. "We wanted a dessert and champagne party for its
elegance, its sinful abundance, and the fact that Tavern
on the Green makes the best white chocolate mousse you
will ever taste in your life." Carmela, the groom's mother,
brought in 200 tiramisu servings in martini glasses
with chocolate curls on top, and the maid of honor Leah

Vestania guested with the Tavern's expert pastry chefs to swirl on the 'C' of their monogram to the cake, the tiramisu, and anything else she could top with her magic touch.

Etta James stepped in to sing Emilie's favorite song "At Last," a special gift from Delilah, and the bride's father danced with his daughter to 'You Are My Sunshine,' a favorite song from Emilie's childhood.

We hold this wedding up not merely as a stylistic trendsetter for its dessert-and-champagne-only focus or the many surprises that led to it, but because this Celebration of Our Marriage returns the focus to where it should be: the marriage between two people who love each other. The destination wedding, the elopement, the surprise for the bride, it all had that same goal in mind. Anthony Cantano saw the true, elevated reason getting lost in the details, so he did something about it. And now the couple returned home, blissfully married and partnered in the most pure and unblemished way possible, still to share joyous celebrating and quality time with all of their most cherished loved ones.

And they did it in fine style, drawing ideas from Emilie's girlhood journal, the notes she took as a young dreamer who wanted pink bridesmaids' gowns and a man who would love her forever. Many dreams came true that night . . . Delilah Winchester's dream of embracing a daughter who's dear to her heart, Carmela Cantano's dream of gaining a daughter who's dear to her heart, a daughter reunited with her father, and a best friend who tells us after her hours in the kitchen to keep an eye out for her name in the future. She's just had an amazing idea.

That sounds like another surprise waiting to happen, and we can't wait.

We send our sincerest wishes for happiness to the loving couple, and to their loving mothers and fathers—for in-

spiring us and skyrocketing the trend of the post-elopement celebration. We're sure many more brides and grooms will follow in their footsteps, returning the focus to where it should be: The joy and blessing of marriage with your best friend, making them family.

WILL SHE EVER GET TO SAY "I DO"?

As the right-hand woman to the most sought-after
wedding planner in the country, Mylie Ford knows
weddings from champagne fountains and twelve-piece
bands to towering cakes and all. But the nuptials of the
decade—those of rich, famous, and truly fabulous stars
Kick Lyons and Celia Tyranova—are not only super
secret, but super stressful . . .

Between an obsessed paparazzo, jealous clients, and
more frequent flier miles than she can ever use, Mylie
is in over her head. And that's before she meets personal chef Russell, a newly divorced single dad who has
everything she's ever wanted in a man—and more.
Such as a six-year-old daughter who detests Mylie on
sight, and the painful ghost of a relationship that's better off dead. Mylie might know weddings, but love is
still a mystery. Suddenly, planning the most famous
wedding in the world seems easy compared to living
happily ever after with the man of her dreams . . .

**You won't want to miss
this new novel by Sharon Naylor,
It's Not My Wedding (But I'm in Charge),
coming next month in trade paperback!**